Praise for

What's Wrong with Dorfman?

"A funny and surprisingly moving story..."
—*The Wall Street Journal*

"The writing is fresh, laced with humor. I definitely recommend it."
—*Women on Writing.com*

"Recommended Reading."
—*Book Magazine*

"Frequently hilarious and unexpectedly touching... Smart, funny characters who actually sound smart and funny... a poignant and finely crafted exploration of the legacies and burdens passed down from parents to children."
—*Publisher's Weekly*

"Top notch. This novel comes highly recommended."
—*Chattanooga Courier*

"A haunting novel of a lost soul, searching for hope and health within his world."
—*Midwest Book Review*

"One of the funniest books I've read in a long time. I couldn't put it down."
—*The Book Reporter*

"Blumenthal's hilariously descriptive language is a delight. Wonderful."
—*The Washington Review*

"Blumenthal has a jaundiced eye and a wonderfully ironic style."
—*LA Daily News*

"One of the 50 Best Books of the year. John Blumenthal's novel is one of those surprising gems...*What's Wrong with Dorfman?* is deeply and completely funny, the plot is tight and the story sings. A winning combination."
—*January Magazine*

... A wonderful achievement, a story told with much humor and truth... the book has elements of Garp's family suffering and Vonnegut's observational humor. It is difficult to find good, clever humor in literature today, but John Blumenthal has done it!"   —*Style*

Millard Fillmore, Mon Amour

"A sardonic story of love among the deeply neurotic... many funny twists and turns."   —*The Hartford Courant*

"Pleasurably light and snappy... Blumenthal is excellent at keeping several plots going at once."   —*Publisher's Weekly*

"An engagingly written comic romance..."   —*Booklist*

"This book is a great read and has the added bonus of making you feel mentally healthy no matter how screwed up you really are."   —*Cathryn Michon, author of*
The Girl Genius Guide to Sex (with Other People)

"That rarest of all literary creations, a comic love story sublimely absurd enough to shovel a glimpse into the soul."
—*Kinky Friedman, author of*
The Prisoner of Vandam Street

"You will laugh. A lot."   —*Bookviews*

"Blumenthal is a master at telling tales of the truly dysfunctional."
—*January Magazine*

Three and
a Half
Virgins

Also by John Blumenthal

What's Wrong with Dorfman?

Millard Fillmore, Mon Amour

The Tinseltown Murders

The Case of the Hardboiled Dicks

Love's Reckless Rash (co-author)

The Official Hollywood Handbook

*Hollywood High: The History of America's
Most Famous Public School*

Three and a Half Virgins

A Novel

John Blumenthal

FARMER STREET PRESS CALIFORNIA

Cover Design by Stephanie Blumenthal
Book typography by Pete Masterson, Aeonix Publishing Group,
www.aeonix.com
Cover image: "cherry" by Madlin from Bigstock.com.

ISBN: 978-0-9679444-1-8
LCCN: 2011939277

Published by
Farmer Street Press
401 California Ave., Suite 8
Santa Monica, CA 90403

Printed in the United States of America

For Ingrid, Julia and Lizzie

It's no use going back to yesterday,
because I was a different person then.
—Lewis Carroll
Alice in Wonderland

Part One

Old Flames

Buns and Lovers

MY NAME IS JIMMY HENDRICKS and I'm a recovering idiot. Twenty years ago, give or take, I did some regrettable things that I'm not proud of today—shameful, shallow, heartless things—and the guilt has been keeping me up nights like an infestation of tenacious bedbugs. What can I say? In those days, like most young, red-blooded American males, my judgment regularly succumbed to a relentless blitzkrieg of uncontrollable hormones. Granted, that's just a feeble excuse for my reckless behavior, but it's the only one I've got.

But I'm getting way ahead of myself.

Flashback to the morning of my fortieth birthday, a month or so before the guilt strikes. I'm sitting alone at the kitchen table, burning my tongue on a scalding mug of Starbucks French Roast, while debating with myself over whether I should indulge in the heavily glazed cinnamon bun that sits on a plate in front of me or go for a slightly bruised banana instead. I'm leaning toward the bun, but I can't seem to escape the thought that the banana will do more to keep my cholesterol within a normal range which, now that I'm forty, has taken on new significance.

As I sit there worrying about my health, I realize that the sudden distress I'm feeling over this particular birthday is silly, but the short leap from thirty-nine to forty symbolizes a milestone that used to seem distant. Earlier that morning, for no rational reason, I spent a good ten minutes gazing critically at myself in the bathroom mirror. Apart from a sprinkling of salt at the temples, a matching set of crow's feet, a slightly less defined jaw line and a subtle trace of a paunch—which I can suck in with stunning alacrity when circumstances require it—looking in the mirror is not an entirely unpleasant experience. Not yet anyway.

Forty. Middle age. Where did the time go?

In any case, while I'm still flirting with the cinnamon bun, Deirdre comes wandering in wearing flip-flops and an oversized T-shirt. After rubbing her eyes with her fists, she opens a cabinet and searches for a mug, but there aren't any because I'd taken the last clean one. Deirdre and I are both spectacularly negligent when it comes to washing dishes, which explains why there's a virtual Everest of mugs, flatware and dishes crowding the sink. Fortunately, we have a housekeeper who comes on Thursdays, but by Monday the place is a mess again.

After cleaning and drying a mug, she heads for the coffeemaker, stopping for a second to yawn, as if yawning and walking should not be done simultaneously, and then moves along to pour herself some coffee.

"You're up late," I observe, glancing at my watch. Deirdre usually sleeps until six and then heads out to the gym, where she works as a personal trainer.

"I took the morning off," she tells me.

She takes a tentative sip of her coffee, testing for temperature, places the mug down on the counter and then shuffles sleepily over to the fridge, where she opens the door and gazes inside.

I clear my throat. "You know what day it is, right?" I ask.

She frowns. "Tuesday?"

"That's right," I say. "Tuesday the fifteenth."

Deirdre nods, then gazes out the window. "Looks like it's going to be sunny," she speculates. "But who knows?"

"It's my fortieth birthday," I say, a little perturbed.

"I know that," she tells me with a devilish grin. "I'm just messing with you. Why do you think I took the morning off? I couldn't let you leave for work without saying happy birthday."

"Oh," I say. "I thought maybe you forgot."

"Of course I didn't *forget*," she says. "Happy birthday, Jimmy."

"Thanks."

I tilt my head and Deirdre gives me a perfunctory kiss on the cheek. Then she studies her reflection in the microwave door and tries unsuccessfully to fix her pillow-tangled hair by patting it down with her hands. It's still a nest of snarls, but now it has symmetry.

"I've decided to turn over a new leaf, Deirdre," I tell her. "I'm joining the gym."

"You said that last year when you turned thirty-nine," she reminds me.

"I'm more mature now," I say. "Plus, I'm going to start eating more salads and go easy on the cholesterol."

"Then why are you staring at that cinnamon bun as if it's got breasts?"

"I'm starting tomorrow."

"Uh huh."

I'm about to add another quip to the banter—something goofy about how forty is the new thirty, thus making twenty the new ten and ten the new embryo—but when I look up at Deirdre, I notice that her eyes have suddenly filled up with tears.

"Something wrong?" I ask.

"What? No," she says, wiping her eyes with the sleeve of her T-shirt. "Just yawn tears." Then she absently picks up the morning paper and squints at it. Deirdre needs to wear reading glasses but she's much too vain. So she squints a lot. A few months ago, at my urging, she tried contact lenses but they made her eyes itch and she kept dropping them down the bathroom sink. Unfortunately, I've been unable to convince her that reading glasses won't really have any significant impact on her appearance. Beautiful women are beautiful with or without lenses and, at thirty-nine, Deirdre could easily pass for twenty-five. But her response to my nagging is always the same: "Who wears glasses at my age?"

Anyway, after trying to focus on the newspaper for about ten seconds, Deirdre finally gives up and looks out the kitchen window, her head turned toward the end of the cul-de-sac, an oddly wistful look in her eyes. I glance at my watch and get up.

"How about a hug?" I ask her.

I approach her and she walks into my outstretched arms. I can hear her yawn as we embrace for three seconds. Then she pulls away and shuffles off toward the bedroom, most likely to begin the morning make-up ritual.

"I'll be home at six," I tell her. "Wear that black dress you just bought, okay? I love that dress."

"Okay," she says dryly.

Once she's gone, I furtively grab the cinnamon bun and put the plate in the sink to hide the evidence. Then I fill my car-thermos with the remaining coffee, sling my sports jacket over my shoulder and head for the driveway. Although the day promises warmth, a pre-dawn mist still hangs in the air, leaving a veneer of moisture on my windshield, so I give it a hasty wipe with a tissue, which only makes it worse and splatters water on my pants. In a few minutes, I'm in my car, mesmerized by the metronomic movement of the wipers. The two-lane road into town is clogged, due to a slow-moving truck, and while I'm sitting in traffic, I devour the bun in about three seconds.

~

In my little town, I have the dubious distinction of being the local electronics magnate. We sell digital cameras, computers, cell phones, routers, speakers, headphones, DVD players, flat screens, Blu-Rays, boom-boxes, keyboards (a recent addition to our inventory), and a vast array of other electronic gizmos, which we also service and install for technologically-challenged people who don't mind being bilked out of forty dollars an hour for something they could probably do themselves if they took the trouble to read the manuals.

Since we're the only electronics store within a fifty-mile radius, business is generally pretty robust. When I started out in this racket twenty years ago, the showroom was less than half its present size, advertising was nonexistent and inventory was limited to stereo cassette players, oversized speakers, used guitars and a few of those quaint relics known as turntables. But over the years, during which I matriculated from salesman to manager to owner, I've expanded the operation, and today it's a thriving, profitable enterprise, partly because I always make a point of hiring geeks and paying them generous commissions. I'd be utterly lost without them. Sadly, I can't make any sense out of a circuit board, and the complex innards of an iPod will always be a complete mystery to me. Somewhere along the line, the technology just raced right past me.

Although I'm clueless about the technology, none of my employees have much business sense, so I manage the books, meet with visiting salesmen, maintain our inventory, oversee shipping and receiving, pay the insurance bills, file quarterly income tax returns and keep a running tabulation on profits and losses. For this I use a calculator, which is two generations shy of being cutting edge.

I'm not a complete loss—I'm a whiz with a laptop. I just don't understand how it works and I'm too lazy to learn. I can't seem to figure out smartphones either, so my cell is a prehistoric flip with no apps. Some people just don't have the aptitude.

Today, since it's still early, the place is empty of customers. I find my manager—an emaciated Asian high school drop-out with an inborn talent for figuring out the intricacies of circuit boards—bopping and jiving in the middle of the showroom to a tune I cannot hear because he's wearing headphones. His eyes are half-closed, so it takes him a moment to return to Earth and notice that I'm standing two feet in front of him.

"Dude," he says, pulling off the headphones.

"Hey Joey."

"What's up?"

I sigh tragically. "Well, Joey, if you really want to know, today I lost my youth and took the first great leap into serious middle age."

"Say what?"

"It's my birthday."

"Awesome."

"It's awesome if you're turning twenty," I tell him.

He extends his fist and I bump it with mine. "Well, happy birthday, dude," he says in his usual monotone.

"Thanks Joey."

His smile falters. "Sorry I didn't get you anything."

"Don't worry about it."

"I didn't know."

"It's okay."

He nods. "So how old are you today, boss?"

"I'm forty, Joey," I say soberly. "Halfway to my grave."

He scrutinizes me, his face moving so close I can see my reflection in his glasses. "Jeez, I thought you were way older than that, dude."

"Thanks so much," I say, wincing slightly.

Joey shoves his hands into the pockets of his black chinos and looks at the floor, probably because he has no idea what to say next and neither do I. Most of our discussions generally end up at this sort of impasse. It's probably just a generational thing, although Joey's a shy kid.

Before I walk off, he offers me the headphones. "Hey, you wanna try these, Mr. H? They just came in yesterday. They're awesome."

"Tempting..." I tell him. "But it's way too early in the day for serious inner ear damage. As long as you think they're good, I'm happy."

"I bet we'll sell a ton of them," he says excitedly.

"That's what I like to hear," I say. "Be nice if we could move one or two of those keyboards too." We're standing next to one, so I idly run an index finger down the keys. On Joey's advice, we started stocking keyboards a few months ago but so far we haven't moved a single one.

Joey lowers his head. I know he feels guilty about having convinced me to take on the stagnant keyboards, so I immediately regret having brought the subject up. He's a sensitive kid and he cares about the store.

I put a hand on his shoulder. "Don't worry about it, Joey," I tell him. "It was a good idea. They'll move sooner or later." But I can see he's still embarrassed so I decide to change the subject. "So you got any plans for the summer?"

"Just hangin' out," he says. "I'm saving up for a motorcycle."

I frown. "Those things are dangerous," I point out. "Make sure you wear a helmet at all times. Promise me."

"Sure," he says. "The thing is, I got a girlfriend now and I can't keep showin' up at her place on my dumb bike. It's kinda dorky." Then he gives me a disconsolate look. "It's a used motorcycle, very cool, but I don't have enough bucks saved up to buy it yet."

"How much do you need?" I ask.

He shrugs. "I don't know exactly," he says. "I've got about nine hundred bucks in my bank account, so I still need about two hundred."

Joey looks forlorn, so I reach into my back pocket and pull out my wallet. As he looks on curiously, I yank out two one-hundred dollar bills and hand them over to him. Speechless, he just looks at them for a second or two, not quite knowing how to react.

"What's this?"

"A summer bonus," I say, turning away toward my office. "Buy the bike, date the girl. *But wear a helmet.*"

While he stands there still looking at the money, I head for the sanctuary of my office where I begin my daily routine, which I punctuate with a series of online poker games, all of which I lose. Business is slow, so I take an early lunch and when I return, Joey greets me at the front door with a bran muffin, a birthday balloon and a huge grin.

~

Before I know it, the workday is over and, after stashing the day's cash in the backroom safe and hugging Joey for the second time that day, I get in my car and pick up Deirdre for my traditional birthday dinner at Oscar's. She looks stunning in her sleeveless, low cut black dress and heels, her blonde hair cascading silkily down to the middle of her back.

On my thirtieth birthday, which was considerably less traumatic, my poker buddies got together and threw a surprise party for me, so I suspect they might be planning to repeat this monstrous act of torture for my fortieth just to see me squirm. I despise surprise parties, and they know this because I've begged them not to even entertain the thought of making me suffer through another one. Nonetheless, I have my suspicions, and if a crowd of grinning idiots in bright conical party hats leaps out from behind various hiding places in the restaurant and startles me out of my wits, my plan is to surprise them back by feigning a massive heart attack. I will clutch my left arm, then the left side of my chest, grimace in pain and crumple to the floor like an abandoned marionette, convulsing theatrically as my horrified friends attempt to resuscitate me with CPR. Hopefully, if someone gives me mouth-to-mouth, it'll be a woman, preferably an attractive one, and not one of the guys from my poker group or my Aunt Louise, who would probably lose her dentures in the process. Not that it matters. Whoever gives me CPR is going to be seriously annoyed when I open my eyes and yell, "surprise!" I may even get strangled if the mouth-to-mouth is performed by one of my burly poker buddies, thus possibly making it my last birthday. The only doctor in the group would probably be Deirdre's gynecologist and gym trainee, Kate O'Toole, a leggy redhead who happens to be stunning. So this strategy might actually have its benefits.

But much to my relief, there's no surprise party this time. Instead, Deirdre and I dine alone at Oscar's, which is considered the best restaurant in our little town and has always been our celebratory venue although I'm not sure why. The prices are too high, the food is mediocre, and there's a certain gloomy Teutonic hunting lodge ambiance about the place, owing to the five moose heads whose expressionless faces stare down at us from every wall. The owner, Oscar Stegmann, sometimes wears lederhosen to give the place an extra air of authenticity, but his thin, hairy legs do not contribute much to the overall dining experience.

After I order a recent-vintage bottle of champagne, Deirdre offers a quick, unimaginative toast and we both lean across the small round table to kiss, which causes the tip of my silk tie to take a short dip in a dish of greasy olive oil and balsamic vinegar. While I wipe it with a wet napkin soaked in Perrier, Deirdre fumbles around in her oversized purse and hands me my birthday present, which turns out to be a complicated-looking electric razor that comes with an owner's manual an inch thick, so I'll definitely have to consult Joey for a private tutorial. He's probably never operated an electric shaver, due to his lack of significant facial hair, but I'm sure he'll figure out how it works in twenty seconds.

Deirdre has a distinct talent for choosing useful gifts. For the last few weeks, I've been using those cheap yellow disposable razors from Walgreens because my old electric one suddenly died on me. Nearly every morning since then, my face has been a patchwork of small ragged squares of toilet paper.

I gush with gratitude (although in truth I would have preferred something more personal) and tell her it's the perfect gift. Then I lean over the table to kiss her again, but this time I keep a protective hand over my tie.

"You're impossible to shop for, Jimmy," she says.

"I know."

"A hobby would help."

"Like what?"

"I don't know," she says. "Golf, tennis, grand larceny?"

"Grand larceny is not a hobby," I tell her, "it's a profession."

Then I put the razor and the owner's manual back into their molded plastic niches and place the box at the edge of the table.

"It's the super deluxe model," she informs me proudly. "It comes with tons of different clippers. I think you can mow the lawn with it."

"I'll tell the gardener."

"There's even a special attachment for nose hair."

"I don't actually have nose hair."

"You will."

"Not every man grows hair in inappropriate places."

"Well, now you'll be prepared," she says, "in case you do."

Deirdre smiles and turns back to her plate, delicately trying to cut though a piece of tough Weiner schnitzel. While she's not looking, I stick an exploratory finger up one of my nostrils and feel around for hairs but, to my relief, there aren't any. At the next table, an elderly woman, who has apparently witnessed and misinterpreted this display, reacts with a disgusted sneer, so I quickly withdraw the finger and give her a sheepish smile.

Meanwhile, Deirdre has finished off her third glass of champagne and starts hiccupping.

"One good thing," she says. "I got a nice discount. I know how you love it when I save money."

I nod appreciatively. In truth, she probably flirted with the sales clerk to get the price reduction. I've seen her accomplish this magical feat with enviable success in the past. It's fascinating really. All she needs to do is edge in a little too close to the guy, lick her lips in a certain way and presto, the sticker price is history. Three months ago, this awe-inspiring tactic caused a youngish car salesman with a double chin and a carefully architectured comb-over, to knock a thousand bucks off a brand new Lexus convertible without consulting the manager. And that included a seven-year extended warranty.

After we finish our dinner, we order dessert and brandy, but before they arrive Deirdre polishes off the last of the champagne, which is unlike her because she usually abstains from liquor, fearing that it will somehow compromise the near perfection of her body. In fact, it's been years since I've actually seen her drunk, but now she appears to be swaying slightly in her chair.

While I contemplate her sudden interest in alcoholic beverages, Deirdre looks up with an odd faraway look in her eyes, which I interpret as a side effect of all the champagne she's consumed so far.

She places her silverware down. "There's something I have to tell you, Jimmy," she says after awhile.

"Shoot."

"I realize the timing isn't the greatest," she says, suppressing a burp. "Actually, it sucks. And I'm truly sorry about that. But I don't really want to drag it out. It wouldn't be fair to you."

"If it's about nose hair—"

"It's not."

I put my brandy snifter down. "Okay, I'm listening."

There's a short pause. Deirdre swallows some of her brandy and then licks her lips. "I want a divorce," she says softly.

"What?"

"It's time," she says firmly, lowering her eyes. "I think it would really be the best thing for both of us."

"Jesus Christ, Deirdre," I say, with mounting anger. "*On my birthday?*"

I look away. At a nearby table, an attractive young woman in a business suit is glowering at her dinner companion as he checks the bill with a pocket calculator.

"I've been meaning to bring it up for weeks, but I keep chickening out," Deirdre admits as she picks up her cocktail napkin and absently begins to shred it. "I guess the champagne has gone to my head or something and I just kind of...I don't know... blurted it out. But there it is. God, what a *relief.*"

"I don't know what to say," I mutter.

"Oh come on, Jimmy. We both knew it would come to this sooner or later," she says, tears forming in her eyes. "In fact, I'm a little surprised you weren't the first one to bail."

"I thought about it," I confess, "but things seemed to be going smoothly."

She looks at me. "You're kidding right?" she asks. "We put on this charade for birthdays and Christmases, but the rest of the time we avoid each other."

Now she's tearing the already torn shreds of her paper cocktail napkin into even smaller pieces.

"Will you stop with the napkin already," I say hotly, "or are you making confetti?"

She places her hands flat on the table, but she's still fidgeting. "It's not like we haven't talked about getting a divorce before."

"True."

"It's just that things are different now, Jimmy." She tries to force a smile and reaches out to put her hand over mine, but I pull mine away, as if I'd just stuck it in a snake pit. "I think you know what I mean."

I narrow my eyes. "It's because of your parents isn't it?" I ask her.

"Of course," she admits.

"Jesus, they've only been dead three months."

"Look at the bright side. You'll be free now," she points out. "Now that my parents are gone, you can play the field."

"I suppose so," I say.

"The fact is..." she begins, but her voice trails off.

"The fact is what?"

Her tone softens. "I don't really know how to tell you this, Jimmy..."

"There's more?" I ask impatiently.

She takes a deep breath, which catches in her throat. "I've met someone," she confesses in a quiet voice.

"*Already?*"

"He wants me to move in with him."

"Who is it?"

"Does it matter?"

"Yes."

"I'd rather not say."

"It's a small town, Deirdre," I remind her. "I'll be sure to find out sooner or later. You can't hide anything for very long here. You might as well tell me now, so I don't have to find out from one of the guys in my poker group or my hair stylist."

"You don't have a hair stylist."

"Whatever," I respond. "So who is it?"

She gives this a few moments of thought. "Okay fine," she says with a weary sigh. "If you must know, it's Dave Barstow."

If I'd had liquid in my mouth at that moment, I probably would have performed a passable Hollywood spit take. Dave Barstow, an effete thirty-year old English teacher at our community college, lives on the cul-de-sac a few doors down from us. Apart from his professorial credentials, he's a tall, muscle-bound guy who sports a goatee, a ponytail and a silver earring. We've only met twice, once when I loaned him a full tank of propane for his barbecue (which he never returned) and once when he came into the store to buy a set of Bose speakers (which he said were overpriced.)

"Dave Barstow, the English teacher?" I ask. "Our fucking *neighbor?*"

"It just sort of happened, Jimmy," she says. "I wasn't looking to mess around. He's always at the gym and—"

"And when exactly *did* it happen?"

"I don't know," she replies with a shrug. "Three months ago maybe."

"*Three months ago?*"

"Give or take."

"So did you start up with this idiot the minute your parents' coffins were lowered into the grave or did you wait until after the memorial brunch?" I ask.

"What's the difference?"

I open my mouth to speak, but I've run out of things to say, so I just stare off into space for a few moments and then signal the waiter for the check. By now, Deirdre has polished off her brandy and I'm staring at the lit candle sticking out of a soggy pierce of Tiramisu the restaurant donated for my birthday.

～

Later, we drive home in silence, both of us staring straight ahead as if there's something fascinating about the road. When we get there, I realize that sleeping in the same bed with Deirdre on this particular night would be awkward, so I grab a pillow and a quilt from the linen closet and spread out on the living room couch. But I can't get to sleep because my brain keeps replaying the same lurid feature film involving Dave Barstow and Deirdre going at it, so I get up and search through a few kitchen drawers for a joint but come up empty. Instead, I down a glass of Scotch, which eventually shuts down the theatre for the night.

Early the next morning, Deirdre throws on her usual Spandex gym outfit and quietly packs a few suitcases, a garment bag, a cardboard box full of books and a huge make-up kit. I'm still a little stunned; this is all happening way too fast for my mind to keep pace with it. Not that I'm surprised—as Deirdre said, we both knew that one of us was likely to ditch the marriage sooner or later. It had always been a charade. I stand mutely in the bedroom doorway, searching for something appropriate to say, but nothing comes to mind. Surprisingly, I'm remarkably calm. There's no reason for me to hang around so I head down to the kitchen. A few moments later, I hear the muffled sound of suitcase wheels banging down carpeted stairs. After making coffee, I sit at the kitchen table and watch through the picture window that overlooks the driveway as she clumsily tosses her luggage into her trunk and drives her Lexus convertible down the street to Dave's almost identical house on the cul-de-sac.

And that's that.

Except it's not. A few days later, I realize that having a wife living nearby with another guy is not a great arrangement because on some occasions, when I'm outside washing my car or looking out my window, I see her leaving for work or jogging with the bonehead she's shacked up with. She sometimes walks his bulldog or waters his lawn when he's off at work teaching Shakespeare or pompously expounding on the craft of writing fiction.

During my first few days of bachelorhood, I can't help but wonder what it is about Dave Barstow that Deirdre finds so appealing. Is he more romantic than I am? Does he coo sweet nothings in her ear and take her dancing? Is it his sexual technique? Superior penile dimensions? The muscular body? I've known Deirdre for a long time and this guy just doesn't seem like her type. Sure, my ego is bruised, and for a while I let myself wallow in self-pity, but all that gradually fades as the prospect of starting anew begins to take hold.

Past Imperfect

UNFORTUNATELY, THE TOWN I live in is pitifully small, so local dating prospects lie somewhere between slim and non-existent. Except for teenagers, most of the town's inhabitants are widowed, happily married or too old to care. For some reason, the divorcees all seem to travel in packs of three or four, thus making advances awkward. For a while, I frequent the only singles bar in town, a joint which features a dance band whose main talent seems to be less about music and more about decibels. But even on week-end nights, the place is sparsely populated with women, except for the bartendress and a retired math teacher named Selma Whitman, who quietly nurses one beer and then goes home.

For my second foray into the world of dating, I decide to buy an introductory membership to Match.com. Eagerly, I upload a color photo of myself that was taken ten years ago and concoct a profile that makes me sound like the CEO of a multinational electronics corporation, a guy with a ludicrously positive outlook on life and an array of interesting hobbies, most of which involve sports that I wouldn't be caught dead engaging in or have never tried. According to my short bio, I enjoy sipping brandy by lit fire-places and relish long romantic strolls on the beach, although our town doesn't actually have a beach unless you count the muddy silt that fronts the shore of our pathetic excuse for a lake. Although

I'm a gymophobe, my profile claims that I work out three times a week; I speak three languages; I adore wine and fine cuisine; I've bicycled through Belgium; I love French movies; I'm a widower; I own a sailboat of unspecified dimensions.

Predictably, this backfires because in a matter of hours my Match.com message box is filled with about a hundred chatty, flirtatious emails from single women with hobbies, interests and outlooks similar to the ones I invented for myself. No doubt my fictitious affluence is an even greater factor in my sudden popularity.

Navigating through all these profiles is torturous, not to mention labor-intensive. Except for a few flakes, most of them seem nice enough, although it's hard to tell for sure. Many have posted more than one photo of themselves, which is confusing because they all look different in each photo. Some are considerably older than I am; others are way too young; a few live too far away (one of them resides in Poland); more than half of them seem to be insanely devoted to their cats or dogs. But the one thing they all appear to have in common is a strong desire to get married. This is not my objective. When I decide to radically alter my profile with details that are closer to the truth, the messages start to dwindle, which is depressing, so I cancel my membership.

My next strategy is to stage a situation in which I can meet someone by chance, so I begin hanging around the produce section of our supermarket, the animal-adoption area of our pet shop and our small library. No success with that plan either, although I end up overstocking my fridge with lettuce, tomatoes, cucumbers and assorted fruits. I even come close to buying a cute little dog, hoping it'll serve as a babe magnet, but I'm allergic to dog dander and picking up dogshit three times a day doesn't seem worth the pleasure of female companionship.

Then an odd thing happens—I find my mind drifting inexorably to the past. I suppose the idea of being with someone I know (or knew) holds more appeal than starting from scratch. Suddenly, I'm consumed by nostalgic reveries involving several women, three in particular, who I dated twenty years ago, before I was married. I soon become obsessed, so one night, having nothing better to do at eleven o'clock, I spend two hectic, semi-deranged hours searching through all the closets in the house for my old yearbooks, pulling out countless shoeboxes filled with old tax returns, insurance policies and quitclaim deeds. I end up finding the objects of my search in a dusty old storage box hidden in the garage. As I flip eagerly through the musty-smelling pages, I soon discover that I still have fond memories of the pleasant days and passionate nights I spent with these three women, all of whom happened, by coincidence, to be virgins when we first met.

With the excitement of an entomologist examining a new species of rose weevil, I study each of their yearbook photographs for hours under the bright glare of a floor lamp that stands beside the living room sofa, trying to recall what it felt like to be alive back then when I was young, carefree and invincible.

First there was Laura, my high school sweetheart, who I dated almost every night during the summer before I headed off to college. Aside from the staged head-and-shoulders shot located in the graduating class section of the yearbook, I manage to find a candid photo of her. She's clad in her soccer uniform with a ball resting at her feet and an uncertain smile on her face. For a fleeting moment, I am transported back to those happy-go-lucky days.

There is only one small photo of Samantha and it's hidden in a back section of the college yearbook reserved for students who transferred to another college, which, in Samantha's case, was the Sorbonne. The expression on her face is deadly serious and characteristically haughty, but her flawless beauty manages to shine through—the black hair pulled back tightly into a ponytail, the patrician features, the dark eyes—and I find myself, once again, overcome with nostalgia.

And then there's Molly, sweet bashful Molly. Unfortunately, the class picture of her is painfully stilted, failing completely to capture her essence, and the single candid shot is so out of focus and overexposed that even a magnifying glass won't bring it into clarity. But, I still have an indelible image of her, so I shut my eyes and coax my mind into wandering back to the day we first met.

My next challenge is trying to envision what Laura, Samantha and Molly might be like now, and before I know it, I find myself engulfed in romantic fantasies. I picture myself falling madly in love with one of them again. We'd run off together to a chateau in the south of France, where we'd grow grapes and make wine. I'd wear a beret and people would call me Jacques; we'd have picnics with brie and long baseball bat-sized baguettes; someone in the background would always be playing the accordion; we'd reek of garlic. Of course, in all these scripted reveries, I can't help but picture us both exactly as we looked when we first met. Hell, if you're going to fantasize, you might as well go the full nine yards.

But soon, these pleasant dreams turn abruptly into guilty nightmares. In my eagerness to reminisce, I'd conveniently forgotten how badly I had treated these women, how I had duped, seduced, deflowered and brusquely jilted each one of them in a callous and heartless manner back in the days when my youthful hormones dictated my behavior. The fact that each of them was a virgin when we met was pure chance, but that alone conspires to make everything infinitely worse. Now I can't sleep for yet another reason. If any one of these women even remembers me at all, her memories are probably laced with simmering hostility. I wouldn't be surprised if they all still despise me.

So now, even those fantasies fizzle.

～

Every other Monday evening, I play poker with a bunch of guys I've known for years, and when our next game night rolls around, I'm tempted to spill my guts about the recent dissolution of my marriage, but something holds me back. It would probably be a little weird and make everyone feel uncomfortable. After all, I was dumped for another guy, which is a little humiliating. So I just play, drink beer, smoke a fat cigar, talk about sports and, as usual, lose practically every single hand. I'm terrible at poker. It's largely a bluffing issue.

But after the game, one of my buddies, a tall, gangly guy named Ira Sanderson, catches up to me as I'm heading toward my car. Ira is soft-spoken and his face is often expressionless, a trait that serves him well at poker.

"So Jimmy," he says cheerfully, "how the heck are you?"

"Super," I lie. "Why do you ask?"

"You don't seem like your old self tonight."

"I have a lot on my mind, Ira," I explain, trying to avoid his inquisitive gaze. "Work stress, you know. The usual crap."

He looks at me suspiciously. Suddenly, he's standing too close to me and our faces are inches apart as his eyes study mine. "You never had work stress before," he observes. "You have those smart kids running the place, like you've told us a million times. So what happened?"

"Nothing much," I tell him. "We're just having problems moving our new line of, um, keyboards."

Ira reaches out, grasps my shoulder and gives it a squeeze. "You can be honest with me, Jimmy," he assures me. "I'm a guidance counselor. I know it's only elementary school, but I can tell when someone's upset. It's my job and I'm pretty damn good at it if I do say so myself. So if there's something on your mind..."

Ira has a boyish face, but his high forehead and round wire-rimmed bifocals give him an air of gravity. He's staring at me now and I'm very tempted to unload.

"It's always good to have a sounding board," Ira continues. "That's why people have therapists."

I scrutinize him for a moment and slowly feel my resistance fading. "Okay, but do me one favor," I say.

"If I can."

"Promise me you won't tell any of the guys. Okay? What I *don't* need right now is more humiliation."

"Scout's honor," Ira vows, holding up two fingers in the Boy Scout salute. Then he grabs my elbow. "Come on, Jimmy," he says, pulling me along. "Let's go get a beer."

So Ira and I caravan to our town's only sports bar, a huge over-crowded circus with about four or five enormous flat screens and a crew of busy young waitresses, most wearing low-waisted jeans that reveal complicated tramp stamps on their lower backs. I have a few too many Coronas and finally tell him the whole story about Deirdre and Dave Barstow. Ira is very sympathetic, nodding solemnly between sips of beer.

"Wow!" he responds when I finish. "That's pretty darn harsh."

"You got that right," I tell him.

"Out of the blue, your wife leaves you," he says, shaking his head in disbelief.

"That's the long and the short of it."

"On your birthday no less."

"Right."

"And then she moves in with a big, muscular young guy too."

"I already know the details, Ira," I say a little grumpily. "But thanks for the recap."

"Sorry," he says. Then he looks me in the eye. "So are you totally devastated?"

Suddenly, I'm not certain whether this little impromptu therapy session was such a good idea, especially since I don't really need therapy, but it's too late to turn back.

"I'm not crazy about being cheated on and I think Dave Barstow is a douche bag, but otherwise I'm okay with it," I tell him. "It was sort of inevitable."

"Oh," he says, apparently taken by surprise. I see the disappointment in his eyes. He desperately wants to help me. I suppose he was hoping for more melodrama.

I feel the need to throw him a bone. "So what's your professional advice?" I ask.

Now he smiles, happy to help. "Can't say I can give you much advice," he tells me, forming a church steeple with his fingers. "The subject of adultery doesn't come up much in my school."

"Somehow I figured that," I respond, wondering briefly why we're even here. "But you've been divorced, right? What did you learn from it?"

Ira scratches his head and looks away. "I learned that you have to move on with your life," he explains.

I wait for him to continue, but he doesn't. "That's it?"

"Pretty much," he confesses, looking somewhat deflated.

"No other penetrating insights?"

"I'm afraid not."

Ira shrugs apologetically and I follow his gaze to an oversized flat screen suspended at an angle above the bar. A baseball game has gone into extra innings and I watch a pop fly sail through the air into foul territory. An outfielder sprints toward it, then hurls himself into the first row of the stands to make a grab, but misses. A little kid in a baseball cap pulls it out of the air and his dad slaps him on the back while he jumps up and down.

Ira punches the air. "Woo hoo!" he exclaims. "Don't you love it when some kid catches the foul?"

"Yeah."

I take a sip of beer and watch one of the sexy waitresses sashay past us with a trio of plates balanced precariously on her forearm.

But then, after a moment of thought, I add, "To be honest, there's something more pressing on my mind."

"I'm all ears," Ira says.

So I tell him about the three virgins and how I've been feeling guilty lately about the way I mistreated them back in the day. I don't go into much detail, but I explain enough of the story to get across the general idea. Ira listens attentively and when I'm finished, he nods somberly a few times.

"So what do you think?" I ask him.

"It's perfectly normal to seek refuge in the past when something like this happens," he tells me. "Those were the good old days, or at least that's what you think now."

"But what do I do about the guilt?" I ask.

"Well," he begins. "Whenever one of the students in my school hurts another student's feelings I always tell them the same thing."

"What's that?" I ask.

"I tell them to apologize."

"Okay..."

"That's right," Ira says enthusiastically. "You'd be surprised how good the apologizer feels afterward. It always works. It's a form of closure."

At the bar, a deafening whoop arises as the score changes and Ira waits for the racket to subside before continuing.

"So what do you think?" he asks.

I shrug because I have no ready answer. Ira's approach has never occurred to me, but I find it intriguing. "Well, now that I think about it, I suppose it wouldn't be too much trouble to send them each an email or write a letter of apology, assuming I can even get their addresses," I volunteer. "Maybe that would help."

But Ira's shaking his head. "I always insist that my students apologize in person," he explains. "It doesn't really work any other way. The indirect approach is too impersonal. The apologizer has to face the victim. Otherwise it's too darn easy."

"So what exactly are you suggesting?" I ask hesitantly.

"I'm not suggesting anything," Ira replies. "All I'm saying is that it's a lot better to apologize in person. For one thing, if you just do it by mail or email and you don't get a response, how do you interpret that?"

I stroke my chin pensively for a few moments. My beer is empty, so I point to my empty glass when our waitress passes by us. "I couldn't possibly do that," I decide. "They all probably hate my guts."

Ira shrugs. "It was just an idea," he says. "I guess I'm not really qualified to advise people about relationships. We don't get a lot of that in my school. Mainly just schoolyard bullies and such."

Predictably, within two weeks, every guy in the poker group seems to know about my marital situation. Word travels fast in my little town. I look across the card table at Ira, but he just shrugs and shakes his head as if to say "don't look at me." Since most of the guys have some of the facts wrong, I fill in the gray areas and tell them the whole story. To my relief, they're all sympathetic, especially the ones who've gone through a divorce or two themselves. One of them, Paul Larson, is envious of my bachelorhood. Steve Auerbach, a tall, stocky guy with a beer gut so protrusive it looks like he's hiding a basketball under his shirt, offers to beat the shit out of Dave until I tell him that, although Dave's an English teacher, he's roughly the size of King Kong, which quickly makes Steve reconsider. Can't say that I blame him, but I make sure he knows that I sincerely appreciate the gesture.

"I just wouldn't feel right letting you commit suicide on my behalf," I tell him. Steve mumbles something and wanders off to get a beer out of the cooler we keep near the card table. "Besides, I don't really care that much."

"I know a guy from New Jersey named Vinnie the Shoe," Eddie Klein volunteers. "I heard he's good at breaking knees and stuff. Just sayin'."

This is a conversation stopper. There's no way in hell that Eddie Klein, a timid, chinless sporting goods salesman with an overbearing wife, would know someone named Vinnie the Shoe unless the guy worked at Florsheim's.

Everybody else just stares at him until Eddie picks up the deck and starts to shuffle it. "Are we going to play cards or what?" he asks.

A Kosher Safari

I SPEND THE REMAINDER of the week contemplating Ira's curious proposal. The fact that it's the advice of an elementary school guidance counselor makes it somewhat difficult for me to determine whether it's astute or flagrantly idiotic. After all, I'm not a troubled eight-year-old looking for a shoulder and there are no bullies in my life. Sure, I'd like to set things right and ease my conscience, but somehow I just can't quite envision myself asking these three women to forgive me nearly twenty years after we dated. On the other hand, there's something oddly captivating about the idea.

All of which is irrelevant because they probably live too far away for me to realistically take on the task of visiting them all. Sure, it's a tantalizing notion, but I'm not flying to Katmandu.

In any case, mainly out of curiosity, I decide to research the whereabouts of my former prey. My first step is to turn to Facebook, where I perform a friend search using their maiden names, but nothing identifiable comes up. After two attempts, I get fifty possibilities, most of them gray heads popping onto the screen. LinkedIn doesn't yield any useful information either.

Next, I subscribe to one of those people search sites, pay the introductory fee and once again write in their maiden names. No success. Clearly, they're either all married or have kept their married names after getting divorced.

For a while, I'm actually a little relieved that I can't locate them.
Game over. No decision necessary. But I can't seem to let it go so I
call my high school and college alumni associations in an attempt—
probably futile—to obtain their home addresses.

Amazingly, the alumni people know everything.

As it turns out, they don't live that far away from me. In fact,
none of them seem to have migrated too far from the area where I
perpetrated my pitiless crimes. According to the college database,
my ex-girlfriends live in Massachusetts, Connecticut and Rhode
Island. Now I have no real excuses left other than abject cowardice.
The alumni people warn me that they can't guarantee one hundred
percent accuracy, but they also assure me that the information is
current and frequently updated.

Then, of course, they ask me for a donation.

~

Given their proximity, I carefully weigh my choices, but my
indecisiveness only worsens my insomnia, which is slowly turning
me into a heavy-lidded, bleary-eyed zombie. Eventually, it dawns on
me that I have no pressing reason *not* to go through with this. After
all, I have no romantic affiliations and I can't see myself spending
the whole summer perpetually awake. I need to get away. I could
use the distraction. Besides, there's nothing like a road trip.

Thinking it might help, I make a list of pros and cons and come
up with the following:

Pros:

1.   I'll ease my conscience.
2.   A flame will be reignited (a long shot.)
3.   I have nothing better to do.
4.   I'll get some sleep.

Cons:

1.   None of them will forgive me.
2.   None of them will remember me.

3. I'll get my ass kicked.

True, the pros outweigh the cons, but con #3 is perhaps the most worrisome. If one of my former girlfriends is married to a big guy with anger issues, this dubious odyssey could get me into some very deep shit which might involve a long hospital stay. The last thing I want to deal is an irate husband or a belligerent boyfriend retaliating for the way I treated their womenfolk so many years ago when I was young and stupid.

How would I defend myself should the situation get ugly? Should I carry a firearm? Take karate lessons before I venture forth? No, that would take too long, plus I can't imagine myself hopping around making violent, unintelligible guttural noises like a Ninja. Nor could I shoot anybody except with a water pistol.

What I need is a type of bodyguard, a frightening behemoth in a dark suit and sunglasses who will stand behind me as I knock on doors, thereby discouraging any enraged husbands or boyfriends from going postal on me. He won't need to carry a firearm or know karate, because his mammoth dimensions will be sufficient to discourage any attempts at physical confrontation. Then, if I decide that the general tenor of the situation is relatively risk-free, my growling grizzly companion could hibernate in a local bar.

Of course, what I *really* need is someone who'll provide me with moral support, a sympathetic travel companion to console me if things don't work out. Besides, it's no fun taking a road trip alone.

I know right away who that someone should be.

~

Morris Berkowitz is my closest friend. He was the best man at my wedding, I was the best man at his, and we've kept up the friendship for the last twenty years. Since neither of us has any siblings, we've always thought of ourselves as brothers, and I guess we're about as close as two men can get without being blood-related or gay. In college, he was a first-string offensive lineman on the varsity football team, where he turned kicking ass into an art form. He weighs in at an imposing three hundred and twenty pounds and stands roughly six feet five inches tall in his bare feet, which incidentally, are incongruously small. He is a mountain of a man. During our senior year, he worked part-time as a bouncer at a downtown bar and I once saw him effortlessly toss three drunk, rowdy frat boys out of the place all by himself. You didn't want to mess with Morris in those days.

Now, however, it's a different story: Today, Morris is an orthodox Jew. Although he was just an ordinary Joe in college, a beer guzzling, pot smoking party animal like the rest of us, once he graduated, he felt that he lacked direction in his life and turned to his local rabbi, who encouraged him to look more deeply into Judaism. He seems to find comfort in the moral teachings and daily rituals of his religion. Morris doesn't wear a black, furry-brimmed hat or have long corkscrew sideburns, but he sports a colorful knitted yarmulke, habitually wears a black suit and observes the Sabbath as well as all the Jewish holidays. He has six children all of whom he fervently hopes will follow in his religious footsteps. Fortunately, he and his family live in Boston which is only three hours from my town, so we try to see each other about five times a year.

Of course, Morris is completely nonviolent. Never swats flies. Leaves crumbs out for cockroaches. Won't slap mosquitoes. If he ever goes to Africa, he'll probably contract malaria. But then, I can't really visualize Morris Berkowitz and his family on a safari unless they serve kosher.

Nevertheless, I'm hopeful that my dilemma might actually interest Morris. From his point of view, I will probably seem to be a man desperate to gain forgiveness, a notion that oozes religious undertones. Actually, he was present at some of my more heartless transgressions in college and always warned me that one day I would regret them. In any case, I'm hoping he will agree to guide me in my search for absolution. My strategy is to emphasize the spirituality of the whole scheme. His sympathy about my impending divorce (I had told him the day after) might also work in my favor. So I call him and plead my case, whining when it seems appropriate. How could he refuse?

Before addressing the subject, Morris voices his concern about my split with Deirdre and inquires about the state of my mental health. I tell him I'm fine.

"In my honest opinion, Jimmy, I think you should really make this pilgrimage on your own," he tells me gently. "You don't really need me."

"Morris I can't," I moan theatrically. "I really want to, but I can't. I'm paralyzed. I need spiritual guidance."

"You're an atheist."

"That's the beauty of it, Morris," I say, my excitement surging. "This could turn out to be a positive religious experience for me. Who knows, it might bring me closer to belief in a higher being."

"When you say 'higher being' do you mean God or somebody who's smoked more grass than you?"

"Ha ha."

"Just go alone, Jimmy," he tells me, sounding a trifle exasperated. "I'm sure you'll survive."

"There's another reason," I say meekly, deciding to attempt an approach that I'm reasonably sure won't appeal to him. "Truth be told, Morris, I'm a little nervous about this whole thing. I need someone large and imposing like you to keep me from getting my ass kicked, should the occasion present itself."

"A *bodyguard*? Me? You're expecting me to hurt people?"

"No, no, no, of course not," I assure him. "You'd be a...visual deterrent. I just need you to stand by me. Who knows what might happen?"

"So you're asking me to do this because I'm a big guy?" Morris asks.

"That's not the main reason," I admit. "The truth is Morris, I can't do it without some moral support. I'm begging you. Please help me out in my hour of need." Then I think of a more persuasive approach. "Think of it as a... what do you call it... a mitzvah."

"More mitzvahs I don't need," he says. "I've done so many mitzvahs, God owes me a credit card."

I'm not sure I get that, but I let it pass. "Like I always say, you can never have enough mitzvahs," I tell him.

"Such wisdom!" he exclaims. "Where does it come from?"

"Mostly fortune cookies," I say.

Morris doesn't laugh. "Does this have anything to do with your divorce?"

"Kind of," I tell him. "I talked to a, um, therapist, and he suggested I take this trip so I can clear my conscience and move on with my life. Plus, I really need to get away, Morris. I need the distraction."

There is silence on the line. I interpret this as a good sign. He is probably ruminating. I can just imagine him stroking his long black beard, lost in thought, weighing the pros and cons.

"Hold on a second, Jimmy," he says.

"Okay."

I hear the clunk of the receiver (Morris doesn't own a cell phone) as he lays it down on a hard surface, and I manage to catch a few disconnected words of dialogue between Morris and his wife, Naomi. Naomi is a soft touch. Two minutes pass as the debate rages on. This is interrupted only once, when a child, probably his youngest, ten-year-old Isaac, blows a competent raspberry into the mouthpiece. There are a few moments of silence before Morris picks up the receiver again.

"Okay, my friend," Morris says. "Given the circumstances—your divorce and all—I'll do it."

"Thank you, thank you, thank you!" I say. "I'll never forget this."

"If you don't mind me asking, exactly how long will this mitzvah take?"

"A week maybe," I say, although I really have no idea.

"Two point three days per virgin?"

"I haven't done the math, Morris," I tell him, "but most of it will probably be drive time, motels, restaurants..."

Morris lets out a deep theological sigh, if there is such a thing. "Fine," he says wearily. "Drive up here next week. I'll go, but no longer than a week. And I'm off on the Sabbath. No cars, no television, no electricity, no air conditioner."

"Agreed," I say. "Thank you Morris. This means a lot to me. You're a real mensch. I'll never forget this."

"You owe me a mitzvah," Morris declares. "Big time."

Part Two

Laura

Laura... Then

MAYBE SHE WASN'T THE MOST attractive girl at Rimbaldi High School, but she had some very appealing features—long wavy red hair with bangs that were cut perfectly straight, a pale complexion that was liberally freckled, light green eyes and an adorable up-turned nose. She wore black-framed glasses and was slightly knock-kneed, but she had gorgeous, succulent lips, the mere sight of which would drive me to lurid fantasies every time I looked at them. In short, I was hopelessly smitten with Laura Beasley the first time I laid eyes on her.

Unfortunately, it was widely known throughout the school that Laura was off-limits for anything even remotely romantic. As far as I knew, she'd never even been on a date. She was as shy as I was and, unlike most of the other girls, the ones who sported daringly tight jeans and revealing tank tops, Laura always wore conservative clothes to school and used no make-up at all.

This sad state of affairs was the fault of her father, Clyde T. Beasley, minister of the First Baptist Church, a self-appointed upholder of the town's morality who had spearheaded a contentious local crusade to ban sex education from our local school system. He and his sanctimonious band of Bible thumpers, all of them dimwitted fanatics who believed that every word of scripture was intended to be interpreted literally, eventually persevered simply by wearing down the local school board. As a result, the only halfway stimulating class at Rimbaldi High was immediately excised from the curriculum. Laura's mother was as bad as her father. She dressed like an Amish person, even in the summer, and made huge embroidered doilies with weird likenesses of Jesus on them. I saw one once—Jesus looked a lot like Elvis Presley with a beard.

After the sex education class was dropped from the curriculum, Laura became an instant pariah at Rimbaldi. I noticed that she would always slink her way to class by staying close to the walls and spend a lot of time staring blankly at the inside of her locker, as if there was something oddly compelling about her textbooks and bag lunch. Frankly, I sympathized, but most of the less judicious boneheads at school blamed her for her father's self-righteous protest even though it wasn't her fault at all. Sometimes, she was cruelly mocked in the hallways or in class. I would have gladly defended her, but I couldn't because that would have given away my secret crush.

The only friends Laura still had after the sex ed ban were three equally unpopular girls: One of them had weight issues, another was plagued by yellow teeth and acne and the third looked like Abraham Lincoln minus the beard. All of them attended Father Beasley's weekly Bible classes. They had no discernible fashion sense whatsoever and resembled a bunch of refugees dressed for inclement weather. The four of them were considered the reject clique. Even the incoming freshmen thought they were gross and kept their distance. I felt genuinely sorry for them.

To be painfully honest, I wasn't exactly Mr. Popularity myself in those days, in spite of my cool name. I had no musical talent, no special athletic ability, no academic skills and no political aspirations, but I was on the chess team and vice-president of the film club. I was excellent in math and English, but I sucked at French, history and shop class, where I once almost sawed off my thumb while struggling to construct a wooden picture frame for Mother's Day. My best class had been sex education, so I was a little annoyed when it was suddenly removed from the roster because it was always an easy A and kept my grade point average high enough to dissuade my parents from taking any punitive action. But I never blamed Laura for that. She wasn't her father. Fortunately, she didn't look much like him either.

I wasn't a member of any cliques at high school, mainly because I wasn't considered cool enough, so I used to hang out with a couple of other fellow misfits, Kenny Moran and Leonard Smiklo. Kenny was a scrawny, bug-eyed guy who wore a French beret and a white RAF scarf to school every day and had a lethal case of halitosis that no mouthwash, breath mint or toilet bowl cleanser could alleviate. He was so self-conscious about it, he would cup his hand over his mouth whenever he spoke, so most of the time you couldn't understand what the hell he was trying to say. Naturally, everybody in school called him "Moron," because his last name kind of leaned in that direction. My other pal, Leonard, was very tall and could probably have been on the varsity basketball team if he hadn't been tragically uncoordinated, not to mention astoundingly accident-prone. He was president of the chess club and shared my obsession with boobs. So did Kenny, I think, but Leonard and I could never discern his opinion on the subject. We assumed he was in favor of them.

Of course, both Kenny and Leonard knew about my frustrating crush on Laura Beasley, and although they were sympathetic and encouraging, I always felt they knew there was no possible way I could ever hope to get her attention, let alone a date. At the time, I suspected that they were right.

"You'd have a better chance of getting Mademoiselle Moreau in bed than Laura Beasley," Leonard said once. "I bet Mademoiselle Moreau knows her way around a bedroom. For sure. She's French."

The woman he was referring to was a sexy blonde French teacher. Half the male population of the school lusted after her, including me, but as a member of the faculty, she was obviously off limits, not that a goofball like *moi* would be at the top of her dance card if the ban was ever lifted.

"Supposedly, she's screwing Cal Torrance," Leonard informed me.

"The lacrosse team captain?" I exclaimed, both surprised and impressed. "No way. Where'd you hear that?"

"Just some gossip that's been floating around," Leonard said.

"Who would tell you gossip?" I asked, eyeing him suspiciously.

Leonard shrugged. "Christ Hendricks, half the seniors are getting blowjobs on a regular basis."

"I know," I said sadly. "That sucks, no pun intended."

Leonard sighed. "Like I told you fifty times, you shoulda dated Melinda Finkel," he said. Melinda Finkel was a girl who supposedly had a crush on me. She was a pigeon-toed girl with scraggly brown hair and a lisp that drove me crazy, particularly since my last name ends in "s."

"Maybe you're right," I said, "but she's really not my type."

Leonard snorted so hard he had to pull a handkerchief out of his pocket and wipe his nose. "Like you're in a position to be picky."

"Hey, just because I'm not devastatingly handsome doesn't mean I don't have certain standards."

Leonard smirked. "Do you believe this guy, Kenny?"

"Shbitrehsvrynustettsetik," Kenny replied.

"That's for sure," I said. Leonard and I had long ago abandoned the task of asking Kenny to repeat the things he said so we just agreed with him, no matter what garbled sounds emanated from his mouth. It was easier that way. In retrospect, I'm not entirely sure what it was I even *liked* about Kenny Moran because I could never decipher the gibberish.

Maybe I wasn't in any of the cool cliques, but I wasn't a total loss in high school. Unlike Leonard and Kenny, I could be shamelessly obsequious whenever I wanted something desperately enough, and I had a distinct knack for persuasion. Except for the phys ed instructor, Coach Dombrowski, who suspected me of trying to subvert the school's gym program (which I was), the rest of my teachers adored me because I always stayed after class to clean the blackboards or volunteered to pick up test papers or sharpened pencils. One day, in an attempt to flex my talents, I approached the vice-principal, Mr. Fence, and informed him that I couldn't participate in gym class anymore because I had a recurrent case of highly contagious plantar wart. Dropping gym class was my second highest priority in those days, the first being a date with Laura Beasley.

"This is so hard for me, Mr. Fence," I whined, "because I absolutely love gym class. I look forward to it everyday. Really. But imagine how awful I would feel if I gave plantar wart to one of the first-string basketball players like Mitch Jones and... and..."

"What is it, son?" he asked sympathetically. "Spit it out."

"And... he couldn't play in the county playoffs."

The truth was, I would have loved to give Mitch Jones plantar wart because he was a nasty, conceited bully who regularly teased poor Laura and took pleasure in taunting the smaller, weaker kids.

Mr. Fence nodded solemnly. "It's nice to see a boy as thoughtful and unselfish as you are, Mr. Hendricks," he said, patting me affectionately on the shoulder, "but if you actually believe I'm buying that load of bullshit you've got another think coming."

~

By the end of my senior year, pointless as it may have been, I had become hopelessly obsessed with Laura Beasley. A few times, I'd had opportunities to talk to her—twice when she was sitting alone in the cafeteria, once when she was doing leg stretches on the soccer field and another time when she couldn't get her locker door to open—but I always chickened out. For a while, I entertained the thought of slipping a note through the narrow slats of her locker, but I couldn't decide what to write. I must have spent three hours at the desk in my room trying to concoct something that would reveal my affection for her in a clever, casual way without being too goofy or smarmy, but I just couldn't seem to find the right words. I certainly didn't want her to think I was a jerk. So I just wasted most of my senior year sulking during the day and locking myself in my bathroom every night, strengthening my wrist muscles while fantasizing about her.

But there was one occasion in which Laura actually spoke to *me*, although she didn't know it was me. Having ditched gym class one afternoon, I headed for the soccer field to smoke a joint under the bleachers. The girls' soccer team was practicing and after lighting up, I spotted Laura running clumsily after the ball, which was slowly heading out of bounds. Beneath her Rimbaldi T-shirt (which featured a picture of the school's mascot, a turtle called "Rimbo"), her breasts bobbed up and down like little animals trying to break out of the confines of her shirt. I was mesmerized by the sight and immediately felt a tent-pole rise in my jeans. It was exquisite really. But, before making contact with the soccer ball, Laura stumbled badly, fell on her ass and then toppled over again while trying to stand up. It was not a pretty sight. Shrill laughter immediately erupted from her teammates and they all pointed at her and mimicked the gracelessness of her fall. No one helped her up. Even the coach seemed to be stifling a laugh. The next thing I knew, Laura was running toward the bleachers, her cheeks streaked with tears, her red hair billowing in every direction, her breasts bouncing with the precision of two pistons.

I froze as she ran awkwardly up the tiers, almost tripping on the way. She sat down carefully on the wooden splintery slats and started to sob, stopping every few seconds to wipe her nose with the tail end of her T-shirt. From where I was standing, I could see her sneakers and her calves, but mainly her ass which was directly overhead. For a moment I was mesmerized again, but then I realized that the smoke from my joint was rising towards her. I put it out as quickly and quietly as I could, but it was too late. For a moment, she was perfectly quiet, but then I heard her sniff the air a few times.

"Is someone there?" she asked, looking first to the left, then to the right, but neglecting to look beneath the bleachers for some reason. "Hello?"

I stood perfectly still. The only sound was my heart racing and her sniffling. At first, it seemed like the perfect opportunity to make contact, but then I realized that I didn't want her to know I'd been a witness to her embarrassment on the soccer field. On the other hand, it might be my only chance.

But then it was too late. The coach blew her whistle and gestured for Laura to return to the field.

∼

In April of that year, I was accepted at Fryman College, a small coed institute of higher learning in Boston, and I heard through the high school grapevine that Laura would be attending a small evangelical Bible college in Georgia, which sounded like a real blast. If I didn't make contact with her during that summer before college, I probably never would. And I knew I would always regret it.

I was also determined to lose my virginity before starting college, but I suspected that Laura Beasley would probably be the last person to help me achieve that goal. Nevertheless, I was dying to take her out.

Then something very odd happened. That summer, I was working at the counter of the town's Baskin Robbins (a dumb job, but better and slightly more lucrative than flipping burgers) to make some extra spending money for college. It was minimum wage plus tips but nobody ever tipped me, not even a quarter, because most of the customers were little kids who usually paid with nickels and pennies and regularly pelted me with M&Ms and spitballs which they fashioned from the napkins. Anyway, one day, Laura's three goofy friends came in for cones and every time I turned my back to them, they started to giggle like a bunch of ninnies.

"What's so funny, ladies?" I asked when I handed each of them their ice cream.

"Oh nothing," one of them said coyly while the other two held their hands over their mouths.

"Do I have a hole in the back of my pants or something?"

"Nope."

"Is there a chocolate stain on my butt?"

"Nope."

I was getting tired of playing games with them, so I just shrugged and went about my work, cleaning up the scoops, wiping the counter, organizing the cones and cups and so forth. I wasn't paying attention to them anymore when the one named Marsha Berger whispered to me while my back was turned.

"Hey Jimmy," she said, trying to stifle a giggle. "You wanna hear something?"

I turned around. "Sure," I said absently. "I guess so."

"It's kind of a confidential secret," Marsha declared.

"That's redundant," I pointed out to her.

"Huh?"

"The phrase 'confidential secret' is redundant."

"Whatever," she said, unconcerned by her grammatical ignorance. "So you wanna hear it or not?"

"Sure."

She leaned across the counter, summoned me to come closer by bending her index finger and whispered in my ear, even though the three of us were the only ones in the place. She said eleven words that almost made me drop the ice cream scoop I was drying: "Laura has a crush on you. She thinks you're really cute."

"Laura Beasley?"

"Duh."

At first I was taken aback. A nanosecond later, I was overcome by an onrush of pure, unbridled bliss, laced liberally with an onrush of hormones that created the predictable reaction in my crotch. *Laura Beasley had a crush on me?* I was almost moved to kiss the three of them on the lips as they watched me with the bemused, conspiratorial grins that often accompany the revelation of gossip. But then the whole thing suddenly seemed so improbable that an iota of skepticism managed to creep in, threatening to spoil my elation. And all these emotions happened within five seconds. Yet I couldn't help but wonder: How come nobody had told me this in high school?

"Get outa town," I said finally, eyeing them suspiciously. "You're bullshitting me. This is some kind of practical joke, right?"

"No it's not," another member of the trio, Linda Fletcher, said.

"You swear?" I asked.

"Yeah," Linda assured me. "Why would we make that up?"

"You might," I said.

"Well, we didn't," Marsha told me. "But don't tell Laura we told you. She'll murder us."

"I doubt that," I said. "Her father's a Baptist minister. The Ten Commandments are pretty clear about murder."

"Whatever. Just don't say anything to her."

"My lips are sealed," I said.

"Okay," Marsha whispered. "Like I said, she'll have a shit fit if she finds out."

"That's for sure," Linda added.

Then they noisily sucked on the bottom tips of their cones,

slapped down a few bucks and some change and headed for the exit. As usual, there was no tip, but I didn't really expect one from them. The news about Laura was the best gratuity I could have gotten anyway.

"Hey!" I called out to them as they were about to leave. "Thanks!" Marsha flashed me the peace sign and then they started their stupid giggling routine again as they stumbled out the door. I didn't realize it until I turned around to face the big mirror behind the counter, but I had a huge, dopey grin on my face.

～

I think I spent the rest of the day happily whistling a dumb Bee Gees song. I really don't remember which one. *Laura Beasley had a crush on me!* When I got home that evening and actually contemplated this intriguing new development in my nonexistent love life, I realized that I was going to have to devise some casual way to actually encounter Laura before the summer drew to a close. Obviously, I couldn't just call her or suddenly appear at her front door one day and ask her out on a date. That would make her suspicious.

But it was already late June so I didn't have much time to waste.

In an attempt to orchestrate a chance meeting, I took to walking the streets of town on my days off, passing all the places where she would be likely to hang out, hoping that I would spot her, but I didn't. She wasn't at the public swimming pool or the mall or the lake or any of the other usual hang-outs. I must have walked fifty miles. It was as if she had disappeared, and I began to worry that her parents had either grounded her for the whole summer for some minor infraction or sent her off to some Bible camp. Leonard and Kenny were out of town for the summer, so I couldn't enlist their help. I was on my own.

Then, one morning, I passed the First Baptist Church on my way to work and spotted something that made me backpedal. On the black outdoor events sign, beneath the corny inspirational Bible passage that was crookedly arranged with white block letters, was an announcement about try-outs for a new summer church choir. Right away, I remembered that Laura had been a soprano in our high school glee club, so I guessed that she'd probably be in her father's church choir too. I wasn't a Baptist and I didn't know a single hymn, but I had a decent voice and the sign didn't specify that you had to be a member of the congregation to join. So I stepped inside and scrawled my name on a roster that was thumb-tacked to a bulletin board in the vestibule.

The next night, I appeared at the church fifteen minutes before the designated time, dressed in a starched white short-sleeved shirt, a sports jacket, navy blue slacks and a pair of shiny brown dress shoes, an outfit that I hadn't worn since my grandmother's funeral two years prior. There probably wasn't a dress code but I didn't want to take any chances. The turn-out wasn't exactly spectacular, maybe six people in all—two old guys, two matronly middle-aged women, a tall, skinny girl who sat alone in a far corner and me. Mr. Beasley was sitting stiffly in the first pew with a clipboard on his lap and a mechanical pencil in his hand. Every now and then he fondled the silver crucifix around his neck.

And then I saw her. Laura Beasley occupied a bench at the church organ that was located behind the pulpit. Her face was bathed in an arc of warm light from a reading lamp situated just above her head. Given the spiritual ambiance, she looked like an angel. I guessed that she was going to be the accompanist for the auditioning singers. Having never spoken to her, I hadn't known that she played the organ, but then I didn't really know much of anything about her. When she glanced at me, I gave her a timid little three finger wave. She waved back with a slight smile and then shyly lowered her head.

When it was finally my turn to sing, I was so nervous my voice cracked twice and I dropped the hymnbook on the floor. I had no idea whether that was considered sacrilegious by the Baptists, so I picked up the thick black book and kissed it. Mr. Beasley rolled his eyes and instructed me to continue. It was torture. My mouth suddenly went dry at one point, but I persevered in spite of the furtive grimaces I was getting from the others every time my voice didn't quite hit the high notes. With Laura five yards away from me at the organ, I just couldn't concentrate. Once or twice, I thought I heard a muffled giggle coming from her direction, but it was difficult to tell because most of the other singers were going through a chorus of unnecessary throat-clearing to mask their discomfort.

After everybody had auditioned, Mr. Beasley approached me and put his hand gently on my shoulder.

"Thank you for coming, James," he said, his thick black eyebrows forming an inverted V. "I don't know quite how to put this but—"

"I know," I interrupted. "I guess I'm not such a hot singer."

"Well, the fact is you might profit from some practice, my son," he advised me in a kindly voice. I guessed this was hard for him. "Perhaps even a lesson or two. But I appreciate your enthusiasm and your dedication to God. I find it...very admirable for a boy your age, very admirable indeed."

"Thanks," I mumbled "Maybe I'll try out again next summer."

"I would encourage you to do that, my son," he told me. "And in the meantime, keep praying."

"You bet," I said.

And then he smiled and headed back into the church.

I loitered in the vestibule for a few minutes, trying to catch sight of Laura, but she wasn't around. Maybe she was in the back removing the black robe, which was an image I immediately began to envision as graphically as I could. The mere thought of her removing clothing was enough to make my heart beat a little faster. In the meantime, Mr. Beasley, who was gathering the hymnbooks, must have been wondering why I was still hanging around, because he looked at me with a curious expression. Finally, I waved at him and left.

The church must have had a back door, because I found her sitting on a bus bench about twenty yards from the church steps, smoking a cigarette. Laura turned her head toward me as I approached.

"Hi Jimmy," she said shyly.

"Hi."

"The busses stop running at six," she told me.

"I wasn't planning on taking a bus," I said. "Mind if I join you?"

"Not at all," she said, patting the place beside her. Then she dug in her pocket and produced a pack of cigarettes. "Want one?"

"No thanks," I told her, sitting down. "I don't smoke."

"You should," she said. "I hear it's great for your lungs."

I laughed. "That was very funny," I said.

"Thank you."

We both turned and smiled at each other.

"I didn't know you smoked," I said.

"It's a secret," she whispered, leaning in closer to me. "If my Dad ever found out he'd probably ground me for a century or make me jump into a live volcano or something."

I laughed again. "Your secret's safe with me," I assured her. "But I don't think there's actually anything about smoking in the Bible, pro or con."

"Do you read the Bible?"

"Religiously."

Then she turned and looked over my ensemble. "You didn't really have to dress up for this," she said.

"I wanted to make a good impression," I told her.

"You look nice though," she observed.

"Thanks, but this starched collar is giving me a rash."

At that, I opened the top two buttons. "Much better," I said. Then I slipped out of my jacket. It was a warm night.

We sat quietly for a moment and I watched her lips form a circle as she blew a perfect halo of smoke. We both followed it float upward until it dissipated.

"So *do* you read the Bible?" she asked me again, flicking an ash.

"Not a big fiction fan."

"You're lucky," she said. "I have to read it every day and memorize these *endless* passages to recite to my Dad all the time. Can you imagine? *Every day?* Like I don't have enough homework. It's such a frigging drag."

"Yeah, I guess that would be a bore," I replied, trying to imagine myself slogging through that torturous task. "But aren't there some cool dirty parts? Like Sodom and Gomorrah?"

"We skip over those."

"Too bad," I said. "Actually, to be honest I don't really understand the Bible. I mean take Noah for example. How did he feed all those animals? What did he do with all the shit?"

"God knows," she said, and I laughed.

Then she delicately removed her glasses and, while squinting, wiped them on her shirt tail. Seconds later, she put them back on, but I remember thinking the squint was kind of cute.

"What?" she asked after noticing that I was staring at her.

"Nothing," I said.

Laura nodded and attempted to blow another smoke ring, but this one never formed into a circle.

"What if your father walks by?" I asked.

"He won't. He usually drives home," Laura said. "The lot's in the back. Plus, our house is in the other direction."

"So why are you sitting here?"

"I don't know." She turned her head away from me. "Actually, I was kind of, um, hoping you'd walk by."

"Really?" I asked. "Why?"

She shrugged. "We never actually met," she said. "I saw you a lot in school, but we never talked or anything."

"I guess that's true," I said. "I wanted to meet you though."

"Then how come you were so weird toward me in school?"

"How do you mean?"

"Um, how come you always avoided me? Every time I passed you in the halls, or saw you in the cafeteria, you looked the other way. It was like I had some awful *deformity* or something."

"Did I do that?" I asked. "I didn't realize it."

"I figured maybe you didn't like me or something."

"The fact is I *do* like you, Laura. I like you very much. I have for years."

"Yeah right," she said skeptically.

"No really," I countered enthusiastically. "I do. It's the God's honest truth."

"Do you believe in God?"

"No," I admitted. "But it's the truth anyway."

There was a long pause and I couldn't figure out how to fill it, so I just smiled at her and she smiled back. She had great teeth. I'd never noticed that before.

"So if you like me so much, why didn't you ever ask me out?"

I shrugged. "I'm kind of shy I guess."

She brought her knees up and hugged them to her chest. I really envied those knees because of their sudden proximity to her breasts. "If you're so shy, why did you audition for the choir?" she asked.

I felt as if I was a witness in court and had just been outsmarted by a lawyer. I hesitated before blurting it out. "Because... I had a feeling... you'd be there."

"No effing way," she said.

"You just heard me sing," I told her. "You think I would have made a total fool of myself just to join a stupid church choir?"

After a moment of contemplation she said, "I guess not."

I glanced at my watch. It was eight o'clock already. I had to take advantage of the situation because there might not be another. But what should I say? I had a joint on me, but I doubted she smoked grass. The legal drinking age in the state had just been lowered to eighteen, but what if she didn't drink? I couldn't take her to a bar.

"So listen," I finally said. "After you finish that cigarette, you wanna grab a burger or something at McDonalds?" McDonalds was about the lamest place for a date, but it was the first option that popped into my head.

She looked at me with a radiant smile that was tempered by amazement, which in turn was tempered by a hint of doubt. "Are you, uh, actually asking me out on a date, Jimmy?" she asked skeptically.

I suddenly felt bold, probably because I already knew it would be a slam dunk, unless her three pals had been putting me on. "Yeah," I said with a nod. "I guess I am. Definitely."

"Cool," she said.

"Then let's go," I told her.

She stubbed out her cigarette on the sole of her shoe and competently flicked it into the street. "I would certainly like that," she said with a smile. "Very much."

~

That night, we sat across from each other in a booth at McDonalds, talking about everything under the sun. Both of us were sipping milkshakes, which suddenly struck me as the kind of dopey thing two high school kids would have done in the 1950s.

But it didn't really matter to me where we were. I was in a stupor of utter happiness just being on a date with her. She thought it was cool that I was going to Fryman College and I told her facetiously that I thought it was cool that she was going to Bible college in

Georgia, which made her laugh because it was such obvious bullshit. Other than that, I agreed with nearly everything she said. If she liked Elton John, I liked Elton John, although I really wasn't crazy about Elton John (Bruce Springsteen was actually my favorite); if chocolate was her favorite ice cream flavor, it was mine too, although my milkshake was strawberry; if she liked looking at sunsets on the beach so did I, even though sunsets bored the hell out of me and beach sand gave me a rash. Nature Boy, I wasn't. But there was one particularly interesting aspect to all this—even though her father was stricter than an aspiring medieval martyr, I soon realized that she wasn't the uptight person I had always imagined her to be. She was just bashful, especially around boys. With a domineering father like hers, who wouldn't be?

"You know one of the main reasons I really like you, Jimmy?" she ventured at one point.

"My wardrobe?"

She shook her head and laughed. "No, silly," she said. "But you dress kinda cute, except your gym shorts were a little too big."

"I know," I said. "They gave me the wrong size."

Me too," she said. "My T-shirt was too small."

I nodded, recalling how sexy she looked in it. "So why do you like me then?" I asked.

"Even though you avoided me all the time—which I *didn't* like— at least you never ogled my tits like all the other boys, when I played soccer and stuff," she explained. "I really hated that a lot. It was kind of... I don't know... annoying."

"That's so obnoxious," I opined self-righteously. Then I added hesitantly, "But you do have a really, um, nice bod."

"You really think so?" she asked.

I put up a hand. "As God is my witness."

She blushed. I was probably the only boy who had ever told her that. "You know something Jimmy," she said hesitantly, "I was kind of hoping you would ask me to the prom. I would have loved to have gone with you."

"Me too, but we didn't really know each other then," I said.

"Yeah."

"Even if we had, I probably wouldn't have had the courage to ask you," I told her. "You might have said no and I would've been totally crushed."

"Of course I would have said yes! Not that it matters anyway," she grumbled sadly. "My father probably wouldn't have let me go, unless I dressed like a nun or something."

Later that night, as I walked her home, she surprised me by taking my hand and I wondered whether she could hear my heartbeat go into overdrive. Her curfew was ten o'clock. When we got to her door, we stood in front of each other on her porch for a few seconds, neither of us quite knowing what to do, both of us looking down at the floorboards for inspiration. After a moment of awkwardness, she fumbled for her keys, and then turned to face me again. Was that an expectant look on her face? Was she waiting for me to kiss her or would that have been too forward? I instinctively stepped a few inches towards her; then she leaned toward me, and before I knew it, our mouths had come together. We were actually kissing! I was making out with Laura Beasley! Surprisingly, she was an excellent kisser, not that I'd had much experience. But it didn't last too long, because after a few seconds, she put a hand on my chest and gently pushed me away. I tried to keep our lips from disengaging by leaning forward as she stepped back until I was afraid I'd lose my balance and fall down on her porch.

Of course, I knew why she'd pushed me away. No doubt, she was afraid her father was peeking out from behind a curtain or something. If he saw us, I'd be toast and she'd be grounded for fifty years which would destroy all my plans. By the time our lips separated, my suddenly rigid pecker was straining almost painfully against the confines of my jockey shorts, but I managed to conceal it by keeping my hands folded over my crotch. Then she smiled bashfully and turned to open the lock on her front door.

"Goodnight Jimmy," she whispered, biting her lower lip. "I had a really, *really* nice time."

"Me too," I said.

"I guess I'll go in now."

"Okay."

"My Dad goes ballistic if I'm two seconds late for curfew."

"Right."

"We have to synchronize our watches before I go out," she told me. "Is that totally stupid or what?"

"Pretty stupid," I said.

Laura didn't open the door. She just stood in front of it for a few seconds, looking into my eyes. Somehow, I knew that this was my cue.

"So, can I take you out tomorrow night?" I stammered. "Maybe we could see a movie or something, or maybe we could—"

"Okay," she said.

"Great. I'll see if I can borrow my dad's car," I told her. "What time should I pick you up? Is sex good?"

"What?"

"Ha ha, I meant 'is *six* good,'" I said, blushing.

"Six is great."

"Okay then," I said with a big grin. "Six it is."

Although I had blurted out the time without thinking, it turned out to be a wise maneuver: If the movie lasted an hour and a half, we'd have plenty of time for some heavy necking and, if I was lucky, petting in my dad's car. I have no idea what was going through her mind, but she lit up with a gorgeous smile. Then she gave me a quick peck on the cheek. "See you then," she said. "I can't wait."

"Me too."

As she stepped inside, I strolled slowly down the flagstone path toward the street and turned to wave at her just before she closed the front door. Then she blew me a kiss. I wasn't sure how to respond, so I made like I had caught the imaginary kiss in my hand, which I immediately realized must have looked fairly idiotic, but it made her smile. And then she disappeared behind the door.

The next night, when I rang her doorbell, it was her father who opened the door, which startled me. He politely ushered me into the foyer and informed me that Laura would be down in a few minutes. She was still getting dressed. Without asking me if I wanted a snack, he walked into the kitchen and returned a minute later with a glass of lemonade and a small stack of stale sugar cookies on a tray that was decorated with what looked like a police line-up of the apostles. Then he led me into the living room—a stark, Quaker-like area featuring several pictures of Jesus. With his hand tightly gripping my shoulder, he sat me down on an uncomfortable chair.

"James," he told me, "I just want you to know that I love my daughter more than anything else in the world, as does Mrs. Beasley."

"Yes sir," I responded.

"She's a tender, innocent young girl," he said.

"I know."

"And I appreciate your interest in getting to know her."

"She has an excellent personality," I said lamely.

"Yes, she does. However…I thought we should have a little chat before you and Laura go," he continued, his prominent Adam's apple bobbing up and down as he spoke.

"Okay."

"You seem like a nice, polite young man, James," he told me.

"Thank you, sir."

"You come from an honest, hardworking family."

"Yes."

"But I am fully aware of the strong hormonal forces that can dominate a young man's mind. Do you follow me?"

"Yes sir."

"So there will be no necking."

"Yes sir."

"No petting."

"Yes sir."

"Nothing of a sexual nature at all."

"I wouldn't dream of it."

"Good, because if you try any funny business with my daughter, *anything at all*, I will track you down if it takes me the rest of my life and personally turn you into a eunuch. Do you know what a eunuch is, son?"

"Yes sir."

"What is it?"

"It's a guy with no reproductive equipment."

"Very well put," he said. "I assume you like having reproductive equipment, James."

"I do. Very much," I said, with a slight gulp.

"So are we clear on that point?"

"Yes sir. Clear as a bell."

Then Mr. Beasley studied me closely for a few seconds trying, I assumed, to gauge my true intentions. I did my best to appear saintly.

"Abstention, James," he said sagely. "Abstention is the key."

"Yes sir."

Of course, I was hardly frightened or deterred by his warning. First, I was way too horny to care what he did to me. Second, I knew it was an idle threat because it would require assault with a deadly weapon. Somehow, I just couldn't imagine Mr. Beasley chasing me around with serrated cutlery.

When Laura finally came downstairs, she glared at her father and could barely look at me. It was obvious why she was embarrassed—her clothes looked as if they'd come from a Victorian Era garage sale. She was wearing a skirt that was unfashionably long, a pair of running shoes with brown socks and an oversized black blousy thing that completely hid her torso and even covered her neck, frilling slightly just under her chin. Poor Laura kept staring at the floor, and I wanted to tell her she looked beautiful in spite of the ridiculous outfit, but her father was standing right in front of us, no doubt checking to make sure all her buttons were closed. Hell, I was so happy to see her, she could have been wearing a circus tent and it would have been fine with me.

"You look quite lovely, sweetheart," Reverend Beasley told her.

Laura just looked at him with a blank expression.

"You kids have a nice time," her father said, making a point of narrowing his eyes at me. I gave him a solemn nod and we were finally out the door. When we were a block from her house, Laura grabbed my hand and we ran down the street until we were around the corner.

"Jesus H. Christ!" she bellowed, her face flushed with anger. "I *hate* my father! I look like the Grim Reaper in this get-up."

"Actually, I think he wears a hood," I said.

"Huh?"

"The Grim Reaper," I said. "I think he wears… never mind."

"Nothing even *matches!*" she exclaimed. "He has no color sense at all!"

"Doesn't matter," I said. "Where's your mother?"

"Tango lessons."

"You're kidding right?"

"Of course," Laura said. "She's at Bible study, where else?"

I hadn't noticed until we got to the theatre, but Laura was carrying an oversized cloth handbag with a shoulder strap. Later, while I stood in line for popcorn and Cokes, she asked me to wait while she visited "the little girls' room". She was gone for about twenty minutes, which made me restless because the movie was supposed to start soon and I knew the rows would be rapidly filling up. But when she came out of the restroom, I suddenly realized what she had packed in that bulging handbag—a whole different wardrobe. Now she was wearing a V-necked sweater, tight blue jeans, ballet shoes, eyeliner and lipstick. She looked utterly stunning and I told her so in one word: "Wow."

"You like it?" she asked, spinning on her heels.

"A lot," I said.

"I got the whole outfit this morning at the mall," she told me. "Just for our date."

"Really?"

"Yeah."

I glanced inside the theatre. It was almost full and I worried that we might not be able to sit together, which would be a disaster.

"We better go in," I said anxiously. "It's filling up."

"Okay."

I quickly took her hand and pulled her into the theatre. We settled in a back row, just in case things got hot and heavy. "You look fucking amazing!"

"Well, thank you," she said, beaming. "You have no idea how hard it was slipping into these tight jeans on the toilet."

"I'll bet."

That night, we held hands in the theatre and munched on popcorn. I wasn't sure how she felt about public displays of affection, but eventually I managed to snake my arm across the back of her seat and encountered no resistance. After the movie, we necked in my dad's car.

"I've never made out with a boy before," she informed me.

"Neither have I."

And then we went at it again. I think she must have pulled my hands off her breasts about six times, although I wasn't keeping score. Each time, she called me "a naughty boy" in such a playful tone that I wasn't sure if she actually wanted me to stop. I think she found it flattering. As it turned out, my relentless aggressiveness didn't seem to really bother her because we ended up dating for the rest of the summer.

The only glitch was her curfew. No matter how heavily we were making out, when nine forty-five rolled around, she would promptly disengage and point to her watch, which meant it was time for us to stop. Then, as I sighed and wondered whether my cum had penetrated through my underpants to my jeans, she would wriggle out of her clothes, change back into the bland Puritanical attire her parents had chosen for her, and wipe off her make-up using the rearview mirror. Of course, I wanted to keep going, but no amount of whining and pouting on my part would change her mind about violating her curfew. Sure, she always apologized profusely, but that didn't do much to quell my sexual agitation. The only benefit for me was that I got to see her in her bra and panties for a few fleeting moments as she got dressed in the back seat (she'd told me to avert my eyes, but I managed to steal a few peeks.) Of course that only made me hornier. Then, on the ten minute drive back to her house, she would take a small mirror out of her handbag and make sure she'd erased all of her make-up. When I took her home, I always parked a few blocks away from her house, just in case the good reverend was spying on us from the front window. Still in the car, we would kiss each other goodnight and make a date to do it all over again the following night.

Then, as soon as I got home, I would lock the bathroom door and hand wash the stickiness off my jockey shorts so my mother wouldn't see it when she did the laundry.

I was deliriously happy to be with her. One evening, I took her out to dinner at a restaurant in the next town, a place that was widely considered to be romantic, owing, I suppose, to the dim lighting, the candlesticks on every table and the horrible violinist who made the rounds from table to table playing schmaltzy love songs from the 1940s. The meal cost me a whole week's salary, but Laura ordered the least expensive entrée on the menu, forgoing a salad, an appetizer and dessert, which I thought was a very sweet gesture, given my limited resources. We played footsie and made goo-goo eyes at each other all during dinner. She giggled a lot. Afterwards, we took a romantic stroll in our local park, holding hands, and I couldn't take my eyes off of her because she looked so beautiful bathed in the lamplight. We ended up necking on a soft bed of grass that was well-hidden behind an area of dense foliage. Although it was much roomier than the backseat of the car, every time there was the slightest sound—a squirrel scurrying up a tree, a breeze ruffling the leaves, unidentified fauna moving in the bushes—Laura would abruptly push me away and sit up, her eyes wide with the fear that someone would discover us.

"Will you please relax?" I beseeched her. "Nobody's around."

"What if a cop catches us?" she asked, smoothing out her dress. "My father knows all of them."

I rolled my eyes. "Everybody knows all of them," I said. "There are only three cops in the whole town and two of them are retarded."

"Really?" she asked. "Which two?"

"They're not really retarded in the true sense of the word," I explained. "They're just a little slow. Besides, there's nothing to worry about. All they do is play checkers and read girlie magazines in their cars all day. Not a lot of crime in town."

"You're right," she said, lying back down beside me and puckering up. "I guess I'm just a little paranoid. Now where were we?"

So that's how we spent our first month together, furiously necking in a variety of places around town, including a dressing room in the public pool cabana and the back room of the Baskin Robbins, both of which could be locked from the inside. Laura seemed to enjoy the adventure of it but, in spite of our intense mutual attraction, she still kept the boundaries clear and whenever I dared to cross the line separating petting from necking, she would adamantly bring my exploration to a close.

One day, there was a miraculous transformation, the cause of which I could never quite figure out, not that I was complaining. Maybe she had convinced herself by then that I was sincere. Whatever the reason, by the end of July, she stopped taking my hands off her breasts and instead encouraged me to fondle them to my heart's content, although she kept her bra on. But by early August, she was voluntarily taking it off, which drove me totally insane with lust; by mid-August we were dry humping, and by the end of August, she actually took my hand and placed it between her legs.

I'm no psychiatrist, but I think part of the reason she was doing all this was to get back at her father. After all, he'd been the one who had single-handedly turned her into an outcast in high school. It was a mixture of revenge and mischief, plus I think she really liked me. Part of it might have been years of repressed passion too. Or maybe she just needed to feel loved. Anyway, she was much, much bolder than I'd ever imagined, and she was no stranger to the art of cursing, especially when talking about her father, who she genuinely despised.

There was also a whole array of tender gestures that endeared her to me. She had this wonderful way of throwing her arms around my neck whenever we kissed and pushing her breasts into my chest. When we walked somewhere, she liked to take my arm and squeeze in close to me and she had this glorious, hearty, throw-your-head-back kind of laugh. Laura Beasley was the most unpredictable girl I would ever meet. For me, it was the closest I had ever come to being in love (although I suspect it was mainly lust) if you didn't count the cocker spaniel puppy my parents had gotten me for my tenth birthday.

Sometimes, I would bring a joint or a six-pack of Bud and after getting high we would go at it for half an hour and then lie on the hood of the car and gaze up at the stars. Laura usually limited herself to half a can of beer and one toke of the joint, but that was usually enough to loosen her up. Of course, before she went home, she would have to use half a bottle of Binaca to conceal her beer breath.

However, on the night of September third, the day before I was scheduled to leave for college, and a date that will live forever in the annals of my personal history, she smoked *half* the joint and consumed *two* beers before we worked ourselves into the usual frenzy in the backseat of the car, which was parked in the lot behind the First Baptist Church. Since mid-August, this had become Laura's favorite place to neck (I suppose she derived some devilish pleasure in the blasphemy.) Anyway, on that particular night, both of us were huffing and puffing, moaning and groaning and getting very sweaty because it was a humid summer night. The combination of the joint and the beers had made Laura more aggressive than usual and before I knew it, she'd stripped down to her panties and socks. Between gasps, I told her that I loved her, which was a lie, but college would be starting soon and I was still determined to lose my virginity before the fast-approaching deadline.

"Do you really love me?" she asked, looking into my eyes.

"Oh God, yes," I said with all the sincerity I could muster. "I *do* love you. I love you soooo much it's making me crazy."

"I love you too, Jimmy," she said, kissing my forehead. "I really do."

"I love you more," I insisted. "I wish I wasn't going away tomorrow, Laurie. I just want to be with you. Forever."

Laura took a deep breath and swept the hair out of her face. "I forgot to get you a going away present," she said with an odd sultry expression.

"That's okay," I told her.

"Don't you want one?"

"Sure," I said.

Then, with a sexy smile, Laura whispered in my ear and told me... *to go all the way.* It seemed so sudden and startling that I wasn't sure I'd heard her right, so I turned down the radio and asked her to repeat it. She did.

"Do you want me?" she asked.

"More than anything in the world!"

"And you'll always be mine?"

"Always," I said.

Like a whirlwind, I began to strip. Then for some reason I hesitated. Maybe it was fear of the unknown or the realization that I was about to achieve the first sexual milestone of my young life, but I suddenly stopped fumbling with my belt buckle. Laura didn't notice because she was struggling to remove her panties.

When she was done, she smiled and gave me a very hard kiss on the lips. "Tell me you love me again," she said.

"I love you again," I told her.

"No really," she said. "I need to know."

I looked into her eyes. "I love you," I said.

"I really want you Jimmy," she cooed. "I want you to be the one. And tomorrow you'll be off to college. So please stop wasting time. It's almost my curfew."

That was interesting, I thought: She had no problem with the sex, but she was worried about her father's stupid curfew.

"I hope you have a rubber," she said.

"Oh yes."

"If I got pregnant..."

"Trust me," I said. "You won't."

Earlier that summer, I'd been optimistic enough to purchase a package of Trojans at the local pharmacy just in case a situation like this might develop, although it seemed unlikely at the time. The cashier, a kid I'd known in high school named Jerry Walker, couldn't seem to stop winking at me, so I paid as fast as I could and hurried out. I kept three of them in my wallet, just behind the cash, and now I took one out and clumsily tore off the wrapper with my teeth, a procedure I had practiced a few times in my room.

"Are you sure it'll work?" Laura asked.

"Pretty sure," I said. "But just to be safe…"

At that, I put the open end of the rubber to my lips and blew it into a balloon. I waited a few seconds, trying to detect leakage, but there was none. Meanwhile, Laura put a hand over her mouth to stifle a giggle.

"Seems to be okay," I said.

"Then let's go before I change my mind."

It was over in a matter of seconds. Then we did it again. Then a third time. I could have gone for four, but I'd run out of rubbers.

Afterwards, we snuggled in each other's arms, both of us content but perhaps a little bit awed, by what we had just done. I desperately wanted to get out of the car and make loud whooping sounds, but I restrained myself.

The next day, I left for college. Laura wept and I held back the tears as we said goodbye at the train station. We promised to write to each other and call at least once a week, and we did for a while. Her letters were penned on pink scented paper, filled with gushy romantic poems and promises of enduring love and crowded with hand drawn pictures of hearts in the margins. I remember her handwriting was loopy and every "i" was dotted with a happy face. They were lovely, emotional letters, and I think I may still have a few of them stuck between the pages of a college textbook. Other times, one of us would call, but those conversations were often interrupted when one of her parents wandered into the kitchen where the Beasley family phone was located and

Laura would whisper a quick, "I love you," then abruptly hang up.

I stopped answering her letters by the end of October. Whenever she called, I told her I was late for a class and couldn't talk or I made up some other excuse. At some point, I had become overcritical of her most superficial imperfections—the thick ankles, the knock-knees, the freckles. Besides, I had achieved my objective. And so, when we were both home for Thanksgiving, I took her out to McDonalds for a burger and broke up with her, citing some lame excuse about the futility of long distance relationships. She didn't react well, but I was adamant.

"I thought you said you loved me," she stammered grimly. "You said we'd be together forever. You said you would always be mine..."

I just shrugged.

"You just used me didn't you?"

I shrugged again.

"I *hate* you!"

It was a cold, heartless, unforgivable thing to do and I did it badly. I was a total asshole. I can still see her, tears running down her cheeks, her lips trembling, as I sat across the table from her, staring at the crumpled bun that crowned my half-eaten cheeseburger. After a moment, she balled up her napkin and threw it at me, but it missed and flew into the booth behind me. Then she ran clumsily out of the diner. I felt an odd sense of relief, in spite of the fact that everyone in the place was staring at me with undisguised contempt. But I coldly shrugged it off. By then, I had bigger fish to fry: College girls.

Laura... Now

A FEW DAYS AFTER I COAX Morris into accompanying me on my potentially humiliating and possibly useless pilgrimage, I drive up to Boston to pick him up. Having only committed to seven days on the road (for which he's cancelled the two Yeshiva classes he teaches every week), Morris is eager to get the whole thing over with. After we have a quick kosher lunch with Naomi and the kids, he grabs an enormous sausage-shaped duffel bag that smells vaguely of food, says goodbye to his family, assures Naomi that he'll call her periodically and follows me downstairs to my car. Once there, Morris tosses his single piece of luggage into the trunk and carefully maneuvers his massive frame into the passenger seat, letting out a few groans as he settles in. I watch him struggle to yank the seatbelt out far enough to accommodate his girth.

"Ready?" I ask, starting the car.

Morris looks at me. "Is this really necessary, Jimmy?" he asks. "I mean, are you absolutely certain you want to go to all this trouble?"

"Yup," I say firmly, "Why? Are you having second thoughts?"

"No, no, of course not. I'm happy to do it. But there's a much simpler method of achieving your goal," he tells me.

"Oh?"

"In my experience, it can be very helpful to turn to God for guidance at a time like this," he suggests. "Your guilt might be alleviated by the simple act of prayer. This would be much easier than a road trip."

"Forget it. God won't listen to me," I tell him. "But you've got an inside line, so if you want to say a prayer for me, feel free. It couldn't hurt."

"I'll take it under consideration," Morris says.

I watch him remove a handkerchief from his breast pocket and wipe his forehead. "So listen Morris, you think this trip will get me a few points with the Big Guy?"

"Points?" Morris replies. "God isn't a game show host, Jimmy."

I decide to drop the subject so I offer no response. This seems to be just fine with Morris, who is no doubt weary of discussing theology with an infidel. I notice that he's still perspiring, so I turn on the air and point the vents toward his face.

"I can't believe Deirdre's divorcing you," he says after a moment. "After all those years. My God."

"You know all the circumstances," I remind him. "It's not a big surprise."

Morris sighs and nods his head sadly. "So who is this Laura Beasley?" he asks me. "I don't remember that one."

"High school sweetheart," I tell him. "Before your time."

So I give him the abridged version of my involvement with Laura and, when I'm done, he shakes his head in disgust. "You know," he says, as I steer the car towards South Boston, "Yom Kippur is coming up soon. You could come to services with me and atone for all this."

"It's not really about atonement, Morris. It's about forgiveness," I reply. "And it has to come from my victims, not God, no offense."

"None taken," Morris assures me, turning in his seat to glance out the back window. "But I'm afraid you're a lost soul, my friend."

I have no idea what he's talking about. "Lost? How do you mean that exactly?"

"You just missed the turnpike on-ramp."

Half an hour later, after a few illegal u-turns, I manage to
maneuver us onto the Massachusetts Turnpike, heading toward
Great Barrington in western Massachusetts, where Laura lives.
I estimate the trip should take about two hours, barring any un-
foreseen obstacles. The closer we get, the more I'm filled with
apprehension. Suddenly, Morris's suggestion that prayer might
be a preferable means of redemption starts to sound much more
appealing to me. It would certainly be less torturous than the
dubious path I've chosen. But Ira's words echo in my ears, so I'm
determined to face the music.

As for Morris, he tries to kill time and cheer me up by rattling
off a litany of ancient one-liners, all of which I've already heard sixty
times. Then he takes a nap, snoring like a congested air conditioner.
I let him snooze until we get within ten miles of our destination.
Then I gently shake his shoulder until he stirs.

"What the fuck?" Morris mumbles as his eyelids pop open.

"Are you supposed to use language like that, being an orthodox
religious man and all?" I ask him.

"Sure," he replies, rubbing his eyes. "It's okay as long as I don't
take the Lord's name in vain."

"Very interesting," I muse. "So basically you can say just about
anything except 'goddamn'. Is that right?"

"Theoretically."

"You think Moses ever said 'shit'?"

"Who knows?"

"Maybe he said 'holy shit' when the Red Sea parted," I opine. "I
certainly would have. What's the Hebrew equivalent of 'holy shit'?"

Morris sighs. "I have no idea, Jimmy," he grumbles. "Can we
just drop the subject please?"

"Right," I say as we pull off the turnpike. I hand him a Map-
Quest map to Laura's house. He looks at it quizzically.

"What the hell?" he asks. "You don't have a GPS?"

"The first one broke," I tell him. "The second one almost directed me over a cliff so I tossed it."

"Even *I* have a GPS," he says. "I'd be lost without it."

This cracks us both up. After the laughter dissipates, we look at each other with affection in our eyes because we've both suddenly been transported back to the old days when we were close college buddies and shared plenty of laughs and plenty of grass. No words need to be exchanged to get that across.

"So use your iPhone," Morris says. "They have navigation right?"

"I don't actually have an iPhone," I confess.

"Android?"

"No."

He looks at me. "You own an electronics store and you don't have—"

"The map, Morris," I interrupt. "Just look at the map."

Morris searches his pockets and produces a pair of reading glasses. "Um... okay, her house is on 1456 West Lincoln Street," he informs me as we approach an intersection. When the streetlight turns green, I look over at him for guidance. "Make a right at the second light," he tells me.

Following his directions, I drive through a sparsely populated residential area, then past an elementary school, followed by a strip mall. After a few more blocks, I stop at a wrought iron gate. When I see the writing on it, I can barely believe my eyes. Lifting my sunglasses, I blink a few times in horror.

"Oh my God," I say incredulously. "This is not good. This is not good at all."

"Look at the bright side," Morris suggests sarcastically. "At least she probably won't injure you and I doubt she'll have a husband or a boyfriend."

"Stop joking around! You have no idea how awful I feel about this," I moan. "I'm probably responsible. Oh God, what have I done?"

"Don't look at me, Don Juan," Morris says. "Not my problem."

"But she's a Baptist," I point out. "Don't you have to be Catholic for this?"

"How should I know?" Morris asks. "I'm a Jew. We have different rules."

"Maybe she converted."

"Could be," Morris says. "Are you going to drive in or what?"

I sigh, but I don't go anywhere right away. I'm in a state of shock and my foot just won't make the short horizontal journey from the brake to the gas pedal. So I just stare at the words on the wrought iron gateway, hoping that I had misread them the first time.

"You want *me* to drive?" Morris offers, with a touch of annoyance. "We might actually get there sometime this month. We're on a tight schedule here."

"No, that's okay," I say uncertainly. "I can do it."

"So why don't you?"

"Don't rush me," I snap. "This is very traumatic for me."

Finally, I drive under the archway and head up a long, winding gravel drive toward a simple white chapel-like structure with a long brick building beside it. I pull to a stop.

"Obviously, you won't be needing me for this," Morris tells me. He pulls a folded newspaper page and a pencil out of his breast pocket and turns to a Sudoku puzzle. "I'm addicted to these," he says. Then he pats me on the cheek. "Good luck, my brother."

"You're a real source of strength, Morris," I say. "Would it kill you to offer a word or two of encouragement?"

"What could I possibly say that would make this better?" he asks.

Then he starts penciling numbers in the puzzle squares and waves for me to go.

I sit there for a moment, trying to decide what the hell I'm going to say to Laura, who is probably *Sister* Laura at this point. Oh God. She may not even agree to see me.

Just as I'm about to step out of the car, one of the nuns emerges from the convent door and slowly makes her way towards me, aided by a gnarled wooden cane. She's maybe eighty, wizened, and her nose is so bulbous and red you might conclude that she has a drinking problem if you didn't know better, although they probably keep a lot of red wine handy for blessings. As she approaches me, I detect a trace of wariness beneath her placid smile. They probably don't get too many civilian guests at the convent, except maybe plumbers, stonemasons, electricians and the occasional pizza deliveryman.

"May I help you?" she asks me. "I'm the Mother Superior."

"Yes," I reply. I'm not sure if I'm supposed to call her "Sister" or "Mother," so I don't call her anything. "I'm looking for one of the Sisters. Her name is Laura Beasley. I need to speak to her. It's quite urgent."

She studies me for a second, peering over the frame of a pair of reading glasses held together by black tape. "Laura Beasley? I'm afraid there's no one by that name here," she informs me.

"Are you sure?"

"Quite sure."

I have no idea what to make of that. Has Laura died? Left the nunnery? Changed her name? Joined the merchant marine?

"This is 1456 West Lincoln, right?" I ask her.

She smiles and shakes her head. "No, young man," she says. "This is 1456 *East* Lincoln."

This bit of good news causes my heart to resume beating at its normal pace again, and I almost hug her, but I control myself. Laura is not a nun! I want to say "thank God," but I figure that's probably inappropriate under the circumstances. Or maybe it isn't.

"Guess I made a little mistake," I confess.

"Don't you have a GPS?"

"Not at the moment," I reply. "Sorry to bother you."

"No worries," she says. "It happens all the time. You want to turn left at the gate, drive past the Burger King and keep going. It's not very far."

"Thank you very much," I say.

"My pleasure," she replies. "Have a nice day."

"Thanks. You too."

"Perhaps you might want to make a donation," she says as I start walking away.

"Yes, of course," I say. I reach into my back pocket and pull a couple of twenties from my wallet.

"God bless you," she says, her eyes widening as she counts the cash.

That'll be the day, I'm thinking. Then she turns and walks back into the building. I climb into the car and sock Morris on the arm.

"What the hell?" he exclaims, dropping his pencil.

"Some fucking navigator you are," I tell him. "This is the wrong fucking address."

"Serves you right," Morris says with a yawn. "Who drives around without a GPS these days?"

I growl and start the car.

~

Ten minutes later, after a short argument about navigation, we're parked across the street from a red brick ranch house, your typical suburban dwelling, featuring a small front lawn mottled with several dry patches, an erratically manicured wall of ivy, a group of plaster gnomes planted in the center of a flower patch and a pair of bikes lying in the driveway. Two kids are playing catch with an old yellow tennis ball in the front yard. Parked in the driveway, behind the bikes, is a dusty late-model SUV with a bike rack on top and the words "wash me" scrawled by someone's finger in the dust. I glance at my watch. It's three o'clock in the afternoon.

"Knock yourself out pal," Morris says.

"Wait a minute," I protest. "You're supposed to be my... deterrent. What if her husband is home and he has an arsenal?"

"Then you might get shot," he says. "I'm here primarily for moral support, remember? I'm not a bodyguard. We discussed this."

"I may need moral support," I whine. "Can you please just walk me to the door?"

"Fine, now we're in second grade," Morris says with a hefty sigh. "Let's roll."

With some huffing and puffing, he struggles to squeeze out of the car. After a moment, I follow him towards the house, but I'm suddenly gripped by fear and seriously consider running away and hiding behind some tall shrubbery. Instead, I stop abruptly on the slate walkway, a few feet from where the kids are playing catch.

"Hey kids," I say pleasantly. "Is your mom home?"

"Yup," one of them responds, tossing the ball straight up in the air and circling under it.

"How about your dad?"

"Nope."

"Is he at work?"

"Yup."

"I'm guessing he comes home around five or six."

The kid catches the ball. "Yup."

"Does he ever come home early?"

"Nope."

As I marvel at the diversity of the young man's vocabulary, Morris pats me on the back and starts walking back to the car.

"Where are you going?" I ask him.

"I'm almost done with the puzzle," he tells me. "It's an easy one."

"So finish it later," I say.

"I really don't think you'll be in any grave danger here, Jimmy," he says. "No husband with a baseball bat. If things don't work out, you can cry on my shoulder later."

He has a point. The only danger will be strictly emotional. On the other hand, maybe she'll be incensed enough to throw a cast iron skillet at me. I can handle that. I have pretty good reflexes. I'll just have to keep a close eye on the cutlery. At least she's not in a nunnery. That's a blessing.

So I march up the walkway like a death row inmate who has an appointment with a syringe, climb the porch steps, think seriously about dashing back to the car, take a deep breath instead and then ring the doorbell.

She's gained about ten pounds and her long red hair has been dyed brown and cut into a kind of suburban Prince Valiant bob, but otherwise she looks about the same. Obviously, I don't, because she doesn't seem to recognize me. But then I notice that she's not wearing her glasses (they're hanging on a chain around her neck) so that might be the problem.

"Can I help you?" she asks, smiling broadly. She's wearing an apron over a shapeless T-shirt, a pair of jeans rolled up at the ankles and blue beat-up running shoes. In her left hand is a vacuum cleaner hose.

I stand there for a moment with my arms slightly away from my sides, as if this will somehow improve her memory. "You don't recognize me do you?" I inquire.

"Should I?"

"Take a good look."

She gives me the once over and then grins. "Are you one of those nice Jehovah's Witnesses who came by last week?" she asks. "Because if you are, I'm still not interested in reading your pamphlets."

"Put on your glasses," I tell her.

Her brow wrinkles. "How do you know I wear glasses?"

"You'll figure that out as soon as you put them on," I assure her. "Plus they're hanging around your neck."

"Oh," she says with a self-deprecating wave of her hand. "Silly me."

She fumbles for the neck chain and carefully slides the glasses on. After blinking a few times, she puts a hand over her mouth and her eyes widen as if she's just witnessed a fatal car crash. I'm waiting for her to punch me in the jaw, but she doesn't.

"Oh my God. *Jimmy?* Jimmy Hendricks?" she exclaims, backing a few steps away from me to take in the whole package.

"Bingo!" I say.

"Holy shit, I don't know what to say! This is such a surprise! Jesus, how many years has it been?"

"About twenty-two, give or take."

"My God has it been that long?" she says shaking her head in amazement.

"That's right."

"Where did the time go?"

"You might want to ask a physicist."

Her laugh hasn't changed a bit. "Still the kidder," she observes. I shrug modestly. "So what the devil are you doing here, Jimmy?"

"It's a long story, Laura," I inform her. "May I come in?"

"Yes, of course. How rude of me. Please."

The inside of the house is all hardwood floors and beige walls. She follows me in after closing the door and then leads me to the living room, which is tastefully decorated with a crowded gallery of family photos on the mantle, an upright Yamaha piano in the corner and a fake ficus tree in front of a picture window. A maroon leather couch, a chair and a brown BarcaLounger surround a flat screen TV. Sporting equipment and a colorful assortment of cat toys litter the floor. As I sit down, I notice that there are no religious icons to be found anywhere, not a single crucifix or portrait of Jesus.

"Can I get you something to drink, Jimmy?" she asks, fidgeting with the hem of her apron and patting her hair. "I have lemonade, beer and Coke. Jesus, I'm still in shock. You're the last person I expected to see today."

"No thanks," I say with a smile. "I'm fine."

"Are you sure?" she asks, leaning the vacuum hose against an armchair. "It's a hot one today."

"Yes. Thank you. Nice of you to offer. Maybe later."

She wipes her glasses on her apron and looks me over again. "You look good, Jimmy," she tells me. "I can't believe I didn't recognize you."

"Yeah well, thanks for the compliment, but the fact is I've gained a few pounds."

"Like I haven't?" she says, giving me a crooked smile. "I never could get rid of this butt after giving birth to the boys. I'm still trying. I go to Jenny Craig once a week and do yoga and Pilates."

"I didn't even notice," I tell her. "You look exactly the same."

"Yeah right."

"No, I really mean it."

"Well thank you very much," she says, skeptically, "but you're totally full of shit anyway."

I'm not quite ready to get to the point of my visit, so I employ a delaying tactic. "How's your father?" I ask earnestly.

"Dad passed away a few years ago," she informs me without much emotion. "Heart attack. Right in the pulpit."

"I'm sorry to hear that."

"Thank you, Jimmy," she says. "I'm surprised it wasn't a thunderbolt. Funny thing is, I'm not all that sad about it. But I guess he's with God now."

"I'm sure he is," I say somberly, wondering whether God would really want a sourpuss like Reverend Beasley skulking around Heaven, preaching abstention and making sure nobody has any fun.

"And your Mom?"

"She has cancer."

"I'm sorry," I tell her.

There's a moment of silence. Laura produces a tissue and wipes her eyes with it.

"I didn't mean to bring up a sad subject," I say.

"Oh it's not that," she says. "It's allergy season."

"Ah."

Laura blows her nose and puts the tissue in her apron pocket. "So you still haven't told me why you're here," she says, struggling to remove her apron. "Not that I'm not glad to see you."

"I was in the neighborhood so I thought I'd stop in."

"Horse shit," she says. "Nobody comes to this neighborhood, unless they go the wrong way and get lost on the way to the convent. Some people are such total idiots when it comes to following directions. Even with a GPS."

"How true."

We both nod a few times as if I had just said something deeply philosophical. "So why are you *really* here?" she asks me again.

I take a deep breath. "Okay, actually it's pretty delicate," I begin, leaning forward, my clasped hands resting between my knees. "The fact is, Laura, lately I've been feeling very guilty about how we left things that fall after high school and I've come here to apologize for my behavior. I should have answered your letters. I should have taken you out when we were on vacation. I was a rat. It was inexcusable. I know that now and I'm sorry."

When I'm satisfied that I've adequately denigrated myself, I sit back on the couch, nervously awaiting her response, but she says nothing.

"It's kind of a conscience thing," I add. "If you're still angry at me, I'll understand. You have every right to be. I just need to know."

"Oh Jimmy," she says, waving her hand as if I'd just said something incredibly trivial. "I'm not angry. Sure, I was really pissed off at the time. In fact, I cried for weeks, but I got over it a long time ago. You were just a horny guy like all guys that age. Always on the make. Brain in your dick. But I really enjoyed our time together. It was a wonderful summer."

For some reason, I'm not satisfied by her response. It's so... casual. "I told you that I loved you to get you to have sex with me," I tell her.

"Of course you did," she says with a laugh. "I knew that."

"You did?"

"Sure," she says.

I can't believe how smoothly this is going. Maybe I've been too hard on myself. "You mean you have no hard feelings at all?" I ask her.

"Not really," she reflects, shaking her head. "Not anymore."

"Are you sure?"

"Yes," she says brightly, although I think I detect a barely perceptible trace of uncertainty in her tone.

"But I took your, um, virginity," I tell her, "and then I dropped you like a hot potato. And now I feel terrible about it. How I treated you and all. I'm here to ask you to forgive me."

She turns her head away and laughs. "My virginity?" she asks. "You didn't take my virginity, Jimmy."

I frown in perplexity and study her face with one eye half closed. Is she in denial? Did somebody get to her before me? Is she delusional? I'm reasonably sure the sex-starved culprit had been me.

"What do you mean?" I ask finally. "It was the night before I went off to college. I remember it vividly."

"Just trust me, Jimmy. You didn't take my virginity."

"I'm sorry, you'll have to explain that," I continue. "I'm pretty sure I did. My memory is still fairly good."

"You really want to know?"

"Yes."

"I don't think you do."

"I do. Lay it on me."

"Okay." She turns her head away again and gazes out the picture window at the kids playing on the lawn.

"That night..." she starts to say. "How can I put this without embarrassing you? That night..."

"That night what?" I ask. "You won't offend me, I promise."

She closes her eyes for a moment as if trying to visualize the situation. "That night, you... were done before you ever got to my..."

"Your what?" I ask impatiently.

Now Laura is blushing. "You know... my vagina."

Now I'm confused. "Huh?" I say. "I don't get it."

She sighs. This is clearly a struggle for her. "You, um... ejaculated before you got past my thighs," she explains, after taking a deep breath. "You were very worked up that night and it was pretty dark. I think they call it premature ejaculation. I read about it in *Cosmo* once in my gynecologist's waiting room. It happens to a lot of teenage boys."

"Oh," is all I can muster.

The expression on my face must have been slightly forlorn because she gives me a sympathetic look. But then I remember something—we'd done it more than once that night. Three times, in fact. I couldn't possibly have screwed up *three times*. Besides, I recall that I'd used all three rubbers. There is no doubt in my mind that I took her virginity, if not on the first pass, then definitely on the second or third. But I decide not to mention it.

"I'm really sorry, Jimmy," she says, lowering her eyes. "I hope I didn't spoil things for you. But that's the way it was. I was intact until I married Kenny."

"Kenny?"

"Kenny Moran."

Now I'm really shocked. "You married Kenny Moran?" I say, trying not to sound too incredulous. "How come I never knew that?"

"We kept it kinda secret when you were in town during college breaks," she says. "He didn't want to tell you on account of the crush you had on me in high school. He thought you'd be hurt. I never told him about our fling. Then we moved out of town."

"Oh," I say. "So how long have you two been—?"

"Twenty years in September!" she says proudly.

"But..."

"But what?"

"Nobody could understand anything he ever said because—"

"He didn't have halitosis anymore when we started dating," she informs me. "A dentist gave him some medication and that fixed it. It was some weird bacteria or fungus or something. He's very sweet and so is his breath. We have two kids. Boys. You must have seen one of them playing on the front lawn. That's Kevin, the one with the moussed-up hair. Kyle's at a friend's house. How about you, Jimmy? Wife, kids...?"

"Pending divorce, no kids," I tell her. "You seem happy."

She thinks about it. "Yeah, I guess," she says without much enthusiasm. "Are you sure you don't want a Coke or something?"

~

Laura insists that Morris and I stay for dinner, so three hours later, we're all gathered around a circular dining room table, wolfing down slices of pepperoni pizza from the neighborhood Papa John's, except for Morris who, for religious reasons, isn't partaking of the pizza. He's consuming a soggy kosher brisket sandwich he'd brought along, which explains the food smell from his duffel. Kenny and I are drinking Coors out of the bottle and Laura is well into her second glass of burgundy. The kids—Kevin and Kyle—sit next to each other, looking sullen and slurping down chocolate milk.

Earlier, when Kenny came home, he didn't recognize me right away either, but once Laura filled him in ("You'll never guess who's here! Jimmy Hendricks!"), he seemed genuinely glad to see me and gave me a hearty hug, slapping my back a few times, as men tend to do when they hug. Then he leaned very close to me, opened his mouth wide and breathed into my face.

"See, Jimmy," he said proudly. "It's all gone. My dentist said I had some kind of fungal bacteria problem or whatever. It's kinda like athlete's foot only in your mouth."

"Laura told me," I said, feigning amazement. "You can actually talk now."

"Cool huh?"

"So maybe later you can translate everything you said to me in high school for four years."

"You're kidding me, right?"

"Right."

Kenny laughed. "Always the kidder," he said.

And then he told me about his job as manager of the local Carpeteria branch which, frankly, wasn't all that captivating, but I was polite and asked him a few random questions about the durability of carpet pile and stain remover. Not that owning an electronics store is exactly all that thrilling. However, I did find it a little odd that he managed a carpet business but lived in a house with hardwood floors. He hadn't really changed much—same basic features, maybe a little larger around the waistline, hairline receding a little. Laura winked at me as she informed Kenny that I was traveling on business in the area and had stopped in to say hello. She referred to Morris as my associate.

As Laura had told me, Kenny didn't know anything about the virginity issue or that Laura and I had even dated. That summer he'd spent a few weeks with relatives, then worked as a counselor at some math camp in Connecticut. I'd left for college before he'd returned. That same summer, my other best friend, Leonard, had spent three months at his uncle's dude ranch in Colorado. Although they'd been my best friends, I hadn't seen either of them much after I'd gone off to college.

So we're all sitting around the big oak table like characters from a Norman Rockwell painting. Very homey. The pizza has been decimated, and now Morris is the only one still filling his face. The kids ask to be excused and disappear into the den to play Xbox. I finish my beer and Laura dutifully scurries to the fridge to get me another, half of which I guzzle down. By now, the alcohol buzz is making me feel all warm and sentimental.

"I don't know about you guys," I say, stifling a burp, "but I sure miss the good old high school days," which is a lie. Nobody misses high school.

"So do I," Laura reflects wistfully, winking at me. I begin to realize that she's probably had one too many glasses of wine because I know she couldn't possibly have enjoyed the old days at Rimbaldi that much. Her wink was a little obvious and I'm afraid that Kenny will notice.

"I hated Rimbaldi," says Kenny. "You know...the breath thing. It was hell. Can you imagine what it's like not being able to communicate with people?"

"Edward Suretzky never communicated with people," Laura points out.

"That's because he was a deaf mute," Kenny counters, with a condescending laugh. "It's not the same thing at all, Laura."

"You're right, Kenny," Laura concedes. She looks down at her plate and starts rearranging her flatware. "It was stupid of me to say that."

We sit in silence for a moment. Kenny picks a few pieces of pepperoni off the cardboard pizza box and eats them, chewing slowly. Then he takes a long sip of beer.

"God, I was such a dork back then," I say. I glance at Laura, who's expressionless. I hear a barely audible snicker coming from Morris.

"We were all dorks," Kenny reflects, pulling some cheese off the box. "Shit, I was the biggest dork in the world. But you were a really great guy, Jimmy, dork or no dork."

"I was?"

"You bet. If it wasn't for you and Leonard, I wouldn't have had any friends at all on account of my... you know... problem."

"I always thought you were very polite and thoughtful," Laura says, pouring herself a third glass of wine. Evidently, she has momentarily forgotten her pact to keep Kenny out of the loop regarding our past relationship. I glance furtively at Kenny. "And you had a great sense of humor," she adds. "I always thought you were very funny, but in a nice way."

"You never say *I'm* funny," Kenny says, perturbed.

"That's because you're not funny, sweetie," Laura replies.

"I can be funny," Kenny counters, shooting her a nasty look.

"Sure you can, honey," Laura says, wiping a drop of wine from her chin with a napkin. "I don't know why I even said that."

Now Kenny eyes Laura suspiciously. "Wait a minute. How did you know he was funny?" he inquires. "You never even met him."

"I um, saw him at the Baskin Robbins once, during the summer after graduation, while you were away," Laura stammers, again winking at me. "He worked there and he was kind of funny."

"That's odd," I say, trying to lend some credibility to her story. "I don't remember you coming in."

"You probably had tons of customers," she says. "It was summer. Lots of people buy ice cream in the summer."

"Lots of people buy ice cream in the summer," Kenny repeats with a snicker. "Now there's an insight."

As Laura shoots her husband a meek glance, I decide to change the subject again. "Okay, I was a funny guy. What else?"

"I would never have passed physics without you," Kenny says, smiling widely enough for me to see that he has some cheese gook lodged in the corner of his mouth. "You practically did all my chemistry homework for me."

"I did?"

"Oh yeah. You don't remember?"

"No."

"Then there was the time you stole the lab rats from Mrs. Pearl's biology class and set them free," Kenny adds, slapping the table. "That was really something, Jimmy. That was like, heroic."

"That I *do* remember," I say.

"You were pretty cool," Kenny tells me.

"I was?"

"A lot of girls had crushes on you," Laura informs me.

"Get out. Like who?"

"Leslie French."

"Leslie French from the softball team?"

Kenny snorts. "She never had a crush on Jimmy," he says. "That's total bull crap Laura, and you know it."

"Yes she did," Laura insists. "Everybody knew about it."

"Is that a fact? So who told *you*?" Kenny asks haughtily. "You weren't even on the softball team."

"I don't know, I just heard it around," Laura replies with a shrug.

"Well I sure didn't," I say. Leslie French was pretty in a way, but her feet were enormous and she walked like a duck.

"People thought you were very *mysterious*," Laura tells me, resuming her critique of my adolescent personality. She glances at Kenny. "Or so I heard."

Laura polishes off her glass of wine and pours herself another, undeterred by the dirty look Kenny shoots her way. She's so tipsy at this point, I'm afraid she's going to teeter off her chair.

I look at the both of them and smile. "But enough about me," I say. "What the hell have you guys been doing since high school?"

So Kenny fills me in: Laura quit Bible school after six months and returned home to live with her parents briefly. To assuage her father's displeasure, she taught Sunday school for a short time, but later she gave up Jesus and got a bartending job at The Inn, which was where she met Kenny, who would go there every night after work, his briefcase loaded with carpet swatches. Six months after they met, while I spent the summer working as a stock clerk for a clothing store in Boston, Laura and Kenny found an apartment in the next town and lived together for two years before getting married. Soon after that, Kenny was offered a better-paying managerial position in western Massachusetts, which he took. Then, along came Kevin and then Kyle...

"What about Leonard?" I ask. "It seemed like he just disappeared."

"Joined the Navy," Kenny says.

"Leonard joined the Navy?" I ask, incredulous.

"He's just a quartermaster," Kenny says. "At least he was the last time I heard, which was years ago. I think he lives on some base in Virginia."

When he finishes the back story, I make a lame toast about the good old days and we all clink, except for Morris, who's way too involved in his second brisket sandwich to notice.

～

After dinner, Kenny and Morris retire to the living room to discuss theology or the Red Sox—I'm not sure which—while Laura and I clear the dishes. By this time, Laura is clearly finding it difficult to walk in a straight line. Instead of washing and drying, which would have been a serious challenge for her, she fumbles in a drawer for a hidden pack of cigarettes and a lighter. Then she grabs my hand and leads me outside to the backyard, where we sit in adjacent rattan rocking chairs on the back porch and quietly gaze up at the heavens. Laura lights up, takes a long drag and blows a series of smoke rings between hiccups. The sky is perfectly clear and I point out

a few constellations just to fill up the silence. After she stubs out
her cigarette and expertly flings the butt into a hedge, she pulls her
knees up to her chest and hugs them, just as she did the night we
first met at the bus stop bench near her father's church. Suddenly,
I'm overcome by a warm rush of fond memories.

"Kenny doesn't like it when I smoke," she explains.

"Oh."

"He's very strict about it," she says. "He's very strict about a lot
of things actually."

Then she shpritzes some Binaca in her mouth, wincing at the
sharp taste. "Hey, you want to see the tree house Kenny and a friend
built for the kids?" she asks, slurring her words a bit. "It's very cool."

Before I have a chance to respond, she snatches my hand, pulls
me out of my seat and leads me unsteadily across the yard to a ma-
jestic old oak, against which a makeshift ladder stands. I follow
close behind her as she wobbles upwards toward the plywood tree
house, missing the occasional rung, and I can't help but notice her
still shapely, but somewhat wider, posterior at it sways rhythmically above me, though the possibility that she could easily fall on
me keeps me alert. In a moment, we're standing in the center of
an elaborate wooden structure nestled in a cradle formed by four
thick, leafy, branches. The place is littered from wall to wall with
camping equipment, including two sleeping bags, a fishing rod and,
incongruously, a soccer ball. Laura promptly trips over a Coleman
stove, pitches forward, and falls into my arms.

"Oops," I say. "Gotta watch your step in—"

"Kiss me," she demands with a goofy, alcohol-induced grin.

"What?"

"You heard me."

I try to take a short step to the right, but she doesn't release
me from the embrace. "Is that really a good idea?" I ask, glancing
toward the back of the house to make sure no one's there. To my

relief, I can see through the living room window that Kenny and Morris are still involved in their discussion "What about Kenny?" I ask her.

"He'll never know."

"Yes but—"

"Just one little kiss, Jimmy," she insists, looking up at me with plaintive eyes. "That's all. I just want to feel what it was like back then, just for a second. Come on."

I hesitate for a moment, staring at the freckles on her nose, but before I can decide what to do, she throws her arms around my neck and kisses me. Her breath smells of wine, cigarettes and Binaca, a little rancid, but not unpleasant. The kiss lasts about thirty seconds and when we separate, her eyes are still closed while mine are glued to the living room window.

"Mmmmm, that was soooo nice," she coos, smiling dreamily. "It feels like I just took a step back into the past."

I smile and Laura finds a tissue and wipes her lipstick from my mouth.

And then we climb back down.

～

When it's time for us to go, Kenny and Laura both implore me to keep in touch and I promise that I will. On the front porch of their house, Laura gives me a quick, innocent peck on the cheek. Apparently still giddy, she offers me yet another sly wink and a crooked smile. I begin to fear the possibility that, in her drunken state, she might blab something to Kenny about our past relationship or our recent moment in the tree house.

While Laura waves from the porch, Kenny walks us to the car.

"So listen," he says quietly. "You're not pissed about Laura and me, are you?"

"What do you mean?" I ask.

"Well, I know you had a crush on her in high school and all," he says.

"Of course I'm not pissed," I tell him. "That was twenty years ago."

"Okay, that's good," Kenny says. "I was a little worried."

"No need," I say. "Now give me a hug, big guy."

Kenny smiles widely and we embrace, which I immediately regret for fear that he might pick up a whiff of Laura's perfume on me, but he doesn't.

Twenty minutes later, Morris and I find a Motel Six. While I unpack my overnight kit, Morris takes a hot shower. Twenty minutes later he's stretched out on top of his bedspread in his boxer shorts, idly thumbing through the Gideon Bible from his nightstand, as if he was looking through the Yellow Pages for a plumber.

"So," Morris says, sounding like a therapist. "Did you learn anything from this experience?"

"I don't know," I tell him. "Maybe I wasn't that big of an asshole after all."

"Don't count your chickens. We still have two to go," he says, placing the Bible on the nightstand. "Turn off the light, will you? I need some shut-eye."

I have a hard time falling asleep because I can't stop thinking about Laura and our strange moment of intimacy in the tree house. I begin to ponder how different my life would have been had I married her instead of Deirdre. Chances are we'd still be happily married, living contentedly on a sunny, tree-lined street in the suburbs. Maybe we'd have a couple of kids; she'd be a member of the PTA; I'd be assistant Little League coach. I'd teach our kids how to ride bikes and swim; we'd vacation at Disney World, maybe buy a timeshare in a house on a lake somewhere. It's an intriguing, but thoroughly unrealistic dream and it eventually lulls me into a deep coma. By the next morning, reality hits me in the eye like the harsh ray of sunlight that filters through the motel window, and I realize that trying to choreograph what might have been, although tantalizing enough, doesn't amount to much more than a good way to get to sleep.

Part Three

Samantha

Samantha... Then

SAMANTHA JANE CONRAD was a purebred, white Anglo-Saxon Protestant from Darien, Connecticut, Switzerland, Biarritz, the Italian Riviera and everywhere else the fabulously wealthy park their Bentleys. She was also probably the richest girl at Fryman College, not that I went around asking women how much they were worth. But you didn't need to ask—her brand new Mercedes, her collection of Louis Vuitton handbags and her ridiculously expensive designer wardrobe told the tale. By contrast, I carried around a battered backpack and my closet boasted four pairs of bleached Levis, six T-shirts, a Rimbaldi sweatshirt, a bunch of mostly mismatching socks and faded jockey shorts, an old parka, two ancient wool sweaters and one weather-beaten pair of running shoes. Also, I had a hideous dented 1982 Chevy Impala that spent about a fourth of its life under the foster care of a tattooed, chain-smoking Ukrainian mechanic named Yegor.

As I learned later, Samantha had been brought up by a series of English nannies, spoke three languages fluently and had attended an exorbitant all-girls' private secondary school in Switzerland, where she'd studied literature. Unfortunately though, her grades were less than spectacular so, when she completed her senior year, her father tried to finagle her way into Vassar by giving the college a huge donation, but I guess the bribe wasn't sufficient enough to

sway the admissions staff. Poor Samantha ended up at lowly Fryman College, where she was compelled to suffer ordinary, unwashed
peasants like me.

Considering her background, it was no surprise to anyone that
Samantha was a snob. Actually, she gave new meaning to the term.
I'd only met one snob in my life, a kid named Edgar Ferguson whose
father owned the leather factory in my town. But never mind that.
The outstanding thing about Samantha was that she was drop-dead
gorgeous: Silky black hair, dark tempestuous eyes, long slender legs,
a perfectly straight nose that spent most of its time in a haughty
sneering position and a spectacular smile, if you could get her to
smile, which was next to impossible. In short, Samantha looked as
if she'd popped out of the pages of *Vogue* and she knew it.

Freshman year, Samantha refused to live in anything as Dick-
ensian as an overcrowded dorm, so her father bought her a huge
penthouse apartment two blocks from the college. She always drove
the short distance, probably so the other kids could salivate at the
sight of her fabulous wheels. She even had her own personal on-
campus parking space, a luxury theretofore reserved exclusively
for members of the faculty and administration. Except for two
other pompous girls whose parents were also nauseatingly well-
heeled, Samantha didn't have any friends on campus, let alone a
boyfriend. The rest of the proletariat gave her a wide berth, since
she practically had the words "buzz off" tattooed on her forehead.
She and her friends seemed to harbor nothing but sneering disdain
for everybody else on campus.

All of which made her unapproachable, at least for someone
of my humble origin. Had I been a yachtsman, a polo player or a
competent shooter of skeet, things might have been different. In any
case, I was not about to waste my time chasing someone I would
never be able to catch.

Or so I thought.

~

I first became aware of Samantha Jane Conrad on my third day at Fryman when I found my dorm roommate, Sanjee Pancholy, drooling over her picture in the freshman class orientation pamphlet. Samantha's photo appeared to have been taken by a professional because she was the only one in the catalogue who didn't look either constipated or bug-eyed. Of course, she wasn't smiling. Her long neck was turned slightly to the side, her eyes were ablaze and her chin was tilted upward, all of which gave her a condescending look. To me, her picture resembled a 1940s Hollywood glamour shot.

Sanjee and I were drinking tall bottles of Taj Mahal beer which had been supplied by his father, who owned a Punjabi restaurant in Chicago and thought it was his responsibility to keep his son well lubricated. A case of it stood beside our shared mini-fridge. Sanjee and I had only known each other for three days and were still struggling to find common territory, a process that partially resolved itself when he filled the space over his bed with a poster of a half-naked Madonna, whose sultry eyes seemed to be staring directly at the centerfold of Miss February that I had taped at approximately the same latitude across the room over my bed.

"She must be Swiss or something," Sanjee speculated, pointing to the pompous title of Samantha's Zurich finishing school—Institute Villa Ste. Jean—which was printed in bold italics below the photo.

I looked over his shoulder. "I don't think Conrad's a Swiss name," I told him. "Sounds kind of English to me. She's probably a Brit."

Sanjee had a dreamy look in his eyes. "I've always wanted to make it with a European girl," he said, dog-earing the page that featured Samantha's picture. "No sexual hang-ups, no inhibitions..." But then a frown clouded his face and he stroked his chin. "You think she shaves her armpits?"

"My guess would be yes, but you never know."

"Legs?"

I shrugged.

"If she doesn't, I can live with that," Sanjee decided. "Hairy armpits or not, she's totally sexy."

"True," I agreed glancing over his shoulder. "But if you ask me, she looks a little..."

"A little what?"

"I don't know," I said with a shrug. "A little snotty."

Sanjee grabbed a magnifying glass from his desk drawer and began to move it up and down in front of the picture until he achieved maximum focus. "You think so?" he asked. "I don't see it."

"Just a guess," I said.

Sanjee closed one eye and looked at me suspiciously. "I've got dibs, Jimbo," he said, closing the pamphlet. "I saw her first."

I had no problem with that—she looked like the sort of girl who was way out of my league anyway—so I walked over to my side of the room, slipped a Springsteen CD into my boom box, plopped down on my bed and started to peruse my own copy of the book, making a check mark beside the name of each girl who looked remotely like a dating prospect. I didn't mention it to Sanjee, but I had a strong feeling that Samantha Jane Conrad couldn't possibly look that good in person.

~

Sanjee was from Evanston, Illinois, and, to hear him tell it, you'd think he had bedded every woman within a seventy-five mile radius of his house. I knew he was full of shit, but I couldn't help but admire the limitless scope of his immodesty. As roommates, we stuck close to each other during those first few months at Fryman, secure in the knowledge that each of us had at least one friend on campus, but also aware that one day we would make new friends and probably drift apart. I would lay awake at night, listening to him reminisce, in far more graphic detail than was actually required, about how he had once gotten laid on a Delta jet at thirty-thousand feet, an endless saga that included such information as what kind of prophylactic he had used and what happens when you accidentally flush a pair of panties down an airplane lavatory toilet. The whole story was clearly bogus but amusing nonetheless.

So it didn't really surprise me when, after two weeks of attempting to make contact with Samantha Jane Conrad, Sanjee had made no measurable progress. Although he was a fairly handsome kid, it was obvious even to me that his technique lacked several key elements, subtlety being the most glaring of the lot. He was too aggressive, too full of himself, too corny. Samantha just ignored him, but then she seemed to ignore pretty much everyone, mostly guys with agendas like Sanjee's.

"You were right, Jimbo," he finally confessed to me one afternoon as we smoked a joint under an ancient elm in the quad. "She is definitely a snob. World class. Won't even talk to me." Then he smiled uncertainly. "But I think the ice is melting."

"What makes you think that?" I asked.

"She sat next to me in political science class," Sanjay said. "There are thirty seats in that classroom, but she took the one right next to me. It's a breakthrough."

"Were there any other seats left?" I asked.

"Three," Sanjee admitted. "But still…"

One night, Sanjee and I crashed a members-only Theta Chi party, which was a fairly simple task, provided you waited long enough for the frat boys to get so wasted that they didn't notice the hordes of party crashers streaming through the front door.

On the way in, Sanjee and I each grabbed a bottle of beer from an enormous cooler and positioned ourselves on a beat up sofa that afforded us an excellent view of the dance floor, where a number of drunken frat boys, most of them either half naked or sporting odd hats and colorful facial paint, were attempting to maintain their balance while gyrating gracelessly to a song that was blasting from a pair of oversized speakers. To our chagrin, most of the women in the room appeared to be spoken for, but the night was young, so we decided to stay for another hour or so, hoping that our dream girls would eventually wander in unaccompanied, eager to find male companionship. Then Sanjee turned his neck to peer behind the couch, and the next thing I knew his elbow was repeatedly stabbing me in the ribs.

"Oh my God. Don't look now," he whispered, excitedly, "but she's standing right behind us."

"Who is?"

"Take a wild guess."

I shrugged.

Sanjee rolled his eyes. "*Samantha,*" he hissed.

Ignoring his command, I promptly swiveled around to take a look. Samantha and her two snotty friends were standing by a wall, holding mixed drinks and chatting, their faces displaying such profound boredom and disdain that I had to wonder why they were even there. It must have been a slow night at the yacht club.

This was the first time I had actually seen Samantha in the flesh. She was even more gorgeous than her photo. I could barely take my eyes off her. Against my better judgment, I was instantly smitten, but I was instantly smitten a lot in those days.

"For Christ sake," Sanjee whispered angrily. "*I said don't look.* Jesus, what's the matter with you, Hendricks?"

I shrugged. "I don't think they noticed," I said. "In fact, if you stuck yourself in the chest with a steak knife right now, they probably wouldn't notice."

Sanjee ignored the remark and chugged his beer until the bottle was empty. "This is my big chance," he said, grabbing my beer out of my hand and chugging that one too.

"What the fuck?" I said.

"I need fortification," he responded.

"Right."

Then Sanjee handed my beer back. "It's showtime," he announced with the cadence of a game show announcer.

"Good luck," I told him.

"Piece of cake," he said.

Sanjee hesitated for a moment, either trying to summon up his courage or harboring second thoughts. He took a deep breath, patted his hair, checked to make sure his fly was zipped up, cleared his throat a few times, rose from the couch and circled back to where Samantha and her friends were holding up the wall. I didn't look, but the music had temporarily stopped and I could hear the entire conversation.

"Hello ladies," Sanjee said brightly.

No answer.

"Come here often?"

No answer.

"Neither do I."

No answer.

"So do you believe in love at first sight or should I walk by again?" Sanjee asked with a chuckle. I winced. This was one of his stock lines, and it never worked.

No answer. Sanjee cleared his throat. I thought about trying to rescue him from certain humiliation, but I didn't know how.

"Listen," he continued, seemingly undeterred by abject failure. "Can I have your phone number? I seem to have lost mine."

Once again, no response. Now Sanjee's voice was wavering. I could visualize the three of them glaring at him.

"Anybody care to dance?"

No answer.

"That's cool."

No answer.

"You speak English right?"

No answer.

"Well it was nice talking to you ladies," he said. "You have a nice night."

I looked behind me and saw Samantha cast him a withering glance which seemed to make Sanjee shrink by about three inches. A second later, he rejoined me on the sofa, where he slouched so low that the back cushions hid him from Samantha and her snobbish friends, not that they were even paying any attention. He looked positively despondent and I couldn't help but feel a pang of sympathy. I handed him my half empty beer bottle, but he just handed it back.

"Fuck this," he said.

～

In the second quarter of that year, I took a creative writing class—Elements of Fiction 102—which was taught by a fortyish woman author named Cecilia Abernathy, who'd won a prestigious award for a book of short stories she'd written about ten years prior. It was a small class, maybe fifteen students altogether, and all we were required to do was write short stories, which the teacher and the class would critique. It was common knowledge on campus that Ms. Abernathy was notoriously lenient about grading and gave practically everybody an A, even if their short stories sucked, which most of them did. All in all, it seemed like a better way to fulfill my English requirement than sitting through endless lectures on Medieval English or plodding through Chaucer.

I had no idea that Samantha had signed up for Ms. Abernathy's course, so I was surprised when I saw her sashay through the door, hugging a few textbooks to her chest, avoiding eye contact. It was the first day of class and she was the last person to show up. A good ten minutes late, she strode right past the teacher, who was in the middle of making some introductory remarks, and settled into a chair directly across from me. The class was held in a conference room and, instead of individual desks, we all sat around a long polished table. Not that I held out much hope, having witnessed Sanjee's catastrophic attempts (he had since given up on her), but clearly Samantha's presence in the class would make it relatively simple for me to flirt with her just for the sport of it.

Or so I thought. No matter how hard I tried, I just couldn't make eye contact with her. It drove me crazy. Every time I glanced over at her, my lips poised to smile, she was looking at something else, usually the teacher, the floor, the ceiling, the framed photograph of F. Scott Fitzgerald on the wall, the middle distance, or her well-manicured fingernails, which she sometimes tapped on the table, an annoying habit that I interpreted as impatience. Clearly, she was an expert at evading eye contact. And she didn't speak much in class when it was time for us to critique somebody's story. I couldn't really decide whether she was timid or if she simply thought the whole classroom experience was just too far beneath her. I assumed the latter.

Stories were submitted in alphabetical order by last name so Samantha was one of the first students required to write something for the vultures in the class to pick apart. We were all given Xeroxes of her story at the start of class. I quickly skimmed my copy right away, hoping it would contain some insight into her soul, assuming she had one. It didn't. To be honest, it was a really hokey mish mash about a polo pony that goes lame and has to be shot by its trainer, an alcoholic Swiss guy named Heinrich. She knew a lot about polo and horses and saddles, but the story had no plot and no point at all and the characters spoke like Victorian fops. The rest of the class savagely trashed it, but Samantha just sat there stoically and sighed a lot, as if she were a duchess listening to a delegation of serfs complaining about high taxes or wretched living conditions. Naturally, I looked at this situation as a golden opportunity.

"I think you're all wrong about this," I declared to the class when it was my turn to comment. "I found the story to be very touching and informative. I didn't know anything about polo before I read this story. I thought it was really very insightful and the characters were quite well-drawn, especially Heinrich."

The whole room went stone quiet as Ms. Abernathy and the rest of the class just stared at me as if I was out of my fucking mind. Two of them actually laughed.

"Now class," Ms. Abernathy said, clearing her throat. "Mr. Hendricks is entitled to his opinion. The story has some... good qualities."

Nobody in the class said anything, but I detected a couple of barely audible snickers and noticed more than a few eye rolls.

But none of that mattered, because when I snuck a look at Samantha, she actually looked back at me, which was a small miracle. She didn't exactly smile. In fact, she appeared somewhat expressionless, but at least we had finally made eye contact. For me, it was a triumph of sorts. I had met the challenge.

On the way out of class, I made sure we exited together so I could collect my reward in the form of her deep, heartfelt gratitude. I was all smiles when she turned to me. "You didn't really *like* that horrid piece of shit story of mine, did you, Larry?" she asked coldly. "You couldn't possibly have, unless you're mentally disturbed. *Are* you mentally disturbed, Larry?"

"It's Jimmy," I corrected her. "And no, I'm not mentally disturbed. The Lithium helps."

I hoped this mild attempt at off-handed wit would get a laugh out of her, but it was if I had just spoken to a giraffe. Her face was a complete blank.

"I don't much care for drollery," she informed me, as I squirmed. "But as I always say, *chacun a son gout. Vous savez?*"

"Yeah well, drollery aside," I went on, "I really thought your story was very... well... avant-garde, a very sophisticated... minimalist approach. Kind of Camus meets Jane Austen. The dimwits in the class obviously aren't bright enough to pick that up."

She gazed at me suspiciously and snorted. She had dark penetrating eyes and I could barely hold the stare. "Obviously, you have absolutely no literary taste whatsoever, Larry," she said. "Camus meets Jane Austen? Hah! That's the most ludicrous thing I ever heard. Evidently, you haven't even read Camus or Austen. My story has no redeeming qualities at all. None. Zero. Unfortunately, I'm a dreadful writer, and if you had half a brain you'd realize that."

"Yes but—"

"I really have to run, Larry. Ciao."

Then she strolled off, leaving me humiliated, incensed and resentful at her condescending behavior. Who the hell did she think she was anyway? At the next class, I simply ignored her. Samantha Jane Conrad, as stunning and fascinating as she may have been, was simply not worth the effort.

~

A week later, it was my turn to write a short story, a prospect that horrified me. I was competent enough at writing term papers as long as I kept the margins wide and utilized as many quotes as possible to fill up the space, but fiction was a complete mystery to me. I had no idea about plot or character development and absolutely no ear for dialogue. I was sure that anything I presented to the class would get royally defoliated. Most of the people in the class thought of themselves as budding writers, wannabe Hemingways who took fiction way too seriously and had no compunction whatsoever about voicing their hostility towards mediocre writing. I certainly didn't want to be on the receiving end of their unbridled scorn. Unlike Samantha, I knew I would find it difficult to maintain a blasé facade in the face of scathing criticism.

Somehow, I would have to write a fairly decent short story. But how could I pull that off? It would be next to impossible for me to write anything even remotely literary. Nevertheless, I sat in front of my portable Olivetti and stared at a blank piece of onion skin paper for about two hours, doggedly hoping that some extraordinary, untapped talent would emerge and make my fingers fill the blank pages with divinely inspired prose. Nothing happened. Even an opening sentence eluded me, not to mention a concept or a plot. I was screwed, and there were only two days left before my crucifixion.

One night, I happened to be loitering around the college library, not so much for studying as shopping for eligible females, when I had a brilliant idea. At least I thought it was brilliant at the time, mainly because the potentially dire consequences didn't immediately occur to me. I dwelled on it for a minute or two, decided it might actually succeed, and then approached the woman at the information desk.

"May I help you young man?" she asked. She had white hair, heavily rouged cheeks and a small birthmark on her forehead.

"Yes," I replied pleasantly. "Does the library have any old copies of *The New Yorker* magazine?"

"Indeed we do," she told me enthusiastically. "We have every single issue all the way back to 1933 or 1934, if I'm not mistaken. They're on aisle 22 through 26 in the magazine section, two rights, a left, another right, then two aisles past the reference books. You'll find them at the very back of the west wing near the microfiche machines." Then she added, with a grin: "It's about twelve miles."

"Next time I'll bring trail mix," I countered.

"There's a campsite about halfway there," she said with a smile.

I thanked her and tried to navigate the impossible maze of shelves for about fifteen minutes until I got dizzy and had to sit down to orient myself. I always seemed to get lost in libraries and often wondered why they didn't just issue maps. Fifteen minutes later, yours truly, Ferdinand Magellan, finally found aisle 22. The magazines were all bound together and organized by year. There were pages and pages of old, musty-smelling, yellowing issues of *The New Yorker*.

Pay dirt.

After wading through about twenty issues, and practically choking on the clouds of dust that flew in my face every time I turned a page, I finally found a short story that seemed as if it might lend itself to plagiarism. It had been written by a guy named Harvey Blitz, whom I'd never heard of. The fact that it had appeared in a 1948 issue of the magazine would probably make it old enough to have escaped Ms. Abernathy's attention, since I guessed she had been born around the time the story had been published. Sure, it was dated, but it wouldn't take much effort on my part to fix that. The plot concerned a college kid who accidentally runs over and kills his own girlfriend and the effects of that tragic incident on the rest of his life. Later, when he's much older, he thinks he spots her on a subway train in New York, but she disappears before he can get to her. It had everything—love, tragedy, pathos and top-notch spelling.

I copied the whole story on my Olivetti, although I altered most of the dated references and added a few minor grammatical errors because I didn't want it to appear flawless, which might arouse suspicion. If I got caught plagiarizing, I'd probably be suspended or possibly even expelled and end up living with my parents, a fate worse than death. But it was worth the chance. At least I thought so at the time.

When I got to class the day my story was scheduled for discussion, Ms. Abernathy didn't distribute copies of it. Suddenly, I got nervous. Maybe she knew who this Harvey Blitz was and was planning to embarrass me in front of the whole group by revealing my heinous act of literary larceny. Maybe Harvey Blitz was a well-known writer and everybody, including Ms. Abernathy, knew who he was except me. What did I know? Just because I'd never heard of him didn't mean anything. I suddenly felt my breakfast slowly begin to meander back up my esophagus and I slinked low in my seat, preparing myself for a well-deserved verbal shellacking. I glanced over at Samantha, but she was busy studying the surface of the table, seemingly bored with the whole tedious routine.

"Class," Ms. Abernathy announced. "Mr. Hendricks has written the best short story I have ever read by a student in all my years as a creative writing teacher."

Suddenly, everybody except Samantha stared my way with either contempt or envy on their faces. Mostly contempt, I think.

"In fact," Ms. Abernathy continued, holding up the manuscript and waving it in the air, "this story is so darn good that I'm going to read it aloud to the class myself, rather than make copies. I don't think there will be any discussion at all. There's really nothing at all to critique, save for a few minor grammatical errors and misspellings."

Then she read Harvey Blitz's tragic tale to the class in its entirety, which was about fifteen typed pages, double-spaced. When she reached the end, a few of the girls were holding back tears. The boys averted their eyes and made coughing noises. Out of curiosity, I looked furtively over at Samantha and, lo and behold, she had the telltale expression of someone struggling desperately to keep emotion at bay.

Ms. Abernathy turned to me and said, "Mr. Hendricks, I think this story is so professional that, with your permission, I would like to personally recommend that my literary agent, Mr. Martin Robbins, send it to *The New Yorker*. What do you think of that?"

I suddenly felt like I was going to projectile vomit all over the table, but I managed to force a smile and croak out the word "cool," with as much excitement as I could fake.

~

Since I was suddenly overcome by fear-induced nausea, I bolted out of the classroom after the session was done and headed for the nearest bathroom, which was on the first floor at the end of a long hallway. Before I was halfway there, I began to notice that someone was calling out for me to wait, but I ignored it until I recognized the voice as Samantha's. So I slowed my pace and let her catch up to me, wondering how she would react if I puked on her shoes.

"That was absolutely *marvelous*, Jimmy," she cried breathlessly, pulling up beside me. I was slightly astounded that she had used my correct name this time.

"Huh?"

"I had no idea what a truly gifted writer you are," she continued. "Your story was really quite emotionally moving. I hate to admit it, but I nearly *wept*. Can you imagine? I never weep."

"Glad you liked it," I replied coolly.

"I would never have guessed you have so much talent. You seem so..." She couldn't find the right word immediately, so she put a finger to her cheek and looked up at the ceiling for inspiration. "... ordinary."

"Gee thanks," I said flatly. Granted, she was beautiful, but her snootiness was seriously starting to annoy me. The nausea was bad enough—I didn't need to be insulted. Then my mind traveled back to the night of the frat party where she had so rudely dismissed Sanjee's well-intentioned efforts to engage her, just as she had done to me the previous week.

"I'm Samantha Jane Conrad," she said. "We met about a week ago?"

"Right," I said dully, shaking the hand she'd extended. "Do you always use your middle name?"

"Yes."

"Why?"

"I don't know. Why do you ask?"

I shrugged. "It seems a little... pompous." I was suddenly feeling very nauseous again. "I have to go," I told her, continuing my journey to the john. "See you around, Samantha Jane Conrad."

I started walking faster, ignoring her struggle to keep up with me. She was cradling a full load of textbooks and loose-leaf binders in her arms and almost dropped a few of them as she scurried after me.

"I know I can't write very well, myself," she admitted, panting a bit, her jewelry making jangling noises. "But I *really* admire people with the literary gift. I absolutely *love* Fitzgerald and Wharton and Sinclair Lewis. Dickens too."

"What's not to love?" I asked, noting that this was a woman who spoke in italics.

"Don't you simply *adore* 'Tender is the Night'?"

"Couldn't put it down."

"So what are you planning to write next?" she asked. Now she was a few half-steps ahead of me, backpedaling as I continued taking long strides forward. Suddenly, I found it hard to look at her. After all, she was a sight to behold. By then, the urge to barf had become slightly less urgent. So I sighed loudly a few times, a ploy which was meant to indicate how tiresome I found the conversation.

"I don't know," I said indifferently. "I thought maybe I'd try a... novel."

Her eyes widened. "*How marvelous! A novel!*"

"Yeah well, I'm not sure I really have that much talent."

"You do, you do!" she insisted. "*I* think so anyway. So does Ms. Abernathy and I suppose she should know, not that I much cared for her pathetic attempt at a short story collection."

I smiled wanly. Somehow, my remark about writing a novel had just slipped out and I had no idea what to say next. I certainly couldn't retract it, but I could make excuses.

"I don't think it's possible to write a whole novel in a college dorm," I ventured. "Too much noise and distraction. Kids throw Frisbees in the halls and snap wet towels at each other all the time. You know how it is."

"Actually I don't," she said. "I don't live in a dorm."

"Is that so?" I replied. "Where do you live?"

"In a little flat a few blocks from this wearisome place they call a college."

"Really?" I marveled. "How'd you swing that?"

"Poppy has more money than God."

"I can see how that might help," I said. "It must be nice having your own place."

"It is!" she exclaimed. "I lay about a good deal and read. I simply *delight* in reading novels. Fiction is my greatest passion in life."

"Yeah, same here," I muttered. Then, for purely sadistic reasons, I decided to take revenge for our first meeting. I was feeling brazen, vengeful and mischievous at the same time. "I'm sorry, what did you say your name was?"

"Samantha," she replied, somewhat annoyed. "I just told you that less than a minute ago."

"Right. Of course," I said apathetically.

Suddenly, we ran out of things to say, so there was a break in the conversation. I did nothing whatsoever to fill in the gap, hoping that it would make her uncomfortable. It did. Watching her squirm was kind of amusing in a fiendish sort of way. I could see her struggling for something to say, but I just kept walking.

By now, she was a little out of breath from trying to stay in front of me as I quickened my pace. At this point, since the nausea had passed and I no longer needed a bathroom, I didn't really know where I was going.

Samantha looked at her diamond-encrusted watch. "I've got about an hour until my next class," she said. "Would you care to accompany me to that horrible place they call the Student Union and have a bite? I know the food is beyond revolting, but it's close by and I'd really *love* to talk to you some more about literature. Obviously, you really know a lot—"

"Gee, I'd love to," I said neutrally. "But I've already got a date."

This was a lie of course, but it caused her to stop dead in her tracks right in front of me and we nearly collided. I'm fairly certain she was shocked. Samantha Jane Conrad was probably not accustomed to rejection, especially not from an uncouth mongrel like me. Shock was written all over her face. It was as if somebody had just told her that her feet were on fire.

So I turned the corner, bidding her a poorly pronounced *"Au revoir"* as she stood there, her mouth slightly agape, wondering what had hit her.

~

Another predicament immediately presented itself: I would have to keep handing in first-rate stories to my creative writing class or Ms. Abernathy would probably begin to suspect that my writing talent was a fraud and start asking incriminating questions. Obviously, I couldn't keep lifting stories from *The New Yorker*—the magazine was simply too high-profile for me to get away with it for long—so I found some other ancient literary journals tucked away deep in the bowels of the library and stole my stories from them. These weren't quite as professional or entertaining as *The New Yorker* stories (in fact, most of them were dark and depressing and way too avant-garde to have any discernable plots), but they seemed literarily professional enough to keep my deception alive for the duration of the course.

"You seem to be growing as a writer," Ms. Abernathy told me in class. "There's some real depth here, although these stories are somewhat... how shall I put it... gloomy and dark."

"I'm moody," I told her.

"Of course," she said. "Your ability to write in so many different styles is impressive. Kudos!"

Having taken my revenge, I had decided to pursue Samantha Jane Conrad just to see if I could pull it off. I like a good challenge and the sexual pot of gold that lay at the end of the rainbow was irresistible. She was heartstoppingly gorgeous and probably had lots of experience in the sack.

One night, I spotted her in the library, where I had gone to find a new short story to lift. She was sitting in an armchair, reading a novel by Henry James in one of the big, brightly lit study rooms, where the fluorescent lights illuminate every pore and pimple grave on your face with disconcerting clarity, although Samantha's complexion was flawless. She was too engrossed in her book to notice me when I entered the room, so I walked right up to her and squatted by her chair.

"Hi Samantha," I said.

She gazed at me. "Hello Jimmy." Her voice sounded a bit cold and distant. Maybe she was still smarting from our last encounter. Or maybe she had simply gone back to thinking that I was just rabble. But then she said, "How's the novel coming along?"

Clearly, this novel charade would have to continue. Without it, Samantha's interest in me would instantly evaporate.

"Actually, not so well," I told her tragically.

"Why?"

"I don't know," I said. "No... inspiration I guess."

"You have to be patient," she instructed me. "It'll come."

"Maybe," I said with a shrug. "Or maybe it won't and I'll just abandon it."

"No!" she cried, slamming her book shut for emphasis, causing a few heads to turn our way. "You simply *mustn't* abandon it. You have so much talent."

"Do you really think so?" I asked

"Yes, yes, yes!" she exclaimed.

I was about to respond, but a guy sitting at a nearby table interrupted. "Shhhh," he hissed at us. "This is a library for Christ's sake. Keep it down."

I mouthed the word "sorry," and turned back to Samantha.

"What a boor," she whispered. "Now where were we?"

I looked at her intensely. "I was about to say that I get so much... inspiration just talking to you, Samantha. You're so... encouraging and you're the only one who's seriously interested in my work. I really appreciate that so much."

"It's my pleasure," she whispered happily. "Art must prosper!"

"Yes, it must," I agreed. Then I took her hand and said, "Who knows, Samantha, if I ever finish the damn thing I might just dedicate it to you."

This perked her up. "*Truly?*" she asked with a delighted gasp.

"Sure," I replied offhandedly. "Why not?"

"But don't you think you should dedicate it to your parents or your siblings?"

I lowered my head in a passing imitation of profound melancholy. "My parents are deceased," I lied, my voice cracking, "and I have no siblings. There's nobody but poor old me and I can't dedicate it to myself."

I think this bit of counterfeit emotion actually touched her. She gave my hand a squeeze. If she'd been standing, she might have hugged me.

"Anyway," I told her, "since you're my muse—"

"Your *muse?*" she asked, her voice filled with excitement. "Me?"

"Sure."

"Oh Jimmy, you're being droll again."

"No I'm not," I assured her. "I mean it."

Her face lit up with a radiant smile. "You have no idea how absolutely *flattered* I am by that, Jimmy."

"Will you *please* keep it down," said the guy at the table. "Go outside if you must talk. Jesus."

Samantha scowled at him.

"Look, maybe we can talk about this somewhere else where we don't have to whisper," I said quietly. "Can I take you to the Union for a burger?"

She didn't answer right away. "What would your girlfriend think?"

"What girlfriend?" I asked. "I don't have a girlfriend."

"What about the girl you took to the Union last week?"

"Oh *her*," I muttered with a look of utter boredom. "It never worked out, so we parted ways. She's not nearly as... mature and intellectual as you, and she has no interest in literature. A relationship like that can never go very far. Also, if you don't mind me saying so, you're much more attractive." I could see her face brightening slightly, although she already knew she was gorgeous. This was not big news.

"I'd love to go Jimmy," she said, standing up.

And so we started to date. Most of the time, we talked about literature. Actually, that's all we talked about. Since I didn't know Zola from Gogol, I had to read practically every available copy of Cliff Notes to appear halfway knowledgeable. I let her do most of the talking, which was not difficult because she loved to talk, but only about books. When I had no clue what she was chattering about, I would interject insipid generic observations such as "he was so insightful," or "the descriptions are so perceptive."

"Do you know what I really like about you, Jimmy?" she asked one afternoon as we sat on the lawn of the quad eating brie and crackers. "You're not arrogant or obnoxious like so many other writers I've read about. You're... very kind and... I don't know... thoughtful and you really seem to... well... like me."

"Of course I like you," I said, taking her hand in mine. "You're terrific, Samantha. How could anyone not like you?"

She looked down sadly. "Trust me," she said. "I'm usually not very popular. I think I frighten people or something. People don't... well... take to me. At my school in Switzerland they used to call me 'The Ice Princess'."

"I'm sure that if people got to know you as well as I do they'd like you," I said sagely.

Then of course, she reverted to style. "Not that I really care," she said.

After a while, I realized, from the way she acted around me, that deep down, Samantha was hardly the arrogant snob she pretended to be. Her aloof façade was just that—a façade. Concealed somewhere beneath that icy exterior was a terrified little girl who had constructed a vast system of impenetrable barriers to mask her true sensitivity. I concluded that the fault lay with her parents, who had coldly delegated her upbringing to a series of nannies, tutors and exclusive private schools. And so, it was virtually impossible for me to pass over the moats, minefields and barbed wire fences that separated us. On the other hand, she was only interested in me because she thought I was a promising novelist. Without that, I'd still be Larry.

And I took full advantage of it, plotting and scheming for a way to get her into bed. Looking back on it, I was, as Samantha might have put it, a cad and a scoundrel. But I just couldn't help myself.

We spent a lot of time together. Mostly, we went to art house movies or ate dinner at fancy gourmet restaurants, all at her expense, since her ten credit cards seemed to have no spending limits and I didn't even have a credit card. She took me to the opera and made me suffer through dull coffee-house poetry readings, piano recitals and two or three interminable author lectures. I drew the line at ballet.

On the negative side, she repeatedly resisted my frequent sexual advances, citing a wide variety of unimaginative excuses such as melancholy, fatigue, migraines, pulled muscles, insomnia or pedicure appointments. Perhaps she imagined we were characters in a Jane Austen novel that flirted and pined for each other all the time, but never made it past first base. Maybe my bogus reputation as a promising young novelist simply wasn't sufficiently stimulating. Or maybe she just didn't find me physically attractive. By week four, I was still kissing her goodnight under the green awning of her apartment building.

At one point, I contemplated the idea of taking her to my hometown for the express purpose of showing her off to all the assholes and bullies who had taunted or ignored me in high school. It was strictly an ego thing. But in the end, I abandoned the idea. For one thing, I had convinced Samantha that my parents were deceased and it would be tricky to avoid them. For another, it would be horribly cruel if Laura were to see us together. Sure, I was an asshole, but even assholes have their limits.

One aspect of Samantha's personality that drove me nuts was her tendency to reveal herself via literary allusions. She called it a "quirk," but it was more of a compulsion. Her mother was Lady Macbeth; her father, Big Daddy. An uncle she liked was Mr. Micawber, a favorite governess, Jane Eyre; a doting professor, Mr. Chips. And so on.

This curious habit of hers quickly made the voyage from eccentric to bizarre when she began to invoke the names of literary characters to describe moments in our relationship. When she thought I was treating her crudely, she called me Wolf Larsen; if I was standoffish, I was Mr. Darcy. She reacted to my obtuse sense of humor by referring to me as Yossarian, and when I dressed too shabbily, I was Tom Joad.

"You're behaving like George Babbitt," she would say whenever I said anything that struck her as hopelessly bourgeois.

"Are you Dr. Zhivago today?" she once remarked when I showed up one chilly night at the library wearing earmuffs. Another time, my taste in headwear caused her to spend the evening calling me Holden. My sexual advances earned me the name Casanova.

I was tempted to ask her if she wanted to join me and a Black friend of mine on a rafting trip down the Mississippi, but I restrained myself.

"Listen Samantha," I told her one day. "Maybe you could start using adjectives to describe me instead of character names."

"But this is so much more fun!" she exclaimed. "Don't you think? Or is it obnoxious? I'll stop if you find it obnoxious."

"No," I said, concealing a sigh. "You're right. It's... um... fun. Very amusing."

"That's a relief," she said. "I derive so much pleasure from it!"

In spite of her various idiosyncrasies and obsessions, I found her fascinating, albeit a little intense. She was beautiful, intelligent and mysterious. Until Samantha came into my life, I had never met anyone who could accurately be described as "cosmopolitan". Sometimes, while she was engrossed in a novel, I would just stare at her, wondering what lay beneath those dark eyes, but suspecting that I would probably never find out. Eventually, I realized that Samantha lived out her emotions in the novels she read. While real life seemed to bore or disappoint her, literature was the only thing that made her laugh or cry or feel anger.

Nevertheless, it was an amazing ego trip. Just being seen around campus with a woman that stunning and sophisticated made me feel like hot shit, especially after four years of relative anonymity at Rimbaldi. My self-esteem had pierced the stratosphere and was heading for the far reaches of the galaxy. Most of the other male students, especially Sanjee, were thoroughly mystified that someone of Samantha's stature and beauty would even deign to notice a worthless insect like me. On campus, it was a very high-profile relationship. Sometimes, I was downright giddy about the whole thing.

Sanjee couldn't seem to get over it.

"You da man!" he would tell me about three times a week, punctuating his excitement with a high five. By this time, he was practically living with a girl from Emerson and I rarely saw him. "When are you gonna tell me your secret?"

"You seem to be doing pretty well on your own," I reminded him.

"That's because I'm hot shit," he would say. "But you..."

It was always the same routine, so I didn't take the insult seriously. More than once, I was tempted to reveal the truth, but decided to keep mum. Sanjee had a big mouth.

"So what's your secret?" he repeated.

"Prayer," I usually told him.

Sanjee smirked. "I'm serious, Jimbo," he would say. "I need to be enlightened. You, my friend, are the Master."

"To be honest, I don't really know," I'd say. "I guess I'm just cute and cuddly. Girls like cute and cuddly."

"Okay, be that way."

Then he would pout for a second or two. "Is the sex still great?" he would ask.

I knew Sanjee wouldn't believe the truth, so I always just said, "Fucking amazing."

~

Unfortunately, as I was soon to discover, Sanjay wasn't the only one on campus who was envious of my relationship with Samantha.

One night, I was sitting alone in the Student Union when one of my creative writing classmates, a guy named Robert Arsenault, wandered in, looked around and pulled up the chair opposite me. He was a tall, gangly guy with intense eyes, long brown scraggly hair and a lopsided Fu Manchu mustache that had a few unfortunate gaps in it. Of all the people in Ms. Abernathy's class, he was invariably the most critical of everybody else's short stories, also the most vicious, and it was no secret that he thought of himself as the most gifted writer in the class. For the entire semester, he'd been dropping hints that he was working on the Great American Novel in his spare time.

After he sat down, I said hello, but he just stared at me. "Something on your mind, Robert?" I asked pleasantly. "You wanna see the menu? There's one on the next table just—"

"You're a fraud aren't you Hendricks?" he said. "Admit it."

"Excuse me?" I replied.

"You heard me," he said frostily.

I inspected my burger. "Goddamn buns are stale again," I said. "Jesus. I mean you'd think—"

"I repeat," he said. "You're a fucking fraud and you know it."

I looked at him. His face was flushed. "I have no idea what you're talking about," I said, although I was beginning to.

He scowled. "That shit you write in class, where do you steal it from?" he asked.

I looked at him, then popped a few fries in my mouth. "If I was the sensitive type, I'd resent that," I told him. "It's not shit and I don't steal it."

"Yes you do," he said.

"No," I said casually. "I don't. The fact is, I don't know where it all comes from. I guess the words just kind of spill out of my head. It's really quite—"

"Bullshit," he said with an unkind snicker. "You couldn't write stuff that good if your life depended on it."

Although I wasn't showing it, I was a little worried. Did he have proof? Was he a Harvey Blitz fan? Had he done some research? Fortunately, there was no Google back then. If there had been, I would've been toast.

"You've got a lot of nerve Arsenault," I said, annoyed that he would even make a presumptuous assumption like that, even though it was true. "Just because I'm a better writer than you doesn't mean—"

"Ever been to Chicago?" he asked.

"No," I said. "Why?"

He smiled in a self-satisfied way. "One of your stories takes place in Chicago," he reminded me. "You mention street names and neighborhoods. How do you know all that shit if you've never even been there?"

I shrugged. "Ever heard of a street map?" I said. "They got them in the library."

"Yeah right."

"No really," I said. "aisle 16, row C12."

"Another one of your stories takes place in London," he continued. "You've probably never been there either."

"Nope," I said, sipping my Coke. "Can't say that I have."

He pointed a finger at my face. "I'm gonna find out, Hendricks," he told me. "You can bet on that. And when I do, I'm gonna make sure everybody knows about it, Ms. Abernathy, the class and your friend Samantha."

I sighed. "So *that's* what this is all about?" I asked. "Jealousy?"

"What? No. Of course not," he stammered. "It's about honesty and the craft of writing. It's about the principle of the thing. You wouldn't understand."

"I understand all right," I said. "It's about sex."

Then he stood up. "I think we're done here," he proclaimed. "Want some advice?"

"Not really."

"Stop plagiarizing," he said. "I'm on to you and pretty soon everybody else will be too. I promise you that. I'm gonna go through every fucking literary magazine in the goddamn school library."

"That would be aisle 22 through 26," I pointed out. "Should take you about a century or two."

He glared at me for a moment, and then stood up and stormed

out. I saw him pass by the window with a foul look of determination on his face. But I wasn't really worried.

~

A few more weeks passed and I still wasn't getting anywhere with Samantha. An eternal platonic literary affair was not really my objective (for one thing, there was too much reading involved), and if I'd wanted to take an art appreciation course, I would have signed up for one. Suddenly, it occurred to me that there was a distinct possibility we would *never* have sex. She was, after all, an ice princess and, although she was nice enough to me, the truly frigid part of her could also involve sex. So I seriously contemplated breaking it off, but then decided that I'd already invested way too much time to impulsively toss it all away. Besides, for some curious reason, I liked her.

Samantha, who was fairly perceptive, may have sensed my impatience. Or maybe she'd just decided it was time to step out of the Jane Austen novel and move on to Henry Miller. One night, while we were strolling hand-in-hand across the quad, Samantha couldn't stop praising a new John Updike novel she'd recently finished reading, so I asked her if I could borrow it. As usual, I walked her to her apartment building, not expecting to be invited in, but she surprised me by saying, "Would you care to come in, Jimmy? I can give you that Updike book if you like."

"I'd love to," I said, trying not to sound too eager. She took my arm and steered me to her private elevator.

Her penthouse was a testament to the potential of interior design when funds are limitless. By comparison, my dorm room was a Neolithic hovel with furniture crafted by a blind carpenter. Samantha's penthouse was a perfect blend of overstuffed chairs and couches, bleached hardwood floors, expensive Oriental rugs, huge fireplaces, and a balcony with enough room to accommodate

a small circus. She led me to an enormous floor-to-ceiling ma-
hogany bookshelf, plucked the Updike book from its niche and
handed it to me.

"Wow," I said, truly awed at the dimensions of her library.
"You've got an incredible collection there."

"Some of them are first editions," she informed me proudly.
"Actually all of them are. A few are even signed!"

"Impressive," I said.

"Well, feel free to borrow anything, anytime you like, Jimmy."

"Thanks."

"Just promise me you won't dog-ear the pages."

"I wouldn't dare," I assured her. "I have way too much respect
for books."

"And try not to crack the spines either," she added.

With Samantha looking over my shoulder, I pulled down a few
volumes and started to peruse them, making the same mundane
comments every now and then about a particular novel I'd never
read. Samantha was so happy at that moment, I thought she was
going to explode.

"One day, your novel will be up there, Jimmy," she said excitedly,
grabbing my elbow and squeezing it. "I'm simply *dying* to read it.
Won't you give me just a little peek? Perhaps one itty-bitty chapter?"

"I'd love to Samantha," I said flatly, still feeling guilty about my
little ruse but, at the same time, marveling at its effectiveness, "but
I'd rather wait until it's a little more, um, polished."

She nodded solemnly. "I understand completely," she conceded.
"No rush. Whenever you're ready. I wouldn't *think* of compromis-
ing your creative process."

I smiled, relieved that I had once again managed to avoid blowing my cover. I was no novelist, but when it came to bullshit artistry,
I was a genius. "May I ask you a question, Samantha?"

"By all means, Jimmy!" she replied. "Ask away."

"Would you be going out with me if I wasn't writing a novel? If I had no literary talent whatsoever?"

As I studied her face, she waved a dismissive hand at me. "Of *course* I would!" she said, unconvincingly. I knew she was lying—it was written in capital letters all over her face. "Why would you even *ask* me such an absurd question?"

"No reason," I answered. "Just curious. Forget it."

"Consider it forgotten."

"Okay."

"So," she said, heading for the kitchen, which had every cooking appliance known to man in it, with the exception of a Weber barbecue grill. "May I offer you a drink, Jimmy? Wine perhaps? I have quite a few excellent vintages. A Cognac? Or perhaps you'd prefer a pint of ale?"

"A glass of straight Scotch would hit the spot," I said.

"Is Glenlivet all right?"

I had no idea what Glenlivet was. "My favorite."

"On the rocks?"

"No, just some ice would be fine."

She looked at me questioningly for a beat before laughing. "That's so very droll," she noted. At some point in our relationship, she had warmed to drollery, or maybe she was just tolerating it for my sake. One never knew with Samantha.

"Old bartender's joke," I told her.

"Have you worked in the bartending trade, Jimmy?"

"No, but I've known a few." This was a lie, but it sounded vaguely Hemingwayan.

"You writers and your infernal drinking," she said, shaking her head with a mixture of solemnity and exasperation. "But I suppose it's all part of the creative temperament."

"Yes," I said morosely. "It's tragic but it's the price we writers have to pay." I guess I'd read that somewhere.

"As I'm sure you know, Fitzgerald died from alcoholism at forty-four," she informed me. "Can you believe it? Forty-four!"

"Think of the books he still could have written. Such a waste," I said, conjuring up a fake bout of profound sorrow. "Such a terrible waste."

"Indeed," she said solemnly. "Hemingway killed himself at sixty-one. Blew his brains out. And of course you know what happened to poor Sylvia Plath, whom I positively *adore*."

I had no idea, but I said, "Such a terrible tragedy."

While she walked off to fix our drinks, I wandered idly around the room. Among the photos and memorabilia on the mantle was a picture of a good-looking blond guy with the strong jaw of a Kennedy, a deep tan and muscular legs. He was dressed in tennis whites and held a racket in his hands. A huge swimming pool sparkled behind him.

"Who's the guy in the picture?" I asked, when she returned with a tray that held a glass of Scotch, a delicate snifter and a bottle of Cognac.

"That's Count Dracula," she said.

Finally! A literary character I was familiar with. "Count Dracula plays tennis?" I asked.

Samantha socked me in the arm.

"Okay," I said. "So who is it?"

"Todd Spencer."

"Boyfriend?"

"Since I was a little girl," she said bleakly. "We're supposed to get married someday, but I'm not sure I really want to. He's very nice, but I'm afraid he's a little... dull-witted. And he doesn't care at all for the Arts. Plus, he makes all these *horrible* grammatical errors when he speaks and it drives me positively *crazy*. I don't think he really understands my passion for literature. Not nearly as well as you do, Jimmy."

I deliberately didn't say a word. I just sat down on the couch.

"And he reads those *awful* trashy horror novels," she added, shuddering. "And thrillers. Can you imagine? It's mortifying."

Samantha poured some Cognac into her snifter and handed me my drink. Then she lit the gas fireplace and sat down next to me on the couch. We drank in silence for a while. She finished her first glass and, like a perfect gentleman, I refilled it for her. She didn't seem to object.

"You know, Jimmy," she said, "your talent for writing is... well... so intellectually *stimulating*."

"Is that right?"

"Yes. Not to mention your simply *marvelous* knowledge of literature."

"You're very sweet, Samantha," I observed, "but I wish I wasn't in such a melancholy mood this evening."

"Melancholy?" she repeated, looking at me quizzically. "How is that, Jimmy? What's troubling you?"

I let out a weary, but very literary sigh, if such a thing actually exists. "To be honest, I've been having a difficult problem with my novel," I told her.

"Oh? I'm so sorry to hear that. Do tell." The deep look of concern in her eyes almost made me ashamed of myself.

"I probably shouldn't bother you with this."

"Oh please do, Jimmy," she said eagerly. "If I can help in any way at all, it would be so very rewarding."

"No," I said. "You'll think it's dumb."

"Nothing you say is ever dumb, Jimmy," she assured me. "Please tell me."

I gazed into her eyes, which were now stationed about ten inches from my face. "Well, you see, it's like this: I need to write a sex scene," I began. "It's vital to the plotline of the story, absolutely vital. But unfortunately I'm still a virgin, so I don't know anything about sex. I can't just base the scene on an experience I haven't had. It would be too... phony and most readers and critics would certainly see through it."

"Yes," she mused. "I understand exactly what you mean, Jimmy. As it happens, I'm a virgin too."

This took me completely by surprise. "No way," I said, eyeing her skeptically.

"I'm afraid so," she moaned. "I have yet to taste the fruits of the act of love."

"What about Todd?"

"He wants to wait until we're married. But, as I explained, I really don't want to marry him. I may have to remain a virgin my whole life."

"Oh come on, Samantha. You must have had *some* experience," I said. "You're so... beautiful and so... worldly."

"I necked once with a ski instructor in Davos," she told me. "I think his name was Beowulf or something. I was a bit tipsy at the time, but I wouldn't let him have his way with me. He was lower class and not terribly bright, I'm afraid. I speak German quite well so I could tell."

I downed the rest of my Scotch, poured her another Cognac and boldly put my arm around her.

"Anyway," I continued with a sigh. "If I don't solve this problem, I may have to just throw the book away."

"Oh no, you simply mustn't! Promise me you won't do that, Jimmy," she cried feverishly.

"But it's so damn *frustrating*," I complained, sitting up and cradling my head in my hands. "I'm just so... stuck. Writers have to write about what they know and, well, I'm completely ignorant about sex."

I glanced at the photo of Todd, wondering why any guy in his right mind would even *consider* delaying sex with this goddess. He must be an idiot. Of course, the idea that he might have scruples never even occurred to me.

"Jimmy, I have an idea!" Samantha suddenly chirped. "Perhaps you should hire a prostitute."

"That would be much too impersonal," I countered. "It wouldn't possibly work."

"Drat," she said. But I could tell she was formulating another solution. "I have it!" she cried. "Maybe you should read some erotic literature! I could make you a list."

Jesus Christ, I thought, how many hoops would I have to jump through to get this show on the road?

"And get my ideas from another writer?" I asked, trying to sound appalled. "I couldn't possibly do that. It would be... um... plagiarism."

"Of course, of course, of course," she said. "Plagiarism is a ghastly crime! How utterly stupid of me to suggest it."

"So I guess it's hopeless," I moaned. "You think I could bring the manuscript over here and throw it in your fireplace?"

"Don't be ridiculous. I would never allow that."

"Fine," I said. "I'll toss it in the dumpster behind the dorm."

But she wasn't paying attention anymore. There was an odd, dreamy look in her eyes. She seemed to be pondering. Either that or she was contemplating a nap.

"Maybe I could help you with your problem after all," she offered after a few moments of silence. She'd had three snifters of Cognac by then.

"How?" I asked, expecting another idiotic suggestion.

Apparently, she'd run dry of idiotic suggestions, because she carefully placed her snifter down on the coffee table and leaned over to kiss me. Her tongue flew around inside my mouth like a fleshy butterfly.

"Wow," I said. "For a virgin, you sure can kiss."

"Thank you," she replied. There was a short lull, and then she said, "If you want more, take me Jimmy. I'm yours."

Then she reached over and finished my Scotch. Without another word, she threw herself into my arms and suddenly we were kissing as if we'd just invented it. She started breathing hard and groaned when I put my tongue in her ear. I didn't really have to do much of anything. She unbuttoned her sweater and then unclasped her bra. Her breasts looked like they'd been sculpted by Michelangelo.

"Maybe you should take notes," she said.

"Huh?"

"Notes," she repeated. "So you'll remember everything."

I looked at her. "Don't worry," I told her, "I'll remember everything."

She nodded and stood up. I thought maybe she'd changed her mind, but she slipped out of her designer jeans and dropped her panties. Then she grabbed my hand and led me into her bedroom. The king size bed had a linen canopy over it. She pushed me onto the mattress, ripped off my shirt and literally jumped on top of me.

The rest, as they say, is history. Or *histoire*, as Samantha would probably put it.

We did it twice that night. She was a veritable tiger, which I didn't expect from someone that inexperienced. Afterwards, she talked about sexual symbolism in French literature for a while and then she dozed off, probably because of all the Cognac she'd consumed. I watched her sleep for a while, thinking proudly that I had just made it to the peak of Mt. Everest.

~

Samantha and I continued to date for the rest of the semester. We had intercourse quite often, in a wide variety of complex positions (she owned a signed first edition of *The Joy of Sex* of course), so I could finish my "research." But I was never entirely sure who she thought she was making love to. On one occasion, in the middle of some heavy duty foreplay, she said, "Fuck me, Victor."

I stopped kissing her. "Who the hell is Victor?" I asked.

"I don't know," she stuttered, a little embarrassed. "Victor Hugo I suppose. I'm re-reading *Les Miserables* in the original French. I'm very sorry Jimmy. Just forget about it. Keep going. I'm very turned on."

The Victor business didn't really bother me that much, although it was a little bizarre being with a woman who thought she was having sex with a dead French writer. But, after a few months, I just grew tired of Samantha. For one thing, the sex had become perfunctory, as if it really *was* just a research project—she didn't seem to enjoy it as much as she had in the beginning. For another, she kept insisting that I let her read my novel and I was running out of excuses. And frankly, I just got bored hearing about literature all the time. To be honest, I wasn't even sure whether she thought I was Jimmy Hendricks or David Copperfield. Sometimes, when we went out to dinner, the literary discussion would run its course and we'd just sit there quietly eating. At some point, I realized that the anticipation of the conquest had been more interesting than the conquest itself. So I finally broke up with her in a very cold and heartless way and began dating another girl who wasn't a virgin and didn't give a shit about literature.

"No," Samantha said emphatically after I suggested we stop seeing each other. "You simply *cannot* break up with me, Jimmy. I just won't allow it."

I avoided looking at her. "I'm sorry Samantha," I said. "I really think it's time for both of us to move on."

"But why?" she asked. "We have so much in common."

"Not really."

"But I thought I was your muse," Samantha said, trying not to appear distraught. I thought I saw her eyes well up.

"You were," I told her. "You are. You always will be." I was tempted to tell her the truth about my bogus writing talent, but there was a strong possibility that she would reveal the truth to Ms. Abernathy (thus getting me expelled and vindicating Robert Arsenault), so that was definitely out of the question. Another, more urgent consequence might have involved her long fingernails and my cheeks.

"But what if you write another novel?" she asked.

"Trust me," I assured her. "That's very unlikely."

"But Jimmy," she said plaintively, "I love you. Maybe... I think... I'm not sure."

Like an asshole, I just shrugged. "You'll get over it."

Suddenly she was glaring at me. "You goddamn writers can be so awfully *cruel*," she said indignantly.

"I guess it comes with the territory," I told her.

She sighed heavily. "Yes, I suppose it does," she said. "At least now you'll be able to write a novel about a tragic love affair."

"If I do, I'll dedicate it to you."

She brightened. "Really?"

"Sure," I said. "Why not?"

"Well, I suppose that's *something*," she reflected. Then she pouted. "So your decision about our *affaire d'amour* is final? It's nonnegotiable?"

"That's correct," I said coldly.

She narrowed her eyes. "Deep down, you're nothing but an egotist," she told me, her eyes filled with a mixture of disappointment and contempt. "You're heartless and spiteful. But I suppose most writers are."

"I'm sorry you feel that way, Samantha," I said, although she had every right to feel that way.

"I despise you!" she hissed.

Then she turned on her heels and casually walked off, trying to make it appear as if nothing of any consequence had happened. But nobody likes to be rejected, not even pampered rich girls. I knew she was upset; maybe she even cried later in private, but she just didn't want me to think that she cared that much. And maybe she didn't. You could never tell what Samantha really thought about anything. That was part of the problem.

My new girlfriend, Amanda Dills, was from Brooklyn, New York, and she'd been around the block more than once. She taught me a few new things about sex, such as how to find the clitoris and what to do with it. It wasn't always so easy to find, especially in the dark, but eventually I got the hang of it. After a while, I became quite the competent sexual sportsman, if I do say so myself, although Amanda showed me the door after three weeks. I had no particular feeling about that at all. There were plenty of fish in the sea.

Fortunately, I even managed to glide through the semester without getting expelled for plagiarism. In spite of Robert Arsenault's obsessive determination to expose me, the secret of my phony literary talent was never revealed. I spotted him one night, sitting on the floor in front of aisle C, sneezing and coughing as he strummed through a dusty old back issue of some long-forgotten literary magazine. Obviously frustrated, he scowled at me when I walked by.

As for the Harvey Blitz short story I'd plagiarized, Ms. Abernathy's agent turned it down. He said it was a little too dated for *The New Yorker*.

Samantha... Now

IT'S A DREARY, OVERCAST Friday afternoon when Morris and I set out for Darien, Connecticut, which is a short hop of about 150 miles from Laura's town in western Massachusetts. Since there's no rush, we decide to take the longer scenic route and when Morris gets hungry we stop at a fast food restaurant, where I have a grilled cheese sandwich and Morris inhales two kosher bagels from his duffel. By seven o'clock, I suddenly have to start driving like a maniac because the Sabbath begins at sunset and we've hit an endless stretch of road with no motels in the area. Morris frets and squirms anxiously, and keeps leaning over me every five minutes to check the gas gauge.

"Will you stop with the fidgeting already? You're driving me nuts."

"We had a deal."

"And I'm living up to the deal," I assure him. "Is it sunset yet?"

"No."

"So we're good then," I say calmly. "Sit back. Relax. Enjoy the scenery. Do a crossword puzzle. Take a nap."

Morris just folds his arms and lets out a low growl.

I look over at him. "I guess we can't do the Sabbath on the median strip," I offer, trying to lighten the mood. "Probably no Biblical precedent."

He ignores me and leans over to check the speedometer. "Maybe you shouldn't drive so fast," he suggests nervously. "The speed limit is forty. What if the cops stop you for speeding? Then we'll never make it."

"Don't worry so much," I tell him. "We'll find a place in no time."

Fifty miles north of Darien, the sun starts to sink dangerously low in the sky and Morris has now worked himself into a snit. We pass farmhouse after farmhouse, but no motels. The two-lane scenic route is now clogged by trucks, tractors and sightseers, so I'm relentlessly honking my horn as we inch along. Morris has broken out into a sweat at this point and doesn't take his eyes off the dashboard clock.

After half an hour of this, we chance upon a cheap motel, one of those dives with a blinking neon sign that boasts TV and air conditioning, as if that was a big deal in this century. It will have to do, so we register and are given keys to a badly lit room that smells like a mixture of toilet cleanser and meatloaf.

Morris hurriedly unpacks two slightly stale loaves of Challah bread covered in Saran Wrap, two napkins, a Jewish prayer book, a prayer shawl, several ceremonial candles with holders and a bottle of red wine. Then he searches for the Tupperware that contains the remainder of his kosher food. After a moment, his eyes widen in horror.

"Oh God," he says.

"What?"

"I must have forgotten to pack the other container of brisket."

"Or you ate it."

"What am I going to do?"

"Look again."

Morris frantically inverts the duffel, and a cascade of underwear, clothes and toiletries tumbles on the bed, but the food is not there. Defeated, he sinks onto the floral bed spread and cradles his head in his hands.

"What am I going to do?" he asks.

"I don't know. How much time do we have?"

Morris gazes out the window, then looks at his watch. "Not much. It's forty minutes before sunset," he cries. We have twenty-two minutes."

"Can't you do it just this once without kosher food?"

"Absolutely not."

"God will understand," I say sagely. "It's not your fault. He'll give you a mulligan on this one."

"You're an idiot."

I take a few deep breaths and start pacing. Then I stop and turn to Morris. "Okay, stay here, I'll be right back."

Ten minutes later, I return with a twelve-pack of Hebrew National kosher beef hot dogs, a bag of whole wheat buns and a mini-jar of Gulden's mustard, all from a nearby gas station mini-mart. Overjoyed, Morris calls me a genius, squeezes my head between his big hands and kisses me on the lips. Then he puts aside the buns and the mustard because they haven't been blessed by a rabbi.

"Women are supposed to perform some of these rituals," Morris explains, "but we don't have a woman so it'll have to be me."

Eighteen minutes before sunset, he switches off the electric lights, shuts down the air conditioner, yanks out the telephone cord and hands me a white silky yarmulke. Then he places two candleholders on the rickety table, lays napkins over the Challah, covers his eyes while lighting the candles, washes his hands by pouring water over them and pulls up a couple of chairs. During this process, he chants a few prayers in Hebrew, explaining their meaning to me as he goes along. There are prayers for every step. Then he lifts the napkins from the Challah loaves and rips off several pieces. Finally, we eat.

After we devour the cold hot dogs, Morris says a few more prayers. By now, both of us are drenched in sweat because the air conditioner is off, so before we turn in for the night, I take a cold shower and open all the windows. Morris falls asleep immediately, but I'm not tired, so I play a few games of solitaire with a greasy deck someone left in a drawer until I drift off.

Since the Sabbath isn't over until Saturday night, we have to keep the room for the rest of the day. I take a long walk down a dirt road that cuts through an endless meadow, buy some strawberries at a fruit stand and spend a few hours at a local diner, reading a newspaper.

Early Sunday morning, we pack up and hit the road again.

~

It's a gray stone monstrosity supported by four Greek pillars. Three fierce-looking sculpted lions guard the entrance. A thick beard of Boston ivy grows up the outer walls. Leading up to a five-car garage is a long circular driveway which winds from the wrought iron gateway, past an acre or two of lush, well-manicured grass, flanked on both sides by pine forests. For some reason, the electric security gate is open, so we drive on through. As we pull up, four gardeners clad in spotless white jumpsuits are blowing leaves around. A pool man's truck sits near a path that leads to the yard.

"Wow," I say to Morris as I park the car near the entrance. "Will you look at this fucking place?"

Morris shrugs. He's not impressed. "Who needs a house that big? If they had any compassion, they'd turn it into a home for foster children. This is disgusting."

I step out of the car while Morris lowers his seat as far back as it will go, then places his rolled-up jacket behind his head and closes his eyes. I lean into the open passenger window and tap him on the shoulder.

"What the hell are you doing?"

"What the hell does it look like?" he says. "I'm taking a nap. That motel room was an oven. I maybe got three hours of shut-eye."

"The motel room was an oven because you turned off the air conditioner," I remind him.

"Jewish law," he says, "although there's some controversy about that."

"Okay, fine," I say. "But you're supposed to support me here, remember? Why do I have to keep reminding you?"

Morris sighs and reluctantly exits the car. A section of his shirttail is hanging out of his trousers and after I point this out, he obediently tucks it in. Then we both head for the huge front door. Morris is still disheveled; his pants are wrinkled, his shirt has a coffee stain on it and his yarmulke is lopsided. No matter. I ring the doorbell and hear a pleasant melody of chimes ringing inside the house.

Nobody answers, so I ring again, but there's still no response. One more ring also produces no result.

"Shit," I say.

"Now what?" Morris asks.

I'm not sure what to do. "We'll wait in the car for ten minutes," I suggest. "Maybe she's in the pool or something."

So we stroll back to the car, but before we get there, a white BMW convertible tears up the driveway and stops next to my Camry with a deafening screech of tires that kicks up a hailstorm of gravel. The driver, a handsome blond guy in Polo tennis whites, jumps over the car door and grabs a tennis racket out of the back seat. I recognize him immediately.

"You must be Todd," I say cheerfully. He removes his sunglasses as he approaches us and gives me the once-over. I extend my hand. After looking at it as if it's crawling with maggots, he gives it a tepid shake.

"Yes, I'm Todd. And you are...?"

"Jimmy Hendricks."

"You're kidding."

"We're not related," I tell him.

"I didn't think so," he says. "You're not Black."

"True enough," I say. Over the years, I've gotten used to the constant aggravation of having to explain my problematical name, but that doesn't stop me from feeling a twinge of resentment towards my parents every time I have to go through the tedious routine.

"Anyway," I continue, "I'm an old college friend of Samantha's. This is my associate, Morris Berkowitz."

Todd's light blue eyes instantly focus on Morris's yarmulke, but his expression seems more like benign curiosity than disapproval. I suppose the inhabitants of Darien aren't accustomed to seeing people walking around the neighborhood in yarmulkes, and as far as I know, Polo doesn't make them. Nevertheless, he gives Morris the same reluctant handshake he gave me.

"How the devil did you know my name?" Todd inquires. He has one of those nasally patrician voices that can't help but sound arrogant.

"In college, Samantha couldn't stop talking about what a great guy you were," I tell him. "It practically drove me crazy. Todd this, Todd that. She had pictures of you all over her apartment."

He smiles, and then frowns. "You were in her apartment?"

"I, um, tutored her in math for a short time."

"Uh huh," he says. "And you came here to see her why?"

"We were just in the area on business," I stammer. "I thought it would be nice to say hello to a fellow Fryman inmate. Rehash old times and whatnot."

"Oh. I see. Well, I'm afraid she's not here. She—"

And then something bizarre happens. Todd puts a trembling hand over his eyes and starts sobbing. I look at Morris who reacts as he always does, with a shrug.

Todd's sudden emotional display doesn't last very long. After a few seconds, he wipes his eyes with his tennis wristband, clears his throat and quickly regains his composure by standing ramrod straight. "I'm awfully sorry," he says. "Why don't you guys come into the house and we'll have a drink. I could sure use some company. It's been fucking lonely around here these days."

It's only around noon, a little early for cocktails, but what the hell? I look at Morris, who reluctantly nods.

So we follow Todd through the mammoth oak front door and into the house. In the foyer, he casually drops his racket on an antique credenza and leads us into an enormous living room roughly the size of a car showroom.

With a weary sigh, Todd flops down on a sofa and indicates that we sit.

"So," Todd says. "What would you guys like to drink?"

"I'll just have a Coke," I say.

"Water," says Morris.

Todd seems a little disappointed that we're abstaining from booze, so I say, "We're both on the wagon."

"I tried that once but it didn't take," he tells us. Then he leaps to his feet and heads for the kitchen. After a moment, he's back and hands us our drinks. He strolls over to a cabinet and fixes himself a gin and tonic. Meanwhile, I'm wondering why there isn't a butler.

"Samantha's in Nantucket," Todd informs me, settling back on the couch. "She's staying at her parents' house there on the Cliffside."

"Vacation?"

"I wish," Todd says, pulling off his wristband. His eyes well up again. "I'm afraid she's decided to divorce me."

I don't know what to say at first. Sure, I'm sympathetic but at the same time the fact that Samantha will soon be single is not an altogether unhappy revelation.

"Gee, I'm very sorry to hear that, Todd," I finally mutter. "I'm going through a divorce myself at the moment. It can be very emotionally draining."

"That's for sure. The thing is, I didn't even know she was unhappy," Todd confesses. "I had no idea at all. She never let on. She seemed perfectly happy reading her damn novels, training her Andalusians, playing tennis, summering in Tuscany, attending benefits, fundraising for charities... I thought things were just fine and dandy between us. Then, all of sudden..."

"It sort of caught me by surprise too," I explain. "We were having a nice quiet dinner one night and BAM... she tells me she's moving in with a younger guy and wants a divorce. On my fortieth birthday no less."

"Ouch," Todd says, wincing. "That is truly appalling. She couldn't have waited another day?"

"Apparently not," I say.

"What's the story with women?" he muses.

"If I knew that, I'd write a book and make a fortune."

Todd chuckles. Suddenly, he seems like a pretty nice guy in spite of his upper crust demeanor. "How've you been dealing with it, Hendricks?" he asks me, leaning back and placing his perfectly tanned arm across the top of the couch. "Your divorce."

"Our marriage wasn't exactly a fairy tale," I reply. "But I consulted... um ... a counselor. For guidance, you know. That helped a lot."

Todd nods, then downs half of his gin and tonic in one long gulp. "It's been about three weeks since she left me."

"Maybe she'll have second thoughts and come back to you."

"Unlikely."

"Don't worry, you'll find somebody else in no time," I counsel him. "You're a good looking guy. You've got lots of money. Cool car... I'll bet women will be lining up to meet you. Me on the other hand..."

After a moment of contemplation, Todd nods. "Thanks for the encouragement," he says, "but right now, everything just seems so... hopeless."

"It'll pass," I offer.

"It's just that we... know each other so well," he says morosely. "Eighteen years of marriage. Starting over just seems so... I don't know... *laborious.*"

Suddenly, I realize I'm feeling sorry for him. "I hear you," I say. "Deirdre and I know each other pretty well too."

"On the other hand," he continues, "she's always been a little on the cold side, but we've known each other since we were kids. We practically grew up together."

Todd turns and plucks a framed photograph off the table behind him. He stares at it. "God, she's so beautiful," he says, tearing up again.

"None of my business," I say, "but did she happen to say *why* she's divorcing you? Just curious. Don't mean to pry."

Todd sighs. "Well, apparently, she's still in love with some jerk she met in college," he says bitterly.

I sit up. "Oh?"

"Some writer asshole."

"Excuse me?"

"I said she's in love with some writer jerk she met in college."

"*Really?*" I say, trying not to sound too interested, because I'm thinking: Who else could this writer jerk be but me? Could Samantha still be in love with me? It seems impossible, given the way I treated her at the end.

"What's his name?" I ask.

"She wouldn't say. Why do you want to know?"

"Maybe I... um... knew the guy in college," I stammer. "I took a few writing classes myself. In fact, Samantha was in one of them."

"Sorry," he says. "I'm afraid I don't know anything about him, not that it matters. Samantha's obsessed with writing and writers, always has been. Frankly, it bores the shit out of me. The house is crammed with books. I may have to donate them to the library or Goodwill. I certainly have no use for them."

I glance at the bookcase that covers one whole wall of the room. "I'm no expert, but they look like first editions," I say. "Must be worth a fortune."

"Who cares?" he says. Shaking his head sadly, Todd tilts his glass to his lips and finishes off his drink. Then he looks at his watch.

"You should probably send them to an auction house," I suggest.

But Todd isn't paying attention. "Listen, I don't mean to roust you fellas out," he tells us, rising from the sofa, "but I have an appointment with my accountant in fifteen minutes. I'm preparing for the divorce settlement. Tons of paperwork. Fortunately, we both signed pre-nups."

"I understand," I say. Morris and I stand up.

Todd leads us back to the front door. "It's been a real pleasure meeting you," he says to me. "As they say, misery loves company."

"How about a hug?" I ask. "You look like you could use one."

Todd hesitates for a second, but then he nods and we embrace and pat each other on the back.

"Take care of yourself, Todd," I tell him. "You'll get through this, I promise you. Most people do eventually, or so my therapist tells me."

"I certainly hope you're right, Hendricks," he says wistfully. "Right now things seem a little bleak."

He follows us as we climb back into my Camry. "Chin up, Todd," I say, opening the car door. "Hang in there."

And then we drive off.

~

Since I didn't bring my laptop and therefore can't access Map-Quest, I have no clue how to get to Nantucket, so we stop at a gas station and purchase a road map of Cape Cod. I also pick up a few packs of Hostess Cupcakes, a couple of bananas and a large bottle of Diet Coke.

"Did you hear what he said?" I ask Morris, as we hit the road again.

"Which part?"

"The part about how Samantha's still in love with a writer from college."

"So?"

"Guess who the writer is?"

"I give up."

"Me."

Morris starts to laugh. He laughs so hard he starts coughing like a car that's running out of gas, and for a minute I'm afraid he's going to choke on his own phlegm. I slap him on the back a few times while I'm driving, which causes the car to swerve into another lane, but eventually he stops.

"Give me a break. A writer?" he says. *"You?"*

"That's right. Me."

"A writer of what exactly?"

"It's a long story," I tell him.

"Tell me anyway, Shakespeare," he insists. "We have plenty of time."

So I spend the next five minutes recounting how I duped Samantha and Ms. Abernathy into thinking I was the collegiate reincarnation of Herman Melville. When I'm finished, he doesn't say anything for a few seconds and just shakes his head sadly.

"You were such a putz, Jimmy," he says. "Such a schemer. Such a louse."

"I know, I know, I'm not proud of it," I moan.

"I'm disappointed in you," he adds. "I may have to reconsider the wisdom of continuing our friendship."

"What can I say?" I whine. "If I could travel back in time, I would do things differently."

"Would you?"

"Knowing what I know today, yes," I say emphatically.

"Well, I suppose we all make mistakes," Morris reflects after a while. "But you kept making the same one over and over."

"My brain was in my penis," I tell him.

"You want to say a prayer of atonement?"

"Not really. I'm an atheist, remember? God would see through it. You can't fake Him out, can you?"

"I've never tried," Morris says.

After a few hours we arrive in the town of Woods Hole, site of the Nantucket ferryboat landing. The docks are bustling with anxious tourists, and after locating the ticket office, we stand in line behind a man wearing madras pants, a bright red Izod shirt and a pink golf cap. Just to the left of us, a young woman in cut-offs and a purple T-shirt, who reeks of marijuana, is frantically searching through a backpack. I'm tempted to ask her if she can spare a joint, but this would not be the place.

Ten minutes later, we're in front of the ticket window, where a woman in harlequin glasses and a Red Sox cap informs us that we will not be able to take the car to the Island because all the spaces on the ferry have already been booked up for the summer season. Most of them, she tells us, were reserved in January.

"How long you planning on staying?" she asks in a Boston accent.

I glance at Morris, who looks at me and puts up his index finger. "A day maybe," I tell her.

"You can park over in the lot by that lobster boat for thirty dollars a day," she says. "We take credit cards."

"That seems like a lot," I tell her.

She shrugs. "Only game in town, unless you want to park ten miles away."

With a grimace, I fork over a twenty and a ten.

"How are we supposed to get around on the Island?" I ask her. "Do we need to rent a car when we get there?"

She laughs derisively and shakes her head. "Are you kidding? You'll never get a rental car, not in the middle of the summer season, not without a reservation."

"Okay, then what would you recommend?"

"Most people rent bikes," she informs us.

So we park the car in the overpriced lot and find a seafood restaurant called the Tail of the Whale, where I scarf down two bowls of thick clam chowder and a fish sandwich, while Morris consumes a soggy hot dog he'd wrapped in one of the Challah napkins. Then he suns himself on an outdoor bench while I throw bread crumbs at a group of shrieking seagulls.

Two hours later, we're roused by the sound of a loud maritime horn signaling the arrival of the ferry. It pulls into its berth and, after the returning passengers disembark, I nudge Morris and we board the vessel via a creaky wooden gangplank with about two hundred other people, all of whom are dressed far more appropriately than Morris, although he doesn't seem to notice. Bright colors that don't match seem to be the common fashion preference among many of our new shipmates, although there are a few kids in flip flops and ragged jeans. A gaggle of tourists in Bermuda shorts snaps pictures with their cell phones as we lumber carefully over the unsteady ramp and onto the vessel.

Unfortunately, by the time we get on board, there are no seats available inside or outside the ship, so we stand at the railing as the ferry pulls away from the dock and slowly floats out of the harbor and into the choppy waters of the Atlantic. Twenty minutes later,

Morris barfs over the edge of the railing, but the strong ocean breeze blows some of it back at us. Now we're both picking stray bits of Morris's half-digested wiener off our clothes. I go inside for a plastic cup of water and some napkins and we thoroughly wet down the stains, but it still smells like puke.

"I've never been on a boat before in my life," Morris admits sheepishly. "Looks like I get seasick."

"You think?" I ask, a little annoyed.

"You don't suppose there's any chance this boat will sink do you?" he asks in a worried tone.

I give him a look.

"Good," Morris says. "I can't swim."

"You played football in college and you can't swim?"

"We rarely played in water," Morris says.

"Can you at least ride a bike?"

"Of course."

"Good to know," I say.

Nearby, a six-year-old boy stands at the ferry's stern, tossing bits of bread at a gathering of eager seagulls, watching gleefully as they all dive bomb in unison to grab the food. The fragrant ocean breeze feels refreshingly cool and clean as it whips my hair in fourteen different directions. Morris looks green as he keeps a hand on his yarmulke to keep it from blowing into the Atlantic.

The trip lasts about two and a half hours. Morris retches over the side a few more times until nothing but spittle and bile emerge. By this time, I've moved about twenty feet away from him to avoid another blowback.

After we dock, Morris and I are delighted to learn that there's a bike rental shop a block from the ferry landing. (Later, we discover that there are about twenty bike rental shops on the Island, so this is no big deal.) After leasing bikes and helmets, I ask the manager if he knows the whereabouts of the Conrad house on the

Cliffside. I figure this is a long shot, but luckily, it's not. Apparently, the Conrad house is renowned among the Islanders.

"You can't miss it," he explains. "It's a huge white house, biggest goddamn one on the Cliff. White Rolls Royce and a yellow Ferrari in the driveway, putting green on the back lawn, tennis court, snotty assholes wandering around..."

Then he gives me a tourist map of Nantucket landmarks—an old jailhouse, a whaling museum and a windmill—and runs off to help another customer.

Unfortunately, the trek to Cliffside is mostly uphill, which should have been obvious since cliffs are usually not downhill from sea level. Morris breathes heavily the whole way, his bike wobbling perilously beneath his body. He looks like a gorilla trying to ride a tricycle. I grimace at the sight of him, afraid that he's going to topple over and hurt himself, but miraculously he manages to maintain his balance.

It takes us about an hour, but we finally find the yellow Ferrari parked in the driveway of the huge house. The Rolls isn't there.

Just as the bike shop manager told us, the place is sprawling and ostentatious, a shingled palace trimmed in white with bay windows that look out over the ocean, flawlessly manicured hedges and four chimneys. Morris, who is now gasping for air, drops his bicycle and leans forward with his hands on his knees, trying to recover from our arduous uphill ride. Then he collapses on the front lawn in the shade of a huge oak tree, pulls off his helmet and wipes his forehead with a pocket handkerchief while I stride to the doorway, ignoring the bright red-lettered NO TRESPASSING sign posted on the front lawn. I'm surprised that there's no security gate that blocks entry to the driveway, but there appear to be very few of these on the Island.

Nobody answers the doorbell on my first try, so I push it again.

She hasn't changed at all in twenty years. It's as if the clock somehow stopped just for her. No wrinkles, no extra weight around the midriff, not even a hint of cellulite on those perfectly shaped thighs. The reason I can tell there's no cellulite is because all she's wearing is a very small and quite fetching white bikini, which contrasts well with her perfect tan. Her body shines from a layer of sunscreen. On her feet is a pair of pink sandals. An iPhone protrudes from the top of her bikini bottom.

She takes off her sunglasses and blinks. After scrutinizing me, the first words out of her mouth are, "What the fuck?"

"Hi Samantha," I say.

"Larry Hendricks?"

"Jimmy," I say, beaming. "Glad to see me?"

"Not even a smidgeon of a smidgeon."

"Yeah right," I chide, smirking.

She ignores the remark. "What in God's name are you doing here?"

"I was in the neighborhood."

"How very droll."

"Can I come in?"

"No, you certainly may *not* come in," she snaps, blocking the doorway. "You can toddle on home and crawl back under your rock."

"You don't really mean that," I tell her. "Be honest."

But she's not paying attention. She's sniffing the air. "You smell like vomit," she observes. "It's positively revolting."

"I know. Somebody on the ferry got seasick."

"Oh," she says, with a weary sigh "I've never been on the ferry. We have a plane of course. So what do you want?"

"I came here to say I'm sorry."

"For what exactly?"

"For, you know, what happened between us in college."

"I'm afraid I don't really recall," she says. "What happened?"

I narrow my eyes. "What do you mean you don't recall? How can you not remember? I was your first lover."

"And...?"

"And then I... um... dumped you. Remember now?"

She laughs scornfully. "Your memory is a little foggy," she says. "I believe it was I who dumped *you*."

"That's incorrect."

"Have it your way," she says coolly.

"Anyway," I continue, "I'm sorry. It was a horrible thing to do. Please accept my sincere apologies."

Samantha yawns. "Look Larry, just do me a *huge* favor and go away," she says, starting to close the door. "I barely even remember you."

"That's not what Todd told me."

She freezes. "Good God, you saw *Todd?*"

"Yes," I tell her. "We had a lovely visit. He's a little upset that you're divorcing him. Actually, he's devastated."

"That's none of your goddamned business," she snaps. "How *dare* you intrude into my personal life?"

"I didn't," I inform her. "He volunteered the information. He's lonely and needed someone to talk to. As it happens, I'm going through a divorce myself so—"

"Did the blabbermouth happen to tell you *why* I'm divorcing him?"

"Yes, he did," I say happily. "He mentioned that you're still in love with a writer you met in college."

"What!" she cries. "That's private. I can't believe he actually *told* you that."

"Maybe so, but frankly I'm flattered," I tell her.

She studies me. "Oh? And why on earth would that be?"

"I think you know."

"I do not," she says, placing a hand on her hip. "Enlighten me."

"Well, obviously it's me. I was a writer in college."

Then she laughs. It isn't an amiable outburst. There is

clearly some serious derision in that laugh. It makes me a little uncomfortable.

"*You?*" she says with a sneer.

"Well, yeah."

This time she throws her head back before she starts guffawing at me again. I suddenly realize that the sun is frying my back.

"Still the arrogant little ass," she says.

"No, that's what I came here to say. I've changed, Samantha. I really have. I've had an... epiphany. I—"

"Epiphany? Ooooooh. Such a big word for a nitwit like you," she observes.

"I've been working on my vocabulary," I tell her. "You know, for my writing."

"Oh really?" she says sarcastically. "Your writing? Funny, I've never seen a novel with your name on it anywhere, not even on Amazon. You're not even on Google. Everybody's on Google. My dog is on Google."

"You took the time to Google me?" I ask. "I'm flattered."

"Don't be," she says. "I wouldn't have bothered, but then, totally out of the blue, I received this curious email."

"Oh? From who?"

"Somebody named Robert," she says. "I forget his last name. Orsinball or Assinhole or something. He sent me a link."

I wince. "No idea who that is," I say, simulating ignorance. "What link?"

"That first short story you *supposedly* wrote for creative writing class? It was written by a person named Harvey Blitz in 1948. *The New Yorker* published it. *You* plagiarized it."

"Of course I didn't *plagiarize* it," I insist with fake outrage. "That's totally ridiculous. Don't believe everything you read on the Internet."

"You're a fucking liar Larry," she says. "I'm closing the door now. Goodbye. Such a pleasure to see you."

"Wait!" I plead. The door is still open. "Okay, okay, it's true. I did it because I wasn't much of a writer and the people in that class were brutal."

"And your so-called 'novel'," she adds. "It was all a hoax to get me into bed, wasn't it, you little worm?"

"Yes it was," I admit. "And it makes me sick to even think about it. But like I said, that's why I'm here. I feel guilty as hell and—"

"You are such an asshole, Larry," she tells me.

"*Was* an asshole," I respond.

She snickers. "If you actually thought the writer that Todd was talking about is *you,* then you are *still* an asshole. In fact you are perhaps the *biggest* asshole I have ever met in my entire life."

"Distinction accepted," I say. "So who's this other writer?"

"Why am I even still having this conversation?" she asks. "It's really none of your goddamn business, but his name is Pierre Delbes."

"Never heard of him," I say.

"Should I give a damn?" she says. "You're a Luddite."

I ignore the slur. "Okay, so I fooled you into thinking I was a writer. I admit that. And I'm truly, *truly* sorry. It was a despicable thing to do. But surely you must have *some* pleasant memories of the time we were together."

Samantha thinks about it for a second. "Hmmm. Let me see," she says, placing a long, well-manicured index finger on her cheek. "Nope. Not a single one."

"That can't possibly be true," I say. "We had *some* good times didn't we?"

But Samantha's not looking at me now. I follow her gaze to the lawn near the oak tree where Morris is basking in the shade.

"Who's the slovenly behemoth sitting on my lawn?"

"That's my friend Morris Berkowitz. We're on vacation together."

"Nonsense. He's wearing a black suit. Nobody wears a black suit on Nantucket in the summer except morticians."

"He has peculiar taste in clothing," I inform her.

"He's not an officer of the law is he?"

"No," I say. "Why do you ask?"

She turns her withering gaze from Morris back to me. "You're trespassing on private property you know," she says.

I'm about to respond when her iPhone chirps. She pulls it out of her bikini bottom and lifts it to her ear. "Hi Muffy," she says. "Yes I *did* hear about it. I can't believe it either. It's positively bizarre. Listen, could you hold on a second?"

Samantha puts her hand over the mouthpiece and turns to me. "I have to take this, Larry," she says. "So you and your fat friend can get on your little bikes and leave now. I don't think we have anything left to talk about."

"Sure," I say, "but if it's not too much trouble do you think you could get us a couple of glasses of water. We're totally dehydrated."

But Samantha doesn't answer. She just goes inside, leaving the door open a crack.

While she's gone, I wipe the sweat off my brow with a tissue and join Morris under the shady tree. I've sweated completely through my dark blue, short-sleeved Izod shirt and my face is completely covered with perspiration. Morris is breathing steadily now and sniffing his armpits. The black suit must be like a sauna. I suddenly notice that his nose is sunburned.

"This isn't going well, is it?" Morris asks.

"No," I say, "but I haven't tried groveling yet."

"So where'd she go?" he asks.

"Important phone call from someone named Muffy."

"I could sure use a glass of water," he says, fanning himself with his big hand.

"I asked her for some," I say, "but I have a feeling she'd rather watch us slowly dehydrate and die on the lawn."

"There must be a hose here somewhere," Morris says, looking toward a hedgerow near the house. "Let's take a look."

Two seconds later, the door bursts open and Samantha reappears with a shotgun in her hands. Before Morris and I can react and scramble onto our bikes, she pulls off the first round, which decimates a layer of bark on the oak tree, but thankfully misses us.

"IN COMING!" I shout as if Morris hadn't noticed.

"Oh God!" Morris shouts back. "Fuck!"

Then I quickly mount my bike and start pedaling as if I was just starting the first leg of the Tour de France. Horrified, Morris grabs his bike and hides behind the trunk of the oak tree when the second shot goes off. But she's not aiming at him, she's aiming at me, so Morris has enough time to clumsily leap onto his seat and catch up to me. The second shot blasts a plaster lawn ornament into smithereens and a piece of the plaster shrapnel almost hits me in the butt. I look back and see Samantha reloading the gun. By this time, Morris and I are back on the pavement, nearly out of range and pedaling like hell for the corner.

By the time we make it back to the bicycle shop in town, we're both soggy with sweat and pumped up with adrenaline. Neither of us has ever been shot at before, at least not with a real gun, and in an odd way, it's exhilarating. But the rush is tempered by the knowledge that we have to get out of Dodge pronto, before Samantha has time to call the police, or gather a posse of irate skeet-shooting, polo-playing relatives and lethal cutlery-wielding groundskeepers.

After hurriedly returning our bikes, Morris and I sprint the twenty yards to the ticket office on the wharf, throw some cash at the clerk and manage to make it to the gangplank just seconds before the last ferry departs for the mainland.

Part Four

Molly

Molly... Then

MOLLY MARTINEZ TRANSFERRED to Fryman as a junior after completing two years at a small community college in Brooklyn, New York. As a general rule, students who transferred as upperclassmen had a hard time adjusting because it was often difficult for newcomers to form friendships. All the cliques and sororities were already in place. Roommates had settled in. Campus friendships had been firmly cemented. On top of that, Molly was quiet, timid and not especially outgoing so, until I came along, she was something of a loner.

At first, I wasn't exactly swept off my feet by Molly, yet there was something oddly captivating about her. She was the product of a Puerto Rican father and an Irish mother, kind of an odd combination of genes that gave her a certain curious mystique. She had light brown skin, a tumbleweed of curly reddish-brown hair that fell to her shoulders, big sad brown eyes that broke your heart and a thin nose with a slight bump in the middle of it. Her full lips, which turned up slightly at the corners, seemed to contradict the poignancy of her eyes and her smile revealed a thin gap between her two front teeth, an orthodontic oversight that contrived to add an appealing touch of quirkiness. There was an aura about her that seemed very exotic to me at the time.

Molly's usual style of dress was also decidedly unconventional, but very cool in some ways. Most of the time, she would wear a man's white shirt (sometimes accented by a colorful tie), baggy jeans and running shoes. Except for oversized earrings, she rarely wore jewelry and her make-up was limited to eye shadow and a subtle shade of lipstick.

Since I knew that she had no friends on campus, it wasn't much of a challenge for me to meet her. I think she was a little desperate for attention during those first few months. I'd observed her walking all alone on the quad or sitting by herself on a bench under a shady tree, reading a book or eating a sandwich. At the Student Union, she was always alone, pretending to be preoccupied with her soda or absorbed in a textbook, madly underlining sentences. Nobody made much of an effort to meet her. She tried to ignore the laughing groups of people that surrounded her. It was heartbreaking actually and, in some ways, she reminded me of Laura. Superficial as I might have been in those days, I felt a very strange thing for the first time in my life: I'm not sure, but I think they call it compassion.

By the beginning of my junior year, thanks to my prior experience as a short story plagiarist, I was able to navigate my way around the confusing labyrinth of the school library so expertly that I could have qualified for head librarian. Because of this talent, my *modus operandi* for meeting girls in those days was to hang out in the library for the express purpose of rescuing frustrated coeds who were hopelessly confused by the complexities of the system. This tactic was usually fruitless.

It was about eight o'clock on a Friday night and she seemed to be utterly lost, walking from one aisle to the next, pulling books out by their spines, inspecting them, flipping the pages, shoving them back in and then turning to the next rack, sighing with frustration as she inched along. She was clearly disoriented so I, Library Man, came to the rescue.

"You seem a little lost," I said pleasantly, as she stood on her tiptoes struggling to push yet another heavy tome back into its tight space on one of the upper shelves. I gently grabbed the book out of her fingers and easily slid it in. When I turned to her, Molly just looked blankly at me for a second or two before whispering "thanks". I had a feeling she was in a state of shock that somebody was actually talking to her.

"May I help you find something?" I inquired. "I know my way around this maze pretty well. I'm a library junkie."

She answered me in such a soft voice I could barely hear her. "Sorry," I said, putting a hand behind my ear. "Could you repeat that a little louder this time or do I need to run home and get my hearing aid?"

"Um, no, I can't say it louder," she whispered firmly. "It's a library. We're not supposed to, um, talk in here. We might disturb the others."

"What others?"

Molly looked around. Except for a geekish library clerk who was wheeling a cart full of books down the aisles, we were the only ones there.

"Don't people study here?" she asked. She was still whispering.

"Sure, but not on Friday nights at eight o'clock," I informed her. "Everybody's out partying or engaging in unspeakable activities."

"You're not," she observed.

"I'm observing the Sabbath."

She smirked.

"Listen," I said, "why don't you raise your voice a few decibels, I'll lower mine a few decibels and we'll meet in the middle."

After a moment of rumination that involved a long consultation with her shoes, she said, "okay" in a normal tone.

"Much better," I said with a smile. Suddenly, I felt the need to say something complimentary, so I added, "You have a nice voice. Very mellifluous, very—"

"You're, um, kidding right?" she asked. "You can barely hear my voice."

"Why would I kid you?" I asked.

"I don't know. We've never, um, met before."

"That's easily fixed," I said, eagerly extending my hand. "I'm Jimmy Hendricks. I'm a junior."

"Is that your real name?" she asked, as she took my hand and gave it a weak, perfunctory shake.

"I'm afraid it is. My parents were big fans."

"Really?"

"Actually, no."

"I'm, um, Molly Martinez," she told me. "I'm a transfer student. I just, um, started here. You're the first person I've actually met so far except for my student advisor and Martha, the woman who works behind the information desk up front."

"Pleased to meet you, Molly Martinez," I said brightly.

She mumbled something that sounded like, "Same here, Jimmy."

"So what's your major?" I asked, this being the standard opening gambit for college students with no imagination.

"Um, Political Science," she told me, gazing at something over my shoulder. "I'm going for my Masters and then a Ph.D. What's yours?"

"Global Studies," I said.

She crinkled her nose. "What is that exactly?" she asked.

"Actually, I have no idea," I said.

"Then why did you choose it?"

I shrugged. "I was late for registration and it was the only major with a vacancy," I said, although the real reason had more to do with the fact that Global Studies was widely known to be unchallenging.

Molly nodded a few times and then looked at her shoes again.

This created a dangerous gap in the conversation which I was determined to fill before she disappeared into the stacks, never to be seen again.

Struggling to engage her, I blurted out the stupidest line I could think of, one that was generally reserved for bars. "So do you come here often?" I asked her.

"Pretty often," she said. "I'm very studious and this is where they keep the books."

"I've noticed that," I told her.

"I'm sorry," she said shyly. "That was dumb."

"Not at all," I said. "I thought it was pretty funny actually."

"How about you?" she inquired. "Do you, um, come here a lot?"

"Yes," I replied.

"To study?"

"Sometimes," I replied. "Sometimes for social reasons. You know, to be around people, make friends and stuff."

"You mean you pick up girls here," she remarked perceptively.

"No, no, no," I said. "Of course not."

"I'm sorry," she stammered. "I shouldn't have said that. It was rude."

"That's okay. To be honest, I'm not much of a ladies' man. I guess I'm a little... bashful and clumsy around members of the opposite sex."

Then, mimicking her favorite gesture, I looked shyly at my shoes.

"Me too," she said, looking over my shoulder again. "I'm kind of... I don't know... "

I turned around to see what she kept looking at behind me, but there was no one there. "You're kind of what?" I asked.

"Nerdy."

"That makes two of us," I told her. "Looks like we have something in common. I'll bet we have a lot in common. Maybe we could explore that some time."

"I suppose," she said blandly. Then she gave me a suspicious look. "Are you trying to pick me up, Jimmy?"

"Of course not," I said, feigning shock. "What makes you say that?"

"I don't know," she replied meekly. "I didn't mean to, um, offend you. It's just that nobody around here has been very interested in me."

"But as long as we're on the subject," I continued, trying my hardest to sound like someone who actually *is* insecure around women, "maybe we could go out sometime."

"But I don't really know you."

"That's kind of the point."

She considered the idea, and for a moment I thought she was going to decline. "I guess it would be okay," she said uncertainly. "If you really want to."

"Why wouldn't I want to?" I asked. "I wouldn't have asked if I didn't want to."

She shrugged and looked away.

"So is now good for you?" I asked.

"Um, no, actually I have way too much studying to do," she responded. This was an obstacle I had never encountered before. The women I usually dated were rarely scholars. "I have a paper to write and it's due on Thursday."

"But that's a week away," I pointed out.

"I prefer to take my time," she muttered. "I don't like to, um, wait till the last moment."

"Okay," I said. "Maybe we can do it some other time then."

"Sure," she said unenthusiastically. "I guess."

"Now what was it you were looking for?"

"What?"

"Here. In the library," I reminded her. "I asked you if you needed some help finding a book, remember? Like I said, I'm a whiz at library science."

"Oh right," she said. "I forgot. I'm, um, looking for a book about Woodrow Wilson and the League of Nations."

"That would be section C, row B," I told her, proud of my knowledge. "Now does this particular book have a title or what?"

～

That was the beginning of my involvement with Molly. We started out by meeting at the library almost every night and soon progressed to the Student Union, where I usually had burgers and fries, and she had salads. Molly was timid around me for a very long time, but after a few weeks, I sensed that she was starting to loosen up. It took me a while to get her to stop saying "um" all the time and to look me straight in the eyes when we talked. Sometimes, when she became too absorbed in her shoes or the surface of a table, I would reach out and lightly raise her chin with my index finger. After a few weeks, I guess she began to trust me, which normally was a mistake. Sometimes, I wouldn't see her for days because she would often hibernate at home to study for an exam or write a research paper or prepare for a class discussion group. Nobody at Fryman, at least nobody I knew, ever prepared for a discussion group except Molly, even though I seriously doubted that she ever overcame her uneasiness enough to actually participate. Apparently, Fryman was a lot more challenging for her than the community college she'd attended. She was very ambitious and strived to keep her grade point average high enough to qualify for a scholarship to Harvard grad school after she completed her undergraduate requirements. That was her dream and I truly admired her unshakeable sense of discipline, probably because it was uncharted territory for me.

The mere fact that Molly considered me less significant than her studies actually intrigued me. I had never been with a woman like that before and I knew she wasn't pulling a hard-to-get routine on me either. Her studies actually *did* take priority.

After a while, for reasons that escaped me, Molly took on the improbable task of helping me with my schoolwork (history in particular), a charitable but completely hopeless exercise, and the only reason I cooperated, was because I liked being around her so much. Obviously, I didn't care about the schoolwork.

"You're not paying attention, Jimmy," she scolded me one night during one of our tutoring sessions in the library. "Do you want to learn this or what?"

"Sorry, Molly," I said, feigning sincerity. "It's just kind of hard for me to concentrate on Herbert Hoover when you're around, although I must say, he has nice eyes."

Molly shook her head wearily. "Staring at me isn't going to help your grade point average," she told me in that no-nonsense tone she used in these situations. "Now pay attention."

"Yes ma'am," I said with a salute. I have to admit, I got a kick out of the way Molly ordered me around like that because it showed how much she cared. None of my other girlfriends had been that interested in my future, except for Samantha but that didn't count because the future I'd painted for myself had been a sham. Futile as it was, Molly had made it her mission to transform me into a scholar. Her tenacity, in the face of certain failure, was remarkable.

Unfortunately, her tenacity in the face of my repeated attempts to get her between the sheets was also remarkable. One night, after about three weeks of platonic dating, I slipped my hand on her thigh under a library table and edged it slowly toward the warmer nest between them. Without taking her eyes off her book, she grabbed my hand and placed it on the table. I tried again. Same response. At night, when we kissed in front of her doorstep or in my car, I'd sometimes raise a hand to cup one of her breasts, but inevitably I was met with instant defeat.

"Is this just all about sex for you?" she asked me one night in the library after I'd tried unsuccessfully to put the moves on her again.

"No," I replied. "That's kind of insulting. I like you, Molly. I like you a lot."

"I like you too," she said. "Kind of."

"*Kind of?*" I said. "Just kind of?"

She gazed at me warmly. "I'm sorry I said that," she told me. "It was mean, but we don't know each other well enough yet. It's only been a few weeks."

I stared at her for a moment. "You look very pretty in this light," I said.

"This is fluorescent light, Jimmy," she pointed out. "Nobody looks good in fluorescent light. And flattery won't work. Just so you know."

After about five weeks of dating her, I began to sense an odd sea change in my character. Was I falling in love or was this simply a temporary lapse of judgment? Or was it lust masquerading as love? To my surprise, my feelings for Molly appeared to be genuine. She just seemed so delicate and fragile and needy that I felt this odd protective instinct whenever we were together. It was weird. Sometimes, I would just sit with my chin in my hands at a table in the library and watch her studying or underlining passages in a textbook with one of those yellow felt tip markers. She had a habit of absently winding strands of her hair around her fingers, a quirk I found thoroughly adorable. Sometimes, she'd look up and give me one of those radiant smiles. After a while, it didn't seem to matter to me that she wasn't exactly my dream girl, because I was in the grip of some strange alteration in my brain chemistry that seemed utterly foreign to me.

"Earth to Jimmy," Molly said one night during one of our many tutoring sessions. She waved her hand in front of my eyes. I'd been staring at her again.

"Huh?"

"You're not even looking at the book," she observed.

"Sorry," I said. "Where were we?"

"Franklin D. Roosevelt and the Great Depression."

"Oh yeah."

Molly sighed. "Don't you care that your parents are spending all this money on your education?"

"Actually, I think they just wanted to get me out of the house so my Dad could put a pool table in my room."

"Not funny."

"I had to go *somewhere* after high school," I told her.

"But you're not learning anything."

"That's not true," I said. "Okay, it's true."

"Why did you even apply to Fryman?"

"I'm not sure," I told her, "but the girl-boy ratio is seven to five."

She shook her head like an exasperated grade school teacher. "You're impossible, Jimmy," she reprimanded me. "That's such a lame reason."

"Okay granted I'm not a scholar," I conceded, "but I happen to know a lot about certain things."

"Like what?"

This stumped me for a moment. "Neurosurgery," I said. "I'm self-taught."

She gave me a look and a sigh.

"Okay, I'm a whiz at library science," I told her. "Nobody knows the Dewey Decimal System as well as I do. It's very complicated."

"Okay, so are you planning to become a librarian?"

"No, but it's a legitimate scholarly pursuit."

"Hardly," she said curtly. "It's not even a real science."

"Okay, maybe I'm not a scholar, but I'm smart, witty, handsome and occasionally honest," I said, watching her roll her eyes. "Okay, maybe not that handsome."

"Don't you care at all about *anything*?" she asked me, bending down to retie one of her running shoes.

"I care about you."

"That's great," she said, "but I meant your life, your career, your future."

"Don't worry about me, I'll muddle through somehow," I assured her. "Maybe I'll marry a rich girl someday, drink gin and tonics all morning, lie around the pool, go to polo matches in my Bentley."

"That's pathetic, Jimmy." I noticed she had yellow ink on the tips of her fingers from all the underlining.

"Okay, so maybe I'll marry you," I said, placing my hand over hers.

"And do what all day?" she asked.

"I don't know," I said. "Sharpen your pencils?"

Molly sighed. "I don't even know why I'm dating you. You can be such an idiot sometimes. You're aimless. You have no goals. You're really not my type at all, not that I actually have a type."

"So why do you keep going out with me then?" I asked her.

A few seconds passed as she studied me. "I don't know," she stammered.

～

In February of that year, Molly had to go home for a week to attend the funeral of her favorite aunt, who had died suddenly of a massive stroke. She was utterly distraught when she received the tragic news and I would hear her suddenly erupt into tears, hidden behind the rows of shelves in the library. Seeing her suffer like that broke my heart, so I did my best to console her. When the time came for her to go home, I drove her to the train station, carried her luggage for her and walked her to the gate. She seemed preoccupied and possibly a little anxious about traveling alone. When the time came for her to board, she gave me a perfunctory kiss on the cheek and disappeared behind the crowds jostling for seats on the train.

While Molly was gone, Morris and Naomi (who was his girlfriend at the time), took pity on me and invited me over to their place for dinner a few times. Morris and I had become fast friends during our sophomore year when, by accident, we'd ended up rooming together. My original plan had been to find an apartment with Sanjee, who'd also decided to move out of the dorms so he could create a bachelor pad for himself. So I managed to find us a small two-bedroom place about five miles from campus, but at the last minute, Sanjee backed out, claiming that he needed privacy. So I was stuck with an apartment I couldn't afford. My only recourse was to advertise for a new roommate so I posted signs on various bulletin boards and trees around campus. Morris was the first and only one to respond. We were an unlikely pair because, at the time, he was a star on the football team and I was allergic to sports. Nevertheless, we bonded and spent many a night sharing joints or drinking beer and prowling for women. But when our lease expired in June, he moved in with Naomi, who he'd met in one of his classes. I found a small studio apartment, where I lived alone.

We remained friends and, during our junior year, after I'd met Molly, we sometimes double-dated. They both took a liking to Molly, although I had a suspicion that neither of them had the slightest clue why a woman that smart, that ambitious and that discriminating would be hanging around with a hopeless nitwit like me, except for purely charitable reasons. Truth be told, I sometimes wondered about that myself.

So, while Molly was gone, I spent a few nights eating at their place.

"If you're smart," Morris told me one night as we stood in his kitchen helping Naomi wash dishes, "you won't screw this one up. I have no idea what this thoroughly delightful woman sees in a schmo like you, but there's no accounting for taste."

"Thanks a bunch, Morris," I replied. "I thought you were my best friend."

"I am," Morris said, putting his huge arm around my shoulders and pulling me toward him. "And I love you like a brother. I just don't see any logical basis for a relationship like this to exist."

"Gee," I said. "Maybe you and I should try to find her another boyfriend."

"Don't be so hard on him, Morris," Naomi scolded him. "Jimmy has a good heart. It's just hidden somewhere."

"Thanks Naomi," I said uncertainly. "I think."

"Just don't blow it, bro," Morris said patting my cheek. "That's all I'm saying. You may never get this lucky again."

I conjured up an image of Molly. "She is great, isn't she?" I said.

"Just try to keep it in your pants," Morris advised me. "For once."

~

Molly returned a week later and I picked her up at the train station. When she saw me waiting at the arrival gate, she threw herself into my arms and kissed me with more passion and intensity than ever before.

"What's this all about?" I asked, nonplussed.

"I don't really know," she said. "I can't explain it. But I really, really missed you Jimmy. More than I thought I would. More than I logically should have."

"Maybe it was something you ate," I suggested.

"I'm serious, Jimmy," she said sternly.

"I missed you too, Molly," I told her. "It was hell."

"Poor boy," she said stroking my cheek. "I thought about you every day. It was actually a little annoying."

"I thought about you too," I assured her. "All the time. Every minute. Even in class."

"Since when do you go to class?"

Later, in my car, while we were stuck in a traffic jam, she turned to me. "You didn't meet anybody while I was gone, did you?" she asked. "Tell me the truth."

"Of course not," I claimed. "Why would you even ask me that? I mean, don't you trust me?"

She looked at me, as if searching my face for some telltale sign that I was lying. "Yes," she said finally, leaning over to kiss my cheek. "I do. I do trust you."

I smiled warmly, secure in the knowledge that there was no chance she would ever find out the truth.

~

Since she'd missed a week of schoolwork, Molly had a lot of catching up to do, so she threw herself into her work and didn't come up for air for several days. But when I did manage to see her for any length of time, she was definitely more affectionate. Typically, I tried to take advantage of this new development. One night in the library, I reached under the table and once again let my hand meander from her thigh to her crotch, fully expecting a rebuff. But I was amazed when she didn't remove it. In fact, she clamped her legs together with my hand securely lodged between here thighs. I looked at her questioningly.

"*We can't do it in the library, Jimmy,*" she snapped.

"Huh?"

"I said—"

"What do you mean by 'it'?" I asked stupidly.

She just gave me a look.

I tried to hide my excitement. "Really? Can we go right now?"

She shook her head, but I could tell she was amused. "Give me an hour. I still have a chapter to read for class tomorrow. Eisenhower and the interstate highway system."

"Gee, I'm flattered," I said. "So it's either me or Eisenhower and you pick Eisenhower." I think I may have even pouted a little.

"You've waited this long," she noted. "You can wait another hour."

"My feelings are hurt, that's all," I whined, and they were.

My tragic look, which was actually legitimate for a change,

must have touched her. She glanced around and did something that really took me by surprise. She put her hand on my crotch.

"That should tide you over," she said, smiling mischievously.

~

Molly lived alone in a tiny one-bedroom apartment in the upper half of a two-story house that was in desperate need of a new paint job and more than a few major repairs. The inside was sparsely furnished with a sad lumpy old couch, a three-legged kitchen table and a desk, all of which looked like garage sale booty. Aside from a few family photos, a subway map of Boston and some posters of Washington, D.C., there was nothing on the walls but a few patchy areas of fresh white plaster awaiting a coat of paint. Her landlord was probably as miserly as mine, maybe worse, but Molly was on a strict budget so it was all she could afford.

When we got there, she told me to sit while she changed, so I plopped down on her sofa and flipped through an issue of the school newspaper, but I couldn't concentrate. It took her about twenty minutes and when she finally appeared, she was wearing a white terry-cloth bathrobe, which was so clean and bright it made everything else in the apartment look even drabber. She lit a few candles and turned on her radio to a channel that featured soft music. Then she went into the kitchen and came back with two chipped Coke glasses, each half full of white wine.

"Do you like white wine?" she asked.

"I like anything with alcohol in it," I told her. "Even cough medicine." She laughed and we clinked glasses and sipped, looking over the rims at each other. The wine was awful, not that I was a connoisseur, although I did know that wine was not supposed to taste like aftershave. I drank it anyway. I didn't want to hurt her feelings.

When we were done with the wine, she stood up, took my hand and led me into her bathroom, which was also rundown, with tiles missing in the shower, a busted towel rack, a cracked mirror and some serious rust stains inside the sink basin. I had no idea why I was in her bathroom. She certainly wasn't giving me a tour.

"You want to take a shower first?" she asked me.

"Just me or—?"

"Together," she said. "It'll save on water."

"Oh," I said. "So it's a conservation thing?"

"No, I've never taken a shower with a boy, but I've always wanted to. It'll be romantic. Don't you think?"

"Shouldn't I seduce you first or something?" I asked. "Somehow it doesn't feel right this way."

"Why bother? You've been seducing me for weeks. Besides, I've already told you I want to do it," she said. "I'm twenty years old. Nobody's a virgin at twenty years old."

So I stripped off my clothes. In fact, I think I broke the world clothing removal record if there was one. Molly turned on the shower and we waited for it to get reasonably warm, which took what seemed to be about three minutes. Then, facing me, she slowly untied the belt of her robe and let it fall to her feet. My eyeballs almost popped out of their sockets, like a cartoon character who just realizes he's five feet beyond the edge of a cliff.

"You're staring, Jimmy," she said.

"What?"

"You're staring."

"Do you want me to stop?"

"I guess not."

"It's just that... I don't understand why you wear those loose clothes all the time."

"My boobs are a little on the big side," she complained.

"I hadn't noticed."

She smirked. "I guess I'm a little self-conscious about it."

"No reason to be."

"I don't like to advertise," she said.

"Why? You think men would be interested in you just because of your body?"

She just gave me a look.

"You have a point," I said.

Then she reached into the shower to test the temperature again. "Okay," she announced. "It's not too hot, not too cold, but if somebody in the building flushes a toilet we could end up in the burn unit."

After about five minutes, following a sensual lathering, she turned off the shower. Then we both quickly toweled off and raced to her bedroom, both of us still stark naked and dripping slightly. The bedroom was just as ratty as the rest of the place, but I didn't care, although the portrait of a somber, bespectacled Woodrow Wilson over the bed didn't add much to the mood. I suppose it could have been worse—it could have been Nixon. Molly lit a few more scented candles. Then we embraced and fell on the bed.

It was over in a matter of minutes, in spite of the annoying distraction of her old rickety bed which made such a cacophony of creaking noises that I was sure it was either going to collapse or cause some annoyed neighbor to bang a broom handle against their ceiling. But nothing happened.

I wanted to have another go at it, but Molly rose from the bed and quickly put her clothes back on.

"Where are you going?" I asked.

Molly smiled and kissed me. "Take a guess," she said.

"Oh God, not the library," I groaned. "Eisenhower and the goddamn interstate highway system again?"

"No, I finished that," she said. "I have to reread his speech about the military-industrial complex."

"Stay," I begged her.

"I'll only be gone an hour or so," she said.

"Remind me to blow up the library tomorrow," I said.

Molly took a deep breath. She glanced at her book bag. I was reaching out to her with my arm, a forlorn look on my face.

Molly glanced at the clock on the wall. "Okay, half an hour and then I have to go," she said firmly. Then, with a smile, she quickly scrambled out of her clothes and slipped back into bed.

⌒

It happened about ten o'clock one morning in spring, two months after I'd introduced her to the wonders of intercourse. Molly was at the library, studying. She usually stayed until eleven if she didn't have a class. But this time, she came home unexpectedly early. I didn't hear her open the door to my apartment, but suddenly she materialized in the doorway. She said, "I forgot my—" and then I heard her gasp as she took in the sight of me, sitting on the couch, dressed only in a bath towel, with my hand up Christine's blouse.

⌒

I hated myself. Begging had no effect on Molly. Neither did groveling. I tried to explain, but it was hopeless. Every time she saw me, she would either do an immediate about-face and walk away, or slam a door on me. Shortly after, she changed the lock on her apartment, got a new phone number and stopped going to the library at night, just to avoid me. I got the message. After two weeks of this, I finally gave up.

Eventually, Molly hooked up with a guy named Dick Morrison, a tall, prematurely-balding Midwesterner who seemed to share Molly's passion for academics. I was despondent whenever I happened to see the two of them walking hand-in-hand around the quad, or sitting under a tree, laughing it up or just reading together. Sometimes I would try to catch her eye, but she always looked away. For the first time in my life, I understood what it meant to be heartbroken. But there was nothing I could do. Once again, I had been asshole. Even if I'd gotten her attention, I had no idea what I would have said. There was nothing to say. I had blown it.

Molly... Now

MORRIS AND I DISEMBARK from the Nantucket ferry and locate my Camry, which has been baking in the sun for the last eight hours. To keep from singeing my hand, I use Morris's sweat-soaked pocket handkerchief to pull open the door. Inside it's a sauna. I turn on the air conditioner and let it blow out the heat for about ten minutes. Then we climb in, careful not to touch anything metallic, and set out for Providence, Rhode Island, where Molly lives.

We're not on the road for more than ten minutes when Morris turns to me. "I'm famished," he says. "I've run out of hot dogs."

"Maybe we'll pass a kosher deli," I suggest.

"Are you joking? In this part of the country?" he says. "I doubt it."

"A supermarket then," I say. "Supermarkets have kosher sections sometimes, don't they?"

Morris thinks about it for a second and nods. "Most of the big chains do," he says. "That's where Naomi usually goes."

"What's the next town?" I ask.

Morris unfolds the map and studies it. "Falmouth."

Twenty minutes later, we're searching the aisles of Falmouth's one and only grocery store which, thankfully, is part of a national supermarket chain. Morris carries a grocery basket as we pass by racks of specialty foods. I spot the boxes of matzoh first and enthusiastically tap Morris on the shoulder. His face lights up when we locate a shelf of pre-packaged kosher sandwiches. He grabs five of them and devours two as we stand in line at the check-out counter.

By the time we roll into Bristol, just south of Providence, it's too late to visit Molly, so we find an inexpensive bed and breakfast on the outskirts of the city. It's an eighteenth-century colonial house with a huge hearth and low doorway lintels, one of which Morris cracks his head on as we approach the uninhabited reception desk. Since it's late, we have to bang the little bell a few times to alert the owner of the place, an attractive woman of about forty or so, who clambers down a dark-stained winding staircase.

"All I have left is the Honeymoon Suite," she tells us, licking the stub of a pencil.

"That'll do," I say, glancing at Morris, who nods his approval. Then I plunk down my Visa card and sign the register.

"Breakfast is at nine," she informs us, closing the guest book. After handing back my credit card, she gives us both a look, which I immediately misinterpret.

"We're not gay or anything," I assure her.

"Doesn't matter to me one way or the other," she replies, handing me the room key, which is attached to a plastic fish-shaped keychain with the name of the inn scrawled on it. "If you pay the bill, I don't care if you bring a couple of sheep up there as long as you keep the noise down and clean up the shit. Whatever floats your boat."

The room is painted a garish shade of pink and the huge round bed has several small, red heart-shaped throw pillows propped against bigger pillows. There's a plaster statue of Cupid poised to shoot an arrow and a bowl of Hershey's Kisses, each one wrapped in red foil, on the bureau. Two pictures on the wall show couples kissing passionately on a beach in the moonlight and a copy of *The Joy of Sex* rests on one of the night tables, alongside a list of pay-per-view porno movies available on the TV, which is hidden in an armoire. It's so romantically oppressive I'm immediately turned on and nauseated at the same time.

"There's only one bed," Morris notes.

"It's the Honeymoon Suite," I remind him. "You think honeymooners sleep in separate beds?"

"Okay, fine," he says wearily. "I suppose it'll have to do."

"It's not like we have a lot of choices," I point out. "Don't worry I'll keep my hands to myself."

"I'm not worried."

Morris takes a hot shower, changes into his pajamas and falls asleep the instant his head hits the pink pillow. This guy could sleep in a rock quarry, *while they're drilling*. I'm a little nervous about seeing Molly the next day, so I have difficulty getting to sleep at first, but Morris's rhythmic snoring eventually lulls me into unconsciousness.

When I wake up the next morning, Morris's arm is draped over my shoulder and his huge hand is resting on my cheek. Very cozy, very romantic, except that he's farting. I gently pull his arm away and quietly get up. By the time I'm finished shaving, brushing my teeth, liberally applying deodorant and combing my hair, Morris is on his feet, chanting his morning prayers. I don't know much about God, but how can He stand this constant litany of praise, the same monotonous, droning passages of adoration twice a day and about ten times on Friday and Saturday? I mean, how needy is He? Doesn't He realize his fawning worshippers have an ulterior motive?

Half an hour later, we hit the road, heading north. I stop for gas and hand the map to Morris.

"Hey Morris," I say. "You think a hearse carrying a corpse is allowed to drive in the carpool lane?"

Morris looks at me. "Are you serious, Jimmy?" he asks. "How the hell should I know? And who cares?"

"Relax, I'm just trying to make conversation."

Morris takes off his rimless glasses, blows warm air on the lenses and wipes them with his handkerchief.

"You know," he muses, "I always liked Molly. I thought you were a goddamn idiot to let her go."

"Don't rub it in," I say with a melancholy sigh.

"She was way too intelligent for you."

"Gee thanks."

"Well," Morris says sagely, "it's all water over the bridge."

"You mean, water under the bridge," I correct him. "It's water over the dam."

"What difference does it make?"

"A lot of difference," I say. "Water can't actually go under a dam unless the dam in question has a hole in it, and if water went over a bridge it would probably be a major catastrophe."

"Thanks so much for clearing that up for me, Jimmy. You're such a fountain of information. You really astonish me sometimes."

"My pleasure," I say. A moment later I pass an on ramp sign for Providence. "I think we're almost there," I tell him. "Could you check the map?"

"Can't we just buy a GPS somewhere?" he asks.

"This is our last stop," I remind him. "Why bother?"

This time, Morris surprises me by successfully navigating us through unfamiliar terrain and it doesn't take us long to find Molly's suburban home. It's a lovely two-story white house, set back fifty yards from the curb, with two chestnut trees in the front yard and a lush, colorful explosion of bougainvillea separating the house from the neighbor's yard. Two ivy-covered wooden columns support a portico at the entrance. A row of azaleas and impatiens borders the driveway. I'm no realtor, but I'd guess the place is worth at least half a million, maybe more.

I don't have to tell Morris to accompany me to the door this time. He just gets out of the car on his own. It's finally sinking in.

We climb the steps to the porch and I ring the bell. After a few gong-like noises from inside, a pretty teenage girl in short-shorts, a bikini top and flip flops materializes in the doorway wearing iPod plugs. I stare at her. Could she be Molly's daughter?

"What's up?" she asks us, carefully pulling the plugs from her ears. "If you're looking for my Dad, he's not here."

"Actually," I say, "it's your Mom I wanted to see."

The girl turns her head and yells, "MOM. Somebody's here to see you. MOM!"

We all wait for a moment but there's no response. The girl rolls her eyes. "She's probably in the garden doing gardening shit," she informs us. "I'll get her. Wait a sec."

"Thanks," I say.

Ten seconds later, a pretty, but somewhat disheveled woman of about thirty-five comes to the door. She's wearing a baggy pair of shorts, a wide-brimmed straw hat, a pair of oversized sunglasses and orange gardening gloves. Beads of sweat cover her forehead and she wipes them away with her sleeve, leaving a streak of soil on her forehead.

It's not Molly.

"Sorry, I couldn't hear the bell," she explains. "I was out in the garden planting petunias. Don't ask me why. It's hotter than hell and I don't even like gardening. They'll probably dry up and die by Thursday. So what can I do for you?"

"Sorry to disturb you," I say pleasantly. "We're looking for a woman named Molly Martinez."

"Who?"

"Molly Martinez?" I say. "I was told she lives at this address."

"Hmmm," she muses, pulling off her straw hat and running a hand through a nest of tangled blond hair. "Doesn't ring a bell. But

we just moved in two months ago, so we don't know the neighborhood that well yet except for the woman next door who brought
us brownies when we moved in, but her name isn't Molly."

"Maybe one of the other houses...?"

"Not a clue," she says with a shrug. "The previous owners were
named... Morrison. A divorce settlement, I think."

I glance at Morris. At first I'm astonished and a little dismayed
to learn that she actually married Dick Morrison, but the good
news is that I won't have to deal with an irate husband. Glad as I
am, my brief moment of relief is tempered by the possibility that
we may never find her. For all I know, she's moved to Brazil. While
I stand there, momentarily stumped, Morris comes to the rescue.

"Do you have a forwarding address for either one of them?" he
asks.

The woman frowns. "Yes, come to think of it, I do," she says. "I
forwarded a couple of tax bills to them. Hold on, it's probably in
my husband's home office."

Just then, a loud motorcycle pulls up at the curb. The driver
guns the motor a few times and suddenly the teenage girl rushes
past us and skips toward the street. Now she's wearing a tight red
T-shirt with the name of a band scrawled on it in gothic-style black
letters, daringly short cut-offs, way too much make-up and perfume
that leaves a noxious trail.

"Whoa! Hold on young lady," her mother says. "Where, may I
ask, do you think you're going?"

The girl rolls her eyes. "Just to the mall," she says.

"Dressed like that?"

"Yeah," the girl says defiantly.

Her mother looks at her skeptically and glances at her watch.
"I want you home by nine," she tells her.

"Whatever."

The girl shoots her mother a dirty look, runs off, climbs onto the boy's motorcycle, puts on a World War One helmet and then they take off. Her mother shakes her head wearily and turns back to us. "I'll be back in a sec," she says.

It's a lot more than sec, but she finally emerges with a scrap of paper, which she hands to me. It has Dick Morrison's address on it.

"Hope that helps," she says.

~

It only takes us a half hour to locate Dick's house. Morris and I walk up the front step and onto the porch, gingerly maneuvering past a few "wet paint" signs. The front door glistens with a fresh coat of semi-gloss. I ring the bell.

There's no answer but, after ringing again, the garage door suddenly creaks open and a new Cadillac backs out slowly with Dick at the wheel, concentrating his eyes on one of the side mirrors. When he notices us, he rolls down the window and peers out, his forehead wrinkling. Morris and I walk over.

"You're Dick Morrison," I say.

"Thanks for the news," he responds, adjusting his tie. "Who are you?"

"We were both at Fryman at the same time," I tell him. "I'm Jimmy Hendricks."

He eyeballs me for a second. "Oh yeah," he says finally. "Jimmy Hendricks. You were the asshole who dated Molly before me."

"That's right," I admit. "I'm that very same asshole."

He slips off his seatbelt, opens the car door and slowly steps out. Fearing that he might sock me in the jaw, I move back a few paces, but he just stands there, puffing up his chest. His white shirt is tucked into a pair of beige dress pants.

"What an unpleasant surprise," he says, looking me over. "So what the hell do you want, Hendricks? And make it quick. I'm late for work."

"I'm trying to find Molly," I inform him.

"And why is that?"

"I just need to see her," I say. "It's a long story. I was hoping you could help me."

"Why the hell should I?"

"Because fellow alumni do each other favors," I declare. "It's a networking thing."

He thinks about it for a moment, inspecting his fingernails. "How do you know she wants to see *you?*" he asks, leaning against the car.

"I don't," I say. "If she slams the door in my face I'll just go away."

He pulls contemplatively at a patch of thin brown shrubbery on his chin that I guess is supposed to be a goatee. Then he notices Morris, who's been standing off to the side.

"Hey, aren't you Morris Berkowitz?" he asks.

"That I am," Morris says.

"Jeez, I saw you take down that gorilla from Tufts my sophomore year," he says. "That was fucking amazing."

"Jack Quinn."

"Yeah, that's the guy," Dick says, shaking his head nostalgically. "Huge motherfucker. So you still playing ball?"

"Bum knee."

"Tough luck," Dick says mournfully. "I bet you could've gone pro."

Morris shrugs. "Not in the cards," he mutters. "But thanks."

"Kinda hot to be wearing black," Dick says.

I clear my throat a few times before Morris can respond. "So listen, Dick," I venture, "in the spirit of collegiate camaraderie, why don't you just tell me where Molly lives and we'll be off on our merry way."

Dick sighs and looks at Morris for approval. Morris nods. "All right," Dick mumbles begrudgingly. "I don't like you much Hendricks, never did, but since you're a fellow classmate and all, I suppose I can tell you. She lives in the city now with our daughter,

Carrie. Condominium. Providence Towers on Buell Street. Across from the University."

"Terrific," I gush enthusiastically. "Thanks so much Dick."

I reach out to shake his hand, but he doesn't respond.

"Guess we'll be off then," I say, turning to leave.

"You going to the reunion, Morris?" Dick calls out as we walk away.

"What reunion?" Morris asks.

"Our twentieth."

"I wasn't planning on it," he says.

"Neither am I," he informs us, which makes me wonder why he even brought it up. "I fucking hate those things."

"Yeah, well thanks again, Dick," I say. "It was nice to see you."

"Take care, Berkowitz," he says, ignoring me completely.

Morris gives him the thumbs-up and we head for the car.

~

It's noon by the time we find Providence Towers, a modern high-rise, very well maintained, all the amenities. A totem pole of signs directs its inhabitants to a health club, spa, pool, hot tub, sauna and massage room. Before we manage to get to the lobby elevators, a uniformed doorman with big ears and thick eyebrows pops out of nowhere and blocks our path.

"Excuse me gentlemen," he says, putting up one of his hands. "You can't just go up. I need to call the party you're visiting."

"It's kind of surprise," I tell him.

"It doesn't matter," he counters officiously. "Rules are rules."

"Fine," I say. "I'm here to see Molly Morrison."

He ambles slowly to his desk and scans a list on a clipboard. "Sorry to disappoint you pal, but there's no Molly Morrison here."

"Try Martinez," I suggest. "That's her maiden name."

He stares at me for a moment and then, after wordlessly displaying his annoyance at having to repeat the process, he scans the list again. Apparently her name is on it because the next thing he says is, "And you are…?"

"Jimmy Hendricks."

He squints at me. "No you're not."

"It's spelled differently," I tell him.

"How's it spelled?"

"What difference does it make?" I ask, my patience waning. "Could you please just ring her for me?"

"Fine," he grumbles. Then he presses a few buttons on a console, picks up a receiver and waits about three seconds. "Ms. Martinez, this is Nick at the desk," he says. "I'm fine, how are you? Yes, it's a lovely day. Is that so? Really? Sure, I'll call him right away. Listen, there's a man here who wants to come up and see you. His name is…uh…"

"Jimmy Hendricks," I tell him for the second time. How does anybody forget a name like that, especially a doorman whose job it is to remember peoples' names?

"Jimmy Hendricks," he says into the receiver. "Uh huh. Uh huh. I see. Okay, Ms. Martinez."

Then he hangs up. He doesn't say anything right away, just takes off his peaked cap and runs a hand over his bald head. So I think: Did she tell him to throw me out on my ass?

"Sixth floor," the doorman finally says, pointing to a bank of elevators. "Apartment 657."

"Thanks," I tell him as Morris and I both move towards the elevators.

"Uh, excuse me, gents," the doorman says, pointing a finger at Morris. "Ms. Martinez only said Mr. Hendricks can come up. Do you want me to ring her again?"

"No, that's fine," I reply, and he shrugs and goes back to his desk. I turn to Morris.

"Look Morris, I really don't think I'll need you this time. She's not married, remember?"

"So what am I supposed to do?" he asks, nodding toward the doorman. "Play canasta with the doorman?"

"Maybe there's a kosher deli nearby," I say. "You could get a bagel or something."

This suggestion seems to intrigue him. "How am I going to find a kosher deli?"

"Maybe the doorman has a phone book," I speculate.

Morris glances at the doorman and sighs. "Okay, that's a good idea. I'll meet you in the lobby in exactly two hours."

"Sounds good," I say.

"Don't be late. You know I'm a stickler for punctuality."

"Not to worry."

"Say hi to her for me."

"Will do."

Morris approaches the doorman while I head for the elevators and push the UP button. After about ten seconds, the doors whoosh open and a thirtyish woman in a pink jogging suit emerges with two Chihuahuas on separate, sequined leashes. One of them yips at me and the woman smiles apologetically as she drags the dogs toward the lobby. After she's gone, I step hesitantly into the elevator. My anxiety has peaked, and my hand trembles slightly as I push the button. I neaten my hair with the palm of my hand and raise my arms to check my armpits which, to my chagrin, are not entirely odor free. Then I flash a smile at the shiny steel elevator doors in an attempt to check my teeth, but the reflection is too hazy. Five seconds later, the elevator stops at the sixth floor and the doors open. Her apartment is a few yards down a long carpeted hallway. I stand motionless in front of her door for a second or two, pull up my pants and suck in my gut. My heart is palpitating, my stomach gurgling. But it's now or never. Showtime. I clear my throat and reach out to knock, but before my fingers make contact with the brass knocker, the door flies open.

"Jimmy!" she exclaims, lighting up with a smile.

"Hi Mol—"

Before I can even finish the sentence, Molly throws herself into my arms and squeezes me tightly, her curly hair positioned right under my nose. Needless to say, I'm nonplussed, and for a moment I'm not sure what to do with my hands. This is not exactly the kind of reception I'd anticipated and it catches me by surprise. Finally, I put my arms around her waist and take in the faint aroma of lilac shampoo. After a moment, we separate.

She takes both my hands in hers, steps back and gives me the once-over. "Look at you," she says.

"Look at *you*," I repeat dumbly.

By now my mouth has gone dry. Molly looks... remarkable. She's not wearing baggy jeans or an oversized shirt. Instead, she's got on a pair of tight designer jeans, white high heels and a loose linen shirt with a plunging neckline that displays a tasteful view of her cleavage. Two thin corkscrew tendrils of hair frame her face.

"You haven't changed much, Jimmy," she says.

"Sweet of you to lie," I respond.

Molly smiles. Then she takes me by the hand and leads me into her apartment, which is stunning, but not showy: White carpeting, plush beige sofas, colorful Bahamian-style paintings on the walls, dark-wood African sculptures and several potted palm trees, lend the space a tasteful tropical ambiance. She ushers me inside and I follow her to the living room. Meanwhile, I'm still wondering why the hell she's so overjoyed to see me, the college asshole who broke her heart twenty years ago.

"This is such an amazing coincidence, Jimmy," she says, sitting down on the couch. I follow suit, sinking into a cozy chair opposite her.

"It is?" I ask. "Why is that?"

"You won't believe this, but I emailed you about five days ago," she tells me.

"Really?"

"Yes!" she exclaims. "The Fryman alumni association gave me your email address."

"I've been, um, out of town on… personal business. I didn't take my laptop and my, um, iPhone has a glitch," I say. Then I'm suspicious. What's she up to? So I ask, "Why would you suddenly email me after twenty years?"

She shrugs. "Remember Dick Morrison?"

"Vaguely."

"We got married after college," she continues. "We're divorced now."

"Oh," I say, deciding to keep mum on my short encounter with her ex.

"Anyway, after the divorce I started to think about the past a lot. Jeez, I even looked at old yearbooks, can you imagine? Why would I even do that?"

"Not a clue," I say.

"Anyway, I thought maybe you didn't want to communicate with me since you didn't email me back," she says, hugging a throw pillow.

"I definitely would have emailed you back."

"I wasn't sure," she tells me. "It's been so long… I didn't know if you were happily married or—"

"About to be divorced," I inform her.

Molly kicks off her high heels, raises both legs onto the couch and slips them beneath her.

"So, what did you say in the email?" I ask.

With her elbow resting on the back of the sofa, she starts rolling a strand of hair around a finger, just as she used to do twenty years ago. Suddenly, I'm overcome with a rush of memories. I can't help but smile.

"I wanted to know if you were planning to go to the reunion," she says. "I'd been thinking about you and how nice it would be to see you again and catch up on old memories."

"I wasn't planning on it but—"

"Please go," she says. "You were the only close friend I had at Fryman."

"Friend?" I say, a little disturbed. "We were lovers, Molly."

"True," is all she says.

Just then, a little girl, maybe four years old, suddenly appears in front of me. She's utterly adorable, curly hair like Molly's, up-turned nose like Dick's, two crooked front teeth. She's hugging a torn, faded blanket to her chest.

She stares at me. "Who's that man?" she asks Molly.

"I'm an old friend of your Mommy's," I reply with a smile. "My name is Jimmy." I extend my hand, but she just scratches her head.

"Carrie, be a good girl and shake Jimmy's hand," Molly says.

Reluctantly, Carrie puts her little hand in mind. "Are you Mommy's boyfriend?" she asks.

I look over at Molly, who just smiles. "Jimmy and I were very good friends when we went to school," she says pleasantly. "That was a very long time ago."

"Did you ever kiss?"

I look at Molly for direction again.

"We were just very good friends, honey," she replies, winking at me.

"Oh," Carrie says.

Then Molly looks at her watch. "I thought you were taking a nap, sweetie," she says. "You were up verrrrry early this morning."

Carrie yawns widely.

"Do you want me to tuck you in?" Molly asks.

"No."

"Okay," Molly tells her. "Give Mommy a kiss now okay?"

Carrie jumps on Molly's lap and kisses her on the cheek. Then she scrambles down and stands in front of me again.

"Daddy's taking me to the zoo tomorrow," she informs me. "I like the hippopotamuses the best. What do you like?"

"The monkeys," I say.

Carrie shrugs. "They're okay too."

"Off to bed now," Molly commands, clapping her hands. "Chop, chop."

Carrie stands in front of me again and I give her a big smile, but she doesn't smile back. With her thumb in her mouth, she turns around and walks back to her bedroom.

"She's a cute one," I tell Molly.

"Do you have kids?" she asks.

"No."

Molly nods. "She's a handful. Very independent, a little precocious," Molly says. "But the divorce has been hard on her. She was pretty close to Dick. He's a good father."

"She looks a lot like her mother," I observe. Then I study her face. "But there's something different about you. I can't quite pinpoint it."

She turns her head to profile position, and I see it immediately.

"The wonders of plastic surgery," she declares brightly. "What do you think?"

"I always liked that little bump on your nose," I say.

"I hated it!"

"It made you seem… exotic."

"Exotic? Are you kidding? I looked like Little Orphan Annie with a beak."

"That would have made me a pedophile," I point out. "Little Orphan Annie is perpetually twelve."

Molly laughs. "So does that mean I'm not exotic anymore?"

"Not at all," I say. "You just look... different."

Instantly realizing the ambiguity of that remark, I'm about to say something more flattering, but Molly suddenly stands up. I'm not sure if this means our meeting is over and I'm supposed to leave or what. Have I offended her? In any case, I stay put in my chair because I haven't told her why I've come to see her yet.

"Can I get you something, Jimmy?" she asks.

"A bowl of lobster bisque would hit the spot."

She gives me a polite laugh. "Sorry, I just finished the last bowl this morning."

"Pity."

"How about a glass of wine? Or a beer?" she asks. "Actually, I don't think I have beer. Dick was the beer drinker. Two six-packs every weekend." Then she grins. "Do you remember that horrible wine I gave you when we first... you know..."

"Distinctly," I say. "My taste buds haven't recovered yet."

She grins. "So what'll it be? I have Coke too."

"Actually, I was thinking more along the lines of a tall glass of Scotch."

She raises her eyebrows. "Hard day?"

"Something like that."

She nods and walks barefooted into the kitchen. I sit alone for a moment, nervously crossing and uncrossing my legs, and then decide to follow her. As I come in, she's standing with her back to me, washing a glass, and I feel a strong urge to sneak up from behind her and circle my arms around her waist. But instead I stand in the kitchen doorway, leaning on the jamb and watch as she uncorks some wine, pulls an expensive-looking wine glass from a cabinet and then pours herself a glass of Chardonnay.

"So Jimmy," she says, squatting down in front of a low cabinet and fishing for a bottle of Scotch. "How did you find me? I just moved here a few months ago."

"Fryman alumni association," I lie.

"Strange that they would know my new address already."

I figure it would be prudent to change the subject, so I say, "Forget the ice. I'll take it straight up."

Then she stands and pours two inches of Scotch into a glass. A second later, when she hands it to me, my fingers brush against hers and it feels positively electric. I down a third of my drink in one gulp.

"Okay," she says, lifting her wine glass to her lips. "Now that you're sufficiently lubricated, tell me what all this is about."

"Okay." I take a deep breath. "The fact is, I came here to apologize."

"Apologize?" she asks. "For what?"

"A lot of things," I reply, clearing my throat. "Most of all, for taking your virginity and then being such a bastard."

She frowns. "You must have a very bad memory, Jimmy," she says. "You didn't *take* my virginity. I wanted you just as much as you wanted me. It was actually *my* decision."

"Maybe so," I concede. "But mainly I want to apologize for being such a complete asshole afterwards. I mean, while you were out of town."

She holds her wine glass with both hands and takes a sip, but keeps her eyes on me. "You shouldn't have done that to me," she says. "I cried forever."

"I'm so sorry," I tell her earnestly. "I didn't mean to do it. It just happened. I'd gone to a movie downtown and there were these gang bangers and—"

"I don't need to know the details," she says, putting up a hand to stop me. "It took a while, but I got over it."

"I was a fool," I say.

"Yes, you were."

Without saying anything more, she exits the kitchen and I follow her back into the living room. We both sit at opposite ends of the same couch.

"Why the sudden apology, Jimmy?" she asks, as we settle down. "It was a million years ago."

"Guilt mostly," I tell her.

"Okay, maybe this will ease your conscience," she offers. "Even though you were an idiot and not even my type, I remember you as being very caring, and a lot of fun to be with. We had some good times. You were the first boy who ever paid any attention to me. You put up with all my studying and my shyness and those godawful clothes I wore."

"But I was such an asshole," I admit.

She shrugs. "*Major* asshole," she tells me. "But you were kind and gentle and I think you really loved me. Besides, you were my first love. I'll always think of you that way even though things ended badly. What woman could forget her first love?"

I look at her skeptically. "You really feel that way?"

"Hey, I let you in didn't I?" she asks me. "I could have had Jagger toss you out the door."

"You mean the doorman?" I ask. "His name is Jagger?"

"Yeah, and get this: His first name is Nick," she adds with a laugh. "Who would name a kid Nick Jagger?"

"Maybe we should start a band."

Molly smiles, then finishes her wine. "So you can let go of the guilt," she says. "Feel better now?"

"Much."

"No point in dwelling on the past," she assures me. Then she lifts her glass and touches mine. "A toast to old romances."

"To old romances," I repeat happily.

~

I spend another two hours with Molly. We reminisce for a while about our first meeting in the library, her dingy apartment with the rickety bed and the portrait of a dour Woodrow Wilson hanging over it, her stubborn insistence that we always whisper in the library and her tenacious but futile attempts to turn me into a scholar. Although I try to avoid the subject, she forces me to tell her about my stupid electronics business, which is a little embarrassing for me, considering she's a full tenured professor at the University of Rhode Island, specializing in international affairs and a consultant for a liberal think tank. (Framed photos of Molly with Madeleine Albright and Bill Clinton adorn her mantelpiece.) At least she's doing something worthwhile with her life, but I always knew her future would be brighter than mine.

"Jimmy," she says sympathetically. "Some of us are cut out for the academic life, others are entrepreneurs like you."

"Andrew Carnegie was an entrepreneur," I tell her with a smirk. "I own a lousy store in a tiny town."

"But you're happy?"

I shrug.

"I'm sorry," she says, reaching over to touch my hand. "You were happy in college weren't you? I mean, you seemed happy when we were together."

"That was the highlight," I tell her. "The education part I could have lived without."

She gives me a crooked smile. I move a little closer to her on the couch.

"I'm serious," I continue. "You and Herbert Hoover were the only ones I ever really cared about."

Laughing, she folds her arms, causing her breasts to rise slightly.

I suddenly realize I'm staring and glance away. "God, I can't believe how great you look, Molly. You must have an aging portrait in your attic or something."

"It's all about maintenance," she tells me. "I go to this godawful gym three times a week. Wanna see my muscles?"

"Sure."

Molly puts down her drink, rolls up her sleeve and flexes a bicep.

"Impressive," I say. "I'm a gymophobe myself."

"I'm on the diet from hell," she tells me. "Think anorexic squirrel."

At this point, I'm eager to move on from the fitness and health seminar into more personal territory. But how to segue?

"I don't mean to pry," I say hesitantly, "but, um, is there a man in your life?"

"Nope. How about you?"

"No man in my life either."

"Good to know," she says.

"I still think about you a lot."

"Liar," she says with a skeptical look.

"I'm not kidding."

"Well I'm glad I made such a lasting impression," she says. "It's been such a long time. Twenty years. Where did the time go?"

Speaking of time, I happen to glance up at her antique grand-father clock and suddenly realize I've been there for three hours. I'm tempted to stay, but Morris is probably very annoyed by now, possibly even hopping mad.

"I hate to say it, but I have to go," I tell her, rising slowly from the couch. "You remember my friend Morris?"

"Of course," she says.

"Right. Well, Morris is waiting for me in the lobby and I'm al-ready an hour late."

"I'd love to see him," Molly says. "I can call Nick and have him—"

"That's okay," I interrupt. "He's probably in a hurry to get home."

I lie because I don't want Morris's presence to spoil a potentially romantic goodbye, which I am hoping will develop at Molly's
front door.

"Are you sure?" Molly asks.

"Yeah."

"Too bad," she says. "Give him my love."

"I will."

We both rise and she follows me to the door. "This has been
really nice," she says, taking my arm. "I wish you could stay longer."

"So do I, but if I keep him waiting in the lobby any longer he'll
sit on my head. He still weighs about 320 pounds."

"Well, I wouldn't want that on my conscience," she says.

When we get to the door, Molly releases my arm and stands
about three feet away from me. I'm thinking: Should I try to kiss
her good-bye? It's tempting, but she's maintaining the distance, so
I decide it would be inappropriate. I would hate to create an awkward atmosphere at this stage. As I approach the threshold, she
plunges her hands in her pockets and starts rocking on her heels.

"If you're ever in the neighborhood again," she says with a wink,
"do please come to visit, Jimmy."

"You bet," I tell her.

"One more thing," Molly says.

"Yes?"

"You never answered me about the reunion," she says. "Do you
think you'll be going? It would be great if you did."

"If you promise to go, I'll definitely be there," I reply.

"Really?"

"Yup."

We both continue to stand there for a moment, looking at each
other, and suddenly I feel like a high school kid on his first date,
trying to decide whether or not to throw caution to the wind and
attempt a goodnight kiss. Images of my first date with Laura flash

by. But Molly's looking down at the floor now, still rocking on her heels. Is she waiting for me to take her in my arms or is she waiting for me to leave? I'm confused, and I search her eyes for some tiny hint, but find them empty. In the end, I take the safe path and do nothing.

"Well, goodbye Jimmy," she says.

"Goodbye Molly." Reluctantly, I step into the hallway.

I hear the door shut behind me. And then I'm suddenly padding toward the elevators, cursing myself for having chickened out when the opportunity was there.

~

As I'd expected, Morris is seething by the time I find him in the lobby near the elevators. If Jewish scripture didn't forbid it, I think he might have strangled me on the spot.

"I've been standing around here for an hour," Morris hisses. "I know the doorman's whole life story and it isn't all that fascinating."

"I'm sorry, Morris," I say. "I just lost track of time."

"He spent twenty minutes talking about his athlete's foot."

"Jeez."

"Fifteen minutes on sciatica."

"Ouch."

"You could at least have called down and said you were going to be late. That would have been common courtesy."

"I didn't think of that," I tell him. "I'm sorry. I really am."

Dismissing my apology with an angry wave of his hand, Morris storms past the doorman and pushes his way through the revolving door while I try to keep up with him. Morris isn't a fast walker, but the anger seems to have invigorated his leg muscles. Without a word, we stride toward the guest parking lot and locate my car. As soon as we're both belted up, I back noisily out of my space. In fifteen minutes we're back on the highway, but we don't speak to each other for at least the first ten miles.

"So," Morris says after he's calmed down a bit. "How did it go?"

"Amazingly well," I tell him. "No grudges, no hard feelings. In fact, I think she still likes me a little. Maybe even a lot."

I look over at him, but he appears to be deep in contemplation, about what I have no idea. No matter. As the Rhode Island landscape flies by, I gaze silently out of my open window, letting the humid sea breeze blow my hair every which way.

An hour later, we're in Boston and, by some miraculous twist of fate, I actually manage to find a parking space less than six thousand miles from Morris's apartment. We both get out of the car to say goodbye.

"You want to come up for a minute?" he asks.

"No thanks," I say, glancing at my watch. "It's getting late and New Hampshire's a long drive."

"Are you sure? I'll bet Naomi still has some kreplach in the freezer."

"I can live without kreplach," I tell him.

"It's an acquired taste."

"But give Naomi and the kids all my best."

"I will."

"Give me a hug, big guy," I say.

Morris steps forward and pulls me into a bear hug. I mean that literally because he's almost the size of a medium grizzly, and I can feel my ribcage creaking like the hull of a ship that's caught in a storm. Then he kisses me on the cheek.

"Thanks for everything, buddy," I say, misting up slightly. "I couldn't have done this without you."

"My pleasure," he replies. "Actually, it wasn't such a pleasure, but at least we got a chance to spend some quality time."

Then he grabs his duffle bag from the backseat, slings the strap over his shoulder and heads up the stairs.

～

On the drive home, I exit at the first highway ramp and take the scenic route, cruising slowly past white farmhouses, red barns and cows lazily chewing grass in lush green meadows. I open a window, take a deep breath and am bombarded by a variety of pleasant country odors—jasmine, freshly cut grass, wood smoke, hay. Even the cow shit smells good. I pass through a few small, quaint New England towns and stop in one to have dinner.

But the scenic drive doesn't help me solve the one big question that's been preying on my mind ever since we left Providence: Do I need to make one last apology?

Part Five

Christine

Christine... Then

FLASHBACK TO MY JUNIOR year in college: With Molly in New York for her aunt's funeral, I suddenly found myself with way too much time on my hands. The days were drab, the nights depressing and lonely. Time passed slowly. Without her, I was listless, lethargic and starving for female companionship. The best I could manage was the occasional furtive date with Mary and her four sisters, a mostly joyless act which I preformed nightly in the romantic ambiance of my bathroom.

What I needed was diversion.

On the fifth day of Molly's absence, I found myself in a seedy part of Boston, where I'd gone to satisfy my now desperate need to observe female pulchritude. The most effective way to do that inexpensively was to take in a few hardcore porno flicks. At that time a lot of Boston's sleaziest X-rated theatres were located in that part of town, so I had to endure an assortment of drooling, demented trolls who sat around me in the sparsely populated theatre. I think one of them was whacking off in an old sock.

Unfortunately, Internet porn hadn't been invented yet and I'd outgrown the skin magazines.

After the movie, I realized that this cinematic adventure had been a mistake because it was freezing cold when I got out and I'd only worn a sweatshirt. So I trotted toward the nearest subway station, oblivious to the fact that I was the only human being in the general vicinity. It was eerily quiet. But after a while, I heard what sounded like a baseball bat being dragged along pavement. Moments later, before I could hope to make the remaining seventy yards to the station, I suddenly became aware of a band of maybe three or four gang bangers rapidly approaching me. To get to my destination, I would have to pass them. Clearly a Fryman sweatshirt was hardly the smartest item of apparel to be sporting in this area. As it was, I was the only guy not affiliated with a gang who was stupid enough to be walking alone on the garbage-littered streets in that particular neighborhood, at that particular time of night. There were no taxis or police cars in sight. In fact there was no traffic at all.

I slowed my pace but we were drawing closer. I could practically smell the feral odor they emitted and see them evaluating me with the squinty eyes of a horde of hungry tigers savoring the epicurean possibilities of a wounded hyena. Obviously, I had to make tracks pronto. Running away, although tempting, was not a realistic option because they would either catch me or I would get lost and find myself in an even worse neighborhood. Or, I'd encounter another gang of heavily armed gladiators walking the other way. If we crossed paths, they would crush me like a pesky bug and I'd spend the rest of my life with the face of a really untalented boxer.

My life was saved by a diner which, luckily for me, happened to be located at a spot exactly equidistant from the approaching Visigoths and me. I ducked inside just in the nick of time, trying to ignore the growls and snarls of the disgruntled warriors as I disappeared from the field of combat.

It was a brightly lit diner and at first I had to hold my hand above my eyes to focus. Once my vision adjusted to the merciless lighting, I could practically feel the grease entering my pores like a layer of sunscreen. The food was probably beyond nauseating, but an acute case of food poisoning was actually a lot more appealing compared to the fate that awaited me on the street should I be insane enough to venture back outside. At the far window of my new sanctuary, I could see the menacing gang bangers standing in front of the glass taunting me, flashing me the bird and shouting angry words, but I knew they'd never dare to kill or maim me in a diner. Too many witnesses.

I took a seat as far away from that particular window as possible and eventually the barbarians stalked off. I guessed that they would either lurk in the shadows until I left the diner, or more likely, move along so they would be punctual when the enemy gang arrived at the designated battlefield for the evening's scheduled confrontation.

From my seat, I could see that there were only three others in the joint—a young waitress, a short order cook and a bag lady who was mumbling something to herself, probably not Shakespeare. There was a menu stuck in a menu holder on the side of my table, so I plucked it out and looked it over, suddenly realizing my hands were shaking. The menu itself was stained with grease and finger-prints and probably hadn't been reprinted since color TVs were invented. I took a deep breath and held my hands out in front of me until the tremor ceased.

Since I hadn't had dinner, I was ravenous. I assumed that most of the entrées on the menu had probably spent the better part of the week festering in a back room, intruding on a family of ver-min that had long ago established their homes there. The meatloaf was probably a bad bet, as were the burgers, the cube steak and the chef's special, which was beef stew. There were even color pictures of all the food, probably for the clientele who couldn't read, but the likenesses made the food appear even more revolting than it prob-ably was, hardly the most brilliant marketing tactic. If I'd had a dog and I'd lost it, I would search for it here.

After a moment or two, the waitress, who was dressed in a

white apron, a red blouse and blue jeans, ambled over to my booth. She appeared to be about my age, possibly a year or two younger, but I was reasonably certain she wasn't a college coed because nobody with half a brain, no matter how desperate, would work in a dive like this.

As she stood by my table, she pulled a pencil out of her shirt pocket and poised it over her order pad. "Ready?" she asked.

"How's the fish sandwich?" I inquired.

"Stale."

"The meatloaf?"

She crinkled her nose. "A little on the greasy side."

"Burgers?"

"Lethal."

"Okay then," I said, putting the menu down and looking up at her with a friendly smile. "What would you recommend?"

"Honestly? I'd recommend you find another restaurant, but most of them are closed."

I nodded. At least she was honest.

"Are you still serving breakfast?" I asked.

"Yup."

"Denver omelet then, not runny."

"Anything to drink?"

"Coke."

"Coming right up," she said amiably. Then she ambled back toward the short order cook, who was stationed behind the counter flipping pancakes with one hand and picking his nose with the other.

A moment or two later, she came back and said, "I forgot to ask, was that a Diet Coke or a regular Coke?"

"Regular."

"Thanks," she said, making a silly cross-eyed look. "I can be kind of a ditz sometimes."

"It's okay. I forget things all the time myself."

I was expecting her to return to the kitchen and fetch my Coke, but she just stood there, shyly studying me as if she wasn't exactly sure what species of animal life I represented. It was a bit unsettling, but I glanced up at her pretty face and gave her body a quick once-over.

"So are you in college?" she asked, glancing at my sweatshirt.

"Yup," I said. "I'm a junior at Fryman."

"So what's a college kid like you doing in a cruddy neighborhood like this at midnight?"

"I, uh, got lost," I lied. "No sense of direction."

"Yeah right," she scoffed. "You probably came down here to see the porno flicks down the block."

"Homework," I told her. "I'm researching a term paper on American cinema verité."

"Uh huh," she said skeptically. "And I'm down here researching a term paper on botulism."

I smiled at this unexpectedly clever quip. "Touché," I said.

"Listen," she ventured, changing the subject. "It's none of my business, but can I give you some advice?"

"Shoot."

"You don't want to be in this part of town this late, especially if you're a rich college boy. You're gang bait."

I was about to correct her regarding her assumption that I was wealthy simply because I attended college, but I thought better of it. If she wanted to believe I was some rich guy's son, why should I spoil the image? The fact was, I found the role strangely appealing, probably because I *wasn't* rich. Plus, I had no designs on this girl, so what harm would come from it?

"I come down here for the cuisine," I told her.

That one amused her because she suddenly erupted with a high-pitched staccato laugh that was so loud it almost frightened me. In the middle of it, she wandered off. I looked around the joint and was relieved to see that the place had a pay phone so someone could call the paramedics if I came down with typhus. There were no cell phones in those days.

About ten minutes later, she returned with a plate in one hand and a tall glass of Coke in the other.

"Hope those eggs are okay," she said. "Chef's blind in one eye."

"They look perfect," I lied.

"Cool."

I studied her for a moment. "So what's a nice girl like you doing in a dive like this?"

"I keep asking myself the same question," she said. "The thing is, my uncle owns the joint and two of his waitresses quit on him last minute, so he needed me to sub for him. The tips aren't bad during the day. I actually live in Somerville."

"Oh."

Then she squinted at me. "What makes you think I'm a nice girl?" she asked. "I mean, I *am* a nice girl, but why would you think that?"

I shrugged. "I don't know," I said. "You just look like a nice person."

"Well thanks," she said with a smile. "You seem kinda nice yourself."

"What makes you say that?"

She shrugged. "I don't know. Good vibes, I guess."

Again, instead of going back to the kitchen, she stuck around. I guessed there wasn't much else for her to do since I was the only customer, except for the bag lady, who was now smearing huge globs of ketchup and mustard on two pieces of white bread.

"It's none of my business, but what's it cost to go to Fryman?" she asked me.

"Well," I replied, "I really don't know because my parents pick up the tab. But I think it's about fifteen grand a year, including room and board and textbooks. I pay for the beer myself."

She whistled. "Wish I could afford that," she said sadly. "I'd love to go to college. It's my dream actually, but I can't swing it. I might sign up for some night classes at the community college when this gig is over, which I hope will be real soon. I'm thinking of doing fashion design. What are you majoring in?"

"Business administration," I told her. Why I was going through this ridiculous charade, I didn't really know. Maybe I was just bored.

"Jeez," she said. "Fifteen grand a year. You must have pretty rich parents."

"Oh yeah," I said. "My Dad invented the Magic Marker."

"No way!" she said. "The Magic Marker?"

"The Magic Marker."

"You're kidding right?"

"Afraid not."

"I'm not an idiot," she told me.

"I never said you were."

She narrowed her eyes at me. "The Magic Marker huh?"

"I swear to God," I told her.

She looked at me skeptically and said, "Uh huh."

"Actually," I continued, "it's sort of embarrassing."

"Yeah right," she said.

"I'm not kidding," I told her. "The other kids at school kind of resent it when you're rich, so I try to be low key about it. My apartment's a dump, my car's an old piece of crap and I dress kind of grubby, as you can see."

I let that little nugget of nonsense sink in and took a bite of my omelet which was, predictably, as runny as a plate of fresh phlegm.

"Omelet okay?" she asked.

"Excellent."

"Good," she said.

"I've never had a better omelet," I declared.

"On a scale of one to ten," she said, "I'd give you a seven for lying aptitude."

"That's odd. I usually score higher."

She smiled, displaying two concentric parentheses at either side of her mouth.

"You're kind of cute," she noted after a while. "What's your name?"

"Jimmy," I said. "Jimmy Hendricks."

"Are you related to—?"

"No."

"I'm Christine," she told me.

"Well, it's a pleasure to meet you, Christine," I said.

"Likewise, Jimmy."

And then we shook hands. I'd expected her palm to be greasy but it wasn't.

"Well, you enjoy that crappy omelet, Jimmy," she instructed me, "and if you need anything else, like a Tums or an ambulance, just holler."

"Got it," I said.

While I forced down my revolting breakfast, almost gagging on the gelatinous muck floating on my chipped plate, she walked off and sat on one of the counter stools, sipping a cup of coffee. Meanwhile, the bag lady was rummaging around in a lumpy Hefty bag.

Ten minutes later, Christine sauntered over to my table again.

"Anything for dessert, Jimmy?" she asked.

"Sure. What do you have?"

"Pie mostly."

"So do you have... cherry pie?" I asked her.

"Actually, we're out of everything but the pumpkin pie."

"Pumpkin pie it is then," I said. "I love pumpkin pie."

"Yeah, me too," she said. "You want whipped cream?"

"Sure."

"Okay," she said. "We have really good whipped cream here. Redi-Wip, but it's fresh. At least nobody's died from it yet. Not that I know of anyway."

"Sounds promising," I said.

She left to get my pumpkin pie and returned a few seconds later. I dug in. Believe it or not, the pie was halfway edible, but there was way too much whipped cream on it.

"You know, Jimmy," she said, taking a seat across from me at the table as she wrote up my check and counted her tips, much of which consisted of change and lint. "It's none of my business, but we close in an hour and the subway stopped running at midnight. How were you planning to get back to school?"

For some reason, this dilemma had not occurred to me.

"Guess I'll just grab a cab," I told her.

"Good luck," she scoffed. "Taxi drivers don't usually come to this part of hell, not at night anyway."

"I can't imagine why."

"So you got a little problem then, don't you?"

"Looks that way," I sighed.

"Listen," she said after handing me my bill. "If you want, you can sleep at my place. I don't live too far from here. Twenty minutes or so, depending on traffic. I've got a sleeper couch in the guest room. In the morning, you can take the subway back to school or, since you're so rich, you could call a cab."

I studied her face for a second. "Are you serious?" I asked, amazed that she would make an offer like that.

"Yeah."

"Not that I'm not grateful, but why would you do that?" I asked, still nonplussed. "You don't know me. I could be the Boston Strangler."

"He's dead."

"Yes but—"

"I'm a Good Samaritan," she told me, "and you really don't have any other choices, do you?"

An hour later, the cook chased the bag lady out and started locking up. Christine flashed me a subtle nod and I met her in the alley at the diner's back door. It was even colder now and the air reeked of spoiled food. Christine scurried in front of me across the potholed pavement toward her car.

She had an old Honda parked behind the diner and it took her about two minutes to get the damn thing to start. Finally, after producing some sickly coughing noises, the engine came alive with a few plaintive sputters and she pulled the car into the deserted street. That's when I started to have doubts about the wisdom of this whole scenario. I kept picturing Molly sitting behind me in the back seat with a disgusted look on her face.

"Um," I said. "Maybe you could just drive me to campus. I'll pay you."

"In this heap?" she replied, with a horsy laugh. "I can hardly get to Somerville without breaking down. Fryman's pretty far. Also, I'm almost out of gas."

I glanced past her at her gas gauge; she had about an eighth of a tank. She caught me looking.

"You think I'm lying, Jimmy?"

"No, no, no, of course not," I stammered. "But I'll be glad to buy you a tank of gas. I'll even throw in a carwash."

She looked at me. "Well aren't you Mr. Generosity?"

"I'm serious," I said

"Sorry to disappoint you Jimmy, but there aren't any stations open this late, not around here, anyway."

"Right."

"Listen, do you want to come to my place or not?" she asked in a tone that had turned decidedly cold. "I could drop you off here if you want, but you'll probably end up with no teeth or worse."

"I'm sorry," I said. "I'd love to come to your place. I'm being an idiot."

"I don't ordinarily do this, you know," she told me sternly. "I'm not like, easy or anything and I don't do one-night stands. But you seem like a nice guy with good manners so I feel like I can trust you in that department. It's just a room for the night, period. You sleep alone, I sleep with a teddy bear."

"Of course," I said. "I knew that."

"Besides," she said with what sounded like a trace of sarcasm in her voice, "you're the son of the guy who invented the Magic Marker. I have great respect for Magic Markers. What would the world do without them?"

Since there wasn't much traffic at that time of night, we were in Somerville in no time. Her apartment building was one of those generic gray brick structures with black wrought-iron bars over every window and a bunch of semi-decrepit cars parked out front, many of them missing bumpers or hubcaps.

Her apartment was tiny, but neat and tastefully decorated. A four-poster bed, covered by a shiny green bedspread with matching pillows of all sizes, dominated her bedroom. The living room was crowded with a bookcase, a loveseat, a chair and a coffee table, which was stacked with fashion magazines.

Christine kicked off her white waitress shoes, untied her apron and led me across the room.

"This is where you sleep," she said opening the guest room door. Evidently, she used this room primarily as a closet. Hidden behind a pile of boxes and assorted clothing was a small brown convertible sofa. "I don't have a lot of guests," she added apologetically.

"It's fine," I said.

"I never have enough closet space," she told me. "Feel free to move the boxes and the other shit."

"Okay."

We stood there awkwardly for a moment. Christine said "okay then," and headed for her bedroom while I walked over the debris in the guest room and approached the sofa bed. I was in the process of trying to open it when I heard her call out to me.

"Are you thirsty?" she asked. "There's beer and soda in the fridge."

"A beer would be great," I shouted.

"Help yourself," she said. "And pour me a glass of wine, wil-lya? There's an open bottle in there somewhere. I can't get to sleep without a glass of wine."

"You got it," I told her. "Now I get to play waiter, huh?"

"Yeah," she said, amused. "I guess you do. Just don't spill anything on the carpeting, okay? It was pretty expensive."

"I'll do my best."

The kitchen was small and a badly situated counter made it almost impossible to open the fridge door all the way. Nevertheless, I managed to stick an arm inside. After blindly searching, I pulled out a can of Budweiser from between assorted boxes of take-out food and several packets of yogurt and cottage cheese. After opening and closing a few cabinets, I found a bottle of red wine and a wine glass and poured it half full.

I'd just put the bottle on the counter when she suddenly appeared in the kitchen, clad in a pair of boxer shorts and a loose T-shirt.

"Thanks," she said, taking the wine glass out of my hand.

I lifted the beer can to my lips and took a swig. "Does that outfit keep you warm at night?" I asked.

"Not really," she said, "but I've got a really good space heater and a down blanket."

Christine put her wine glass on the kitchen counter and unpinned her hair, which fell to the middle of her back.

"By the way," I said, pulling my wallet out of my back pocket. "I think I forgot to leave you a tip."

I offered her a ten-dollar bill, but she just looked at it with a scowl.

"That's not cool, Jimmy," she scolded. "I'm not a hooker. You should know better than that. Where are your manners? Jeez."

"No, no, no. You're misunderstanding me," I stuttered. "It's just a tip for service... at the restaurant."

"Jimmy, your meal didn't even cost that much."

"I'm a generous tipper."

"Whatever," she said peevishly. "Just put it away. I don't want to see that wallet again."

"I apologize," I said.

"Apology accepted."

"I didn't mean to—"

"Just forget it," she said.

Jesus, I thought, why was I being such a complete dolt? She was just a nice girl with a kind heart and I was making a total ass of myself, although insulting her had not been my intent. Fortunately, she hadn't noticed that the ten was the only bill in my wallet. Ten bucks was barely enough for cab fare to Fryman.

She took a slow sip of wine, closed her eyes for a moment and licked her lips. "So what do you think of the place?" she asked.

"It's nice," I said.

"Yeah right," she responded. Then, with an ambiguous chuckle, she said, "The closet in your mansion is probably bigger than my whole apartment."

"Look," I said. "About this whole Magic Marker thing..."

"What about it?"

"Never mind."

I was going to come clean, but then I suddenly realized that I couldn't very well tell her I'd been lying the whole time, especially after I'd just insulted her. And what would I do if she threw me out?

Shrugging, Christine turned off the kitchen light and I followed her into the living room. After carefully placing her wine glass on a coaster on the coffee table and making sure I used a coaster for my beer, she gestured for me to sit on the loveseat and, after I'd plopped down, she settled into an armchair that faced the TV. Then she grabbed her glass of wine and drank about half of it. I followed suit with my beer. We sat in silence for a moment.

I produced a yawn. "Well, I guess I'll turn in now," I said. "I'm kind of tired."

"Yeah, me too," she said. "Long shift."

When she got up, she accidentally tipped her wine glass onto the floor. She looked down in horror.

"Shit, *shit*, SHIT!" she screamed. "This is brand new carpeting! *Fuck!*"

At that, she dashed into the kitchen. She was back in a few seconds, carrying a roll of paper towels and a sponge soaked with dishwash liquid and water. Wasting no time, she got on her knees and started dabbing and scrubbing.

"I had it Scotch Guarded but—"

"Let me help," I said, sinking to my knees beside her. I grabbed a wad of paper towels from her and started cleaning. "Don't worry, we'll get it out," I assured her, although I had no idea.

And so we both scrubbed. After a while, the stain began to fade. Still down on our knees, I turned my face towards hers. Instinct took over and I moved in to kiss her. She didn't resist. The kiss lasted about eight seconds but then she disengaged.

"I *said* there would be no sex," she said firmly. "Didn't you hear me?"

"I'm sorry," I told her. "It won't happen again."

"Good."

We turned our eyes back to the rug and continued scrubbing. Once the stain was gone, Christine got a hair dryer from the bathroom, plugged it in and pointed it toward the wet spot on the carpet.

While she worked, I plopped back down on the loveseat and watched her. It took her about ten minutes. She was very thorough. When she was finished, she returned the blow dryer to the bathroom and closed the door. I picked up a magazine and started idly flipping through the pages.

She was in there for quite a while, maybe ten minutes. While I was absorbed by a fashion photo of a half-nude magazine model, the bathroom door opened, but I didn't look up right away.

"Ahem," Christine said.

I raised my eyes. She was stark naked.

I frowned. "I thought you said—"

"I had a change of heart," she told me. "That kiss *really* turned me on."

"But—"

"Plus I'm horny as hell and my fucking vibrator battery just died."

"Oh."

"I mean, we're both adults, right?"

I hesitated for a moment. Flickering images of Molly were filling the silent movie screen in my brain. But the guilt didn't last very long because I was suddenly on the loveseat with Christine perched on my knees.

We kissed for a few minutes and I fondled her breasts, which were at eye-level. Soon we were both moaning, almost in synch, which produced a sound that reminded me of a Gregorian chant. Suddenly, I was lying on top of her on the loveseat, which was much too short to comfortably accommodate us in that position and I almost knocked over a table lamp. As it wobbled, Christine pulled away.

"Be careful," she said, reaching over me to steady the damn thing. "It's an antique."

"Sorry."

Then we started up again. Christine unbuttoned my shirt, and yanked my belt off. Then she stood up and I followed her into her bedroom. She lay down while I struggled to find a rubber. Fortunately, I kept a couple of Trojans in my wallet for emergencies like this one.

Christine was a competent lover but the missionary position seemed to be the only routine in her repertoire, at least at first. But then she got bolder and more experimental and suddenly she was all over me. Obviously, my guilt regarding Molly had temporarily vanished, but I had a nagging feeling it would return very soon.

When the second time came to an end, I rolled off her, breathed a contented sigh and stared at a long serpentine crack in the ceiling, thoroughly disgusted with myself.

She leaned on an elbow and gazed at me. "You don't look too happy," she observed.

"Just tired," I told her.

"Are you thirsty?" she asked brightly.

"Actually, I am," I said. "That was quite a work out."

"It sure was!" she exclaimed, swiveling out of bed. "Be right back. Don't go anywhere, okay?"

"Where would I go?"

I watched her ass as she strolled into the kitchen, and could barely take my eyes off the silhouette of her body as she leaned over the sink. Then I closed my eyes and started punching a pillow, angry at myself for having given in to temptation. About a minute later, Christine returned with two glasses of water.

"What the hell are you doing?" she asked.

"Huh?" I said, dropping the pillow. "Nothing."

Christine rolled her eyes and lay back down on the bed. For a moment, neither of us said anything.

"Sooo… was it good for you?" she asked me. "Tell me the truth."

"It was great," I replied dully, wishing that it had never happened.

"Phew," she said. "I wasn't sure."

"You're very sexy," I told her. "Was it good for you?"

"Yeah…" she said uncertainly. "I guess."

"*You guess?*" I turned on my side and looked at her. Remorseful as I felt, I still had an ego. "Are you saying it *wasn't* good?"

"No. It was fine. I really liked it," she said, "but I just wasn't sure what to… I don't know… expect."

"What do you mean?"

"Nothing," she said "Let's change the subject."

"No let's *not* change the subject," I insisted.

"I have some leftover pizza," she told me. "I could heat it up."

She got up, but I grabbed her arm. "You didn't answer my question," I said.

Christine sighed and sat on the edge of the bed for a moment, facing the wall. Then she turned to me. "I didn't mean to insult you," she said. "It's just that… I don't have anything to compare it to."

"How do you mean?" I asked.

She paused. "I've never actually… done it before."

I was silent for a moment, trying to imagine if her answer could possibly have any other meaning. Then I sat up.

"Are you saying you're a virgin?"

"No," she said. I breathed a sigh of relief. "I was a virgin half an hour ago. Now I'm not."

"You're putting me on, right?" I asked her.

"No."

Naturally, I was stunned, but after a moment of reflection, I grew skeptical. Christine was far too sexy to have maintained her virginity this long. No way. Not a chance. I was sure I couldn't have been the first horny refugee from the porno theatres who had ever flirted with her at the diner.

But then I remembered something she had whispered to me just before the initial penetration: "Be gentle, Jimmy." At the time,

I thought it was just sex talk, but maybe I'd misinterpreted those words.

"So you're saying you've never had sex with a man before?" I asked.

"Pretty pathetic, huh?"

"No experience whatsoever?"

"I once did some heavy petting with a guy in high school," she told me. "We were both drunk. But I was only sixteen. It was junior year."

"So why me?" I asked. "We only just met."

"I don't know. You're cute and you seem like a nice guy."

And my father invented the Magic Marker, I wanted to add.

"It's no big deal," she muttered. "I'm almost nineteen. It was time. Now do you want some pizza or what?"

~

Christine slept deeply that night, her soft breath tickling my upper arm, but I tossed and turned, worrying about the whole situation. What if she was the clingy type and insisted on seeing me again? After all, I'd taken her virginity. That could be disastrous if Molly ever caught us together. She would never tolerate an act of infidelity, no matter what creative excuse I invented. I could end up spending the rest of my college life a lonely bachelor. More importantly, I didn't want to lose her. *How could I have been such an asshole?*

My only potential excuse, a bald-faced lie, was that I'd been seduced against my will, but I had a strong feeling that would never hold up in court. Under cross-examination, I'd fold like an origami seagull.

Of course, there was really no cause for anxiety because Christine would never be able to find out where I lived. I wasn't listed in the phone book and the college administrators never revealed that information to anyone unless there was an emergency. Student addresses were considered confidential—at least to non-alumni and other students— for a number of obvious reasons, this being one of them.

While Christine slept soundly, I stealthily slipped out of bed and quietly put on my clothes. Then I tiptoed into the kitchen and wrote her a note saying I had an early class, and thanking her for saving my life. I was sure she would understand—after all, it had only been a one-night stand. Then I carefully opened her front door and left her apartment.

~

Three months passed with no word from Christine, so I forgot about the whole episode. By this time, Molly and I were talking about living together the following year. Things were going swimmingly.

Molly was at the library when my apartment buzzer sounded with its usual halfhearted bling. Having decided to cut my French Lit class, I was taking a long shower and I didn't hear it at first. But whoever was ringing it was persistent, so I put a stained bath towel around my waist, pushed my wet hair out of my face and opened up, thinking that maybe Molly had forgotten her key, which she sometimes did. She could be absentminded at times, especially when she had a test coming up. And she was always misplacing her purse.

But it wasn't Molly.

"Christine?" I said, trying not to sound too shocked.

"Jeez," she said. "What the heck took you so long? I rang like five times."

"I was in the shower," I explained, although that should have been obvious since I was still wet and wearing nothing but a towel.

"Glad to see me?"

"Yeah," I said trying to smile. "Of course I am."

She searched my face. "You don't look glad to see me."

"It's just such a surprise," I told her.

"Okay, then how about a hug?" She opened her arms and I reluctantly put my hands around her waist.

"You know, I was kinda hoping you'd call," she said, gently pushing me away.

"You never gave me your number."

"I would have," she said with a tinge of anger in her voice, "if you'd stuck around long enough."

"Like I said in the note, I had an early class that day and—"

"Bullshit."

There was no believable excuse, so I didn't offer one.

"So are you going to ask me in or what?"

"Sure," I said. "Jesus, I'm sorry."

"Good God, what a stinking dump," she noted, glancing around the place. "Don't you clean up after yourself, Jimmy?"

"Once a year."

Of course, by now, my heart was pumping so fast, I felt dizzy.

"Christine, it's not that it's not great to see you and all, but what exactly are you doing here?" I asked, hoping to make this visit as short as possible. "I mean, it's been months."

"Mind if I have a seat?" she asked.

I swept a mountain of dirty shirts, underwear and pants from the couch, even though I really didn't want her to make herself at home. "Don't take this the wrong way, Christine," I said, "but how'd you find me? I'm just curious."

"That night at my place, your wallet fell out of your pocket," she explained. "You were in the bathroom, so I picked it up to put it back in your pocket. But I sneaked a look at your driver's license, just to see if you were really who you said you were. I mean, who names a kid Jimmy Hendricks?"

But I wasn't listening. I glanced at my watch—Molly wouldn't be back for another hour or so.

"In a rush, Jimmy?" she asked.

"I have a class in fifteen minutes," I lied.

"I think you're going to have to miss that one."

"I can't."

"Sit down Jimmy," she instructed me.

"I really should dry my—"

"Remember that night three months ago when we made love?"

"Yes, of course," I said. "How could I for—"

"Will you please sit down, Jimmy," she said again.

"I'm fine standing."

"Suit yourself," she said. Then she sighed deeply. "I'll make this short."

A moment passed as she gazed out the window and then turned her eyes back to me. "I'm three months pregnant. I just found out yesterday."

"Well congratulations," I told her.

She sighed. "You're being kinda dense," she said, waiting for my expression to change from perplexity to comprehension. "Figure it out."

I frowned. "No way."

"You're the only suspect."

"That's crazy," I said. "What makes you think it's mine?"

"You were the only one I've been with," she said angrily. "I'm not a whore."

"That's not what I meant," I said. "But I used rubbers."

"Obviously not very good ones," she said.

I suddenly felt like someone had punched me in the solar plexus. My heart was pounding and I felt flushed. I wanted to double over and barf. Words would not come out of my mouth. I felt like a character in a daytime soap who just found out he was adopted. I sank down on the couch next to her.

"You don't look too thrilled," Christine observed.

"It's kind of unexpected," I mumbled.

"I know, I know," she said excitedly. "I can't believe it myself. I didn't think virgins could get pregnant. Guess I was wrong."

"Christine," I stammered, "I'm way too young to be a father."

"Of course you are," she said. "We're both too young."

I breathed an inaudible sigh of relief.

"But it's kinda cool. You want to feel my belly?"

"Huh?"

"My belly. Do you want to feel it? I mean, there's not much to feel yet, but every now and then I could swear something's moving inside."

"Um…"

Christine rose, loosened her skirt and pulled up her blouse. Then she sat down again, right beside me. She wasn't wearing a bra, but sex was the last thing on my mind at that moment.

"Come on Jimmy," she said. "Right here. Feel it. It's so… *weird.*"

When I didn't react, Christine huffed impatiently, took my hand and placed it on her abdomen, which was slightly distended.

"And my breasts are a little bigger too," she said. "Wanna feel them?"

I was still in a daze, so, before I could answer, she took my hand and slipped it under her shirt.

That was when Molly walked in.

~

There were two women sitting across from us, both of them strumming idly through ancient copies of *Mademoiselle* and *Vogue*, which were the only magazines available. One looked to be in her twenties; the other was a little older. Both were alone. The younger one sipped at a can of Coke. It was early in the morning. Christine, who was sitting next to me, started fidgeting with the gold crucifix that hung around her neck, so I put my hand on her knee.

"It'll be okay," I told her softly.

Christine nodded and tried to smile, but I could tell she was upset.

It was a modern waiting room, clean, orderly and pleasantly lit. Two framed photographs of ocean sunsets decorated the wall in front of us and there was a fish tank off to the side. Soft, unidentifiable music emanated from a hidden speaker. Very calming. Behind a wall of glass, office attendants sat at their desks, typing or talking on phones or kibitzing, and the occasional nurse popped in to search for paperwork on a wall rack sagging from the weight of medical charts.

"Really," I said, taking her hand in mine. "This was the right decision."

"I know," she whispered.

"We're too young."

"I know."

"It wouldn't be fair to the baby."

"I know."

As it turned out, Christine was actually a few weeks short of her first trimester and, although she agreed that neither of us was old enough to be a parent, it had taken me some time to persuade her to go through with the abortion. I knew that she was conflicted about it. As a Catholic, she'd been taught her whole life that abortion was murder and if her family ever found out about her decision there would be hell to pay. My viewpoint on the issue was decidedly more liberal, yet I wasn't entirely happy about it either.

To pay for it, I'd had to sell my car and wash dishes for a week at the Union, but I didn't reveal any of that to Christine. After all, she still thought I was a rich kid and the time wasn't right for me to reveal myself as a liar. Scrounging up the money on my own was the only answer.

Just then, a teenage girl entered the room, accompanied by an older woman who I took to be her mother. The girl was chewing gum and seemed indifferent, but her mother was wiping her eyes with a handkerchief. As they headed for the receptionist's desk to sign in, I tried to divert Christine's attention to the colorful fish darting around inside the tank.

"They say it'll only take about a half hour," I told Christine. She seemed mesmerized by the fish.

The door that separated the waiting room from the examination rooms suddenly opened and a nurse with a surgical mask around her neck appeared in the doorway. She was holding a clipboard and after glancing at it, she called out a name. One of the women sitting across from us tossed her magazine on the table in front of her, stood up and, with a sigh, followed the nurse who smiled warmly at her. Then they both disappeared behind the door.

That was when Christine noticed the plastic model that sat on the end of the receptionist's desk. Its colorful parts depicted a fetus curled up in a uterus. I followed her gaze and then looked at her face, dreading what I would see there. Her eyes had welled up and a lonely tear streamed slowly down her cheek.

She stood up and turned to me. "I can't do this, Jimmy," she said. "I just can't. I'm sorry."

Then she headed for the door and I followed her out.

~

Of course, I tried to talk sense into her, but Christine had made up her mind and refused to discuss it. At one point, I suggested that we consider putting the baby up for adoption and at first Christine seemed open to the possibility. But as the pregnancy progressed, her interest in that option waned.

Although we had vowed to keep it a secret, Christine confessed everything to her sister Ellen, who ended up making the tragic mistake of revealing the whole thing to her parents.

Dominick and Mary DeLuca—both devout Catholics—hit the ceiling, horrified that Christine had engaged in pre-marital sex and even more outraged that she had even *contemplated* having an abortion. There were a series of fierce, arguments for a while. They were disappointed in her, they said. She had incurred the Lord's wrath and would burn in hell unless she received forgiveness. They consulted their priest who admonished her, but provided guidance. I tried to take the blame and got my head chewed off as well, but at least I managed to deflect some of the heat from poor Christine.

As I was soon to discover, Christine's parents were worse than I had imagined. They both held pre-Neolithic positions on a wide variety of social and political issues. The bigger and more vocal fanatic of the pair was her father, a construction foreman with a military haircut, a neck the size of a tree trunk and a huge fist that he repeatedly stuck under my nose to emphasize a point. He threatened to track me down and pull out my liver with his bare hands if I didn't do "the right thing," which was to marry Christine as soon as possible. He reminded me of a more seriously deranged version of Reverend Beasley. But he refused to budge on the marriage issue. He was a rock where that was concerned.

Later, Dom accused me of raping his daughter and threatened to report me to the authorities if I made a fuss about marrying her. Unfortunately for me, aside from his own violent tendencies, Dom DeLuca was *supposedly* related to a guy who made his living breaking other people's knees without anesthetics. I wasn't sure I believed this tale, but why take a chance? For a while, I seriously considered escaping to some remote corner of the world, maybe Fiji or Tibet, but I didn't have the funds to travel that far. Dominick and his friend would probably track me down anyway.

One day, he told me exactly how he felt about the situation. "I don't like you Hendricks," he hissed, spitting the words in my face, his breath a noxious mixture of garlic and ineffective breath mints. "I don't like you one little bit. And if you hurt my little baby girl, if you even *think* of cheating on her or running out on her, I will personally make your life miserable. You got that, college boy?"

"Loud and clear," I said.

Once his daughter had been absolved of sin and I had agreed, albeit reluctantly, to marry her (not that I had a choice), I think Dominick started to like the idea of being related to my father, the man who'd invented the Magic Marker. I tried numerous times to disabuse him on that score, but no one believed me when I insisted that my father was actually an electrician and my mother gave piano lessons to eight-year-olds.

The DeLuca clan promptly caught on when my parents appeared at the wedding in their Chevy instead of a stretch limo. My father wore a starched shirt, trousers that were about an inch too long and a clip-on tie. My mother had on a dark purple pant suit and a string of fake pearls. They were hardly the picture of elegance. I had a distinct feeling that Dominick wanted to strangle me on the spot, but somebody had to marry his daughter and he'd already paid for the cake, the flowers and the one-man band (an ex-Las Vegas lounge singer named Dino Rossini), so it might as well have been me, regardless of the bogus Magic Marker fortune. Oddly enough, Christine didn't seem to care that her dreams of an affluent lifestyle had suddenly vanished.

Our wedding took place at a small Catholic church on the outskirts of the DeLuca's town. Since Dom was embarrassed that his little girl had gotten pregnant out of wedlock, the guest list was limited to close relatives. I wanted to run away into the woods when the priest said the words that condemned me to life with a woman I barely knew: "Do you, James Robert Hendricks, take Deirdre Christine DeLuca to be your lawful wedded wife?"

I almost choked on the words "I do" but as soon as I'd said

them, Dominick shot me a glowering look while my mother, who was weeping with joy, smiled through her tears and kissed my father on the cheek. I hadn't explained the circumstances to them yet.

After the wedding, we set up a household in a small town in New Hampshire where housing was inexpensive and anonymity secure. Obviously, I had to quit school, which didn't exactly break my heart. But since I lacked a degree, all I could manage to find was a minimum wage job at the electronics store that I now own, although in those days, it was little more than a rundown Mom and Pop business, and Mom and Pop were cheapskates. To help make ends meet, Deirdre, who would have preferred going to the local community college to study fashion design, reluctantly enrolled at a dental hygienist school in the next town. I'm not sure why, but she suddenly decided to use her first name—Deirdre—rather than her middle name, which had always been favored by her parents. She never actually told me why.

Since I was still seething with resentment at having been railroaded into marrying her, we didn't speak to each other unless we had to. I respected her space and she respected mine and we both went about our business with a minimum of conversation, limiting our interactions to neutral territory such as financial matters and the like. Initially, we slept in separate beds. Since our apartment was a tiny one-bedroom, my bed was actually the living room convertible sofa, an item of furniture with a mattress so lumpy that I invariably spent my days with an aching back, a persistent pain that only intensified my embitterment over being condemned to serve an unjust sentence in a marital penitentiary.

Of course, I was dying to stage a prison break and embark on a series of wild extra-marital affairs, but it would've been nearly impossible to maintain the necessary secrecy in a town as small as ours. Dom's icy warnings managed to keep me in line.

When Deirdre suffered a miscarriage, which her sanctimonious father predictably interpreted as the Lord's payback for our extra-marital escapade, we were both surprised at how disconsolate the loss made us feel. The resulting grief and mourning gradually drew us closer.

Nevertheless, once the pregnancy issue had resolved itself, I assumed that Deirdre and I would finally be free to get divorced. But Dominick made it abundantly clear that he would disown his daughter if she even contemplated divorcing me, in spite of the fact that he hated my guts. And that was a light sentence compared to the pain and suffering he threatened to inflict upon me should I attempt to wriggle free of the marriage.

With divorce off the table, Deirdre and I decided to separate, but Dominick treated us to another example of his impeccable logic. He announced that he didn't approve of marital separation because the Lord wanted married couples to stay together and that living apart would inevitably lead to promiscuity. Sure, he was a bonehead, but I lacked the courage to cross him. I'd gotten used to having kneecaps that didn't bend in four directions.

Somehow, Deirdre and I muddled through it all. Having no choice but to make the best of it, we managed to tolerate each other and for the most part, we were polite and considerate. Eventually, we shared a bed and had regular sex. I had no complaints in that department. Deirdre was a passionate lover with a healthy libido and no shortage of energy. Of course we had our share of blistering arguments, which usually ended with me taking up temporary residence in a friend's guest bedroom, but eventually those incidents became less frequent. After a while, most of our arguments ended with spectacular make-up sex.

The years passed. Deirdre gradually became a caring and affectionate wife, and I found myself slowly warming to the role of her husband. In spite of everything, we seemed to be drawing even closer, sharing intimacies, tolerating each other's quirks, supporting each other during trying times, acting, in short, like a reasonably happy couple, although there was always a pool of resentment lurking beneath the surface.

Six years after our marriage, my father died of a cerebral aneurysm. Deirdre and her parents attended the funeral and during the memorial service, Mrs. DeLuca actually wept. As I stood near the gravesite holding my mother's clammy hand, I found myself suddenly overcome with emotion and it took all my strength to keep from falling apart. Of course, most of it was a deep sadness at the loss of my father, but on another level, I was equally grief-stricken by the realization that I had made a complete and utter mess of my life. My youth was slowly slipping by and here I was, married to a woman I didn't really love, working a lousy minimum wage job and living in a tiny apartment. All of this had come to pass because I had lacked the strength of character to remain faithful to the one woman I did love. In effect, I had botched up my life because I could not resist the temptation of a pointless one-night stand. I was, in short, a fool.

When the funeral service was over, my mother took me aside for a private word. She was wearing a white blouse, black slacks and the same string of fake white pearls she'd sported at the wedding. She held an unfiltered Camel between her yellowed fingers.

"Listen Jimmy," she whispered, blowing smoke out of the corner of her mouth. "Last night, I was putting a bunch of your father's clothes and things together for the Salvation Army and I started rummaging around in the safe."

"So, did you find anything good?" I asked.

"Yeah. At the bottom of this drawer, I found a life insurance policy your Dad had taken out about twenty years ago."

"That was very thoughtful of him," I said.

"He never told me a thing about it."

"Well, it'll help you get by," I told her.

"I won't need an income anymore," she said. "The policy is kind of big."

"How big?"

My mother dropped her cigarette and carefully rubbed it out with the tip of her shoe. "Five hundred grand," she said.

I almost fell on my ass. My quiet, unassuming father had secretly insured his life for half a million bucks?

"I don't know why he didn't mention it in his will," my mother added calmly, tapping a fresh pack of cigarettes against the palm of her hand.

"Maybe he just forgot," I ventured.

"I guess so," she said. "Kinda hard to forget something like that though."

On top of that, my parents' modest two-bedroom house, for which they'd originally paid forty thousand dollars in the early Eighties, happened to be located in a section of town that was quickly becoming gentrified by a group of Wall Street investors, so the land value had skyrocketed. My mother sold the place for over four hundred thousand dollars to a land speculator who razed it to make a condominium complex.

Ironically, my mother was suddenly a rich woman. Maybe she wasn't the wife of the man who held the patent on the Magic Marker, but she was more than comfortable.

Meanwhile, I was still struggling to accumulate enough cash to buy the store I now managed for eight dollars an hour. I estimated that it would take me maybe six years to accomplish that goal if Deirdre (who had quit school to become a personal trainer) and I both saved about a third of our salaries each year. But I guess my mother sympathized, and one day, out of the blue, I received a check for two-hundred thousand dollars in the mail from her.

So I bought the store, and a year later, I took out a sizeable mortgage on a vacant building on our main drag and doubled my floor space. Sure, it was risky, but as it turned out I had a fairly good head for business. Who knew?

Deirdre and I were suddenly very well off which made both her and the rest of the DeLuca family jubilant, although her father's unfavorable opinion of me never wavered and probably never would. A year after I bought the store, we moved to a brand new tract house in the Heights, twenty miles north of town. It wasn't ostentatious, but it had a small pool, a circular driveway, four bedrooms and a spectacular view of the mountains.

I have to say that we were fairly content together for quite some time once our financial problems had vanished. We were growing up together and creating a history. Love didn't seem to be much of an issue anymore. Unfortunately, the miscarriage had mangled Deirdre's reproductive equipment and she would never be able to bear children, so we compensated by devoting more time to each other. We vacationed in Florida, New Orleans and Las Vegas and took cruises to Greece and Alaska. For a while, we even considered adopting a child, but Deirdre confessed that she didn't want to sacrifice her job for full time child-rearing.

Then, suddenly, we hit a snag. I'm not sure why, but as we approached our nineteenth anniversary, the marriage we had worked so hard to construct out of bitterness gradually started to crumble. It began, as so many marital crises do, with a skirmish about nothing and snowballed into a continual series of pitched battles, interrupted by short periods of reconciliation. But eventually, we ended up the way we had begun, resentful and bitter, two polite strangers occupying the same house. Although we were both civil, and often even pleasant to one another—especially on holidays—it was clear that our marriage was cracking. I deluded myself into thinking we would eventually negotiate a lasting treaty and somehow soldier on. I'm not even sure I understand why I felt that way.

Three months before Deirdre announced her intention to move in with Dave Barstow, Mr. and Mrs. DeLuca both died in a car accident involving a deer and a skidding Brink's truck, and Deirdre suddenly felt free to divorce me. Apparently, she hadn't feared the wrath of God as much as she'd feared the wrath of her father.

Christine (Deirdre)... Now

I'M NOT ENTIRELY CERTAIN I have any compelling reason to apologize to Deirdre, given her decision to leave me for the biggest jerk in town. Yet, in spite of her infidelity and my resentment over it, I still can't help but feel guilty about the Magic Marker deception. If it hadn't been for that foolish ruse, I'm convinced that she would never have sacrificed her virginity that night. But the worst part is that I had snuck out of her apartment the next morning like a burglar. For that crime, I feel even guiltier.

When I finally get home from Boston, the first thing I do is check in at the store. I find myself staying late, poring over the books, paying a few delinquent bills and checking inventory, all because I can't bear the thought of clanking around like a tormented poltergeist in a big empty house. I suddenly miss Morris. This loneliness business is new to me, and I suppose I'll need some time to adjust.

I peruse Molly's email over and over, searching for some hidden meaning behind her words, but they hold no subtle encouragement and are just amiable. I don't delete it because I find myself clinging to the remote possibility that we might one day begin anew and because this email is the only link I have to her.

I must admit that Ira was right. So far, my quest for forgiveness has been more than therapeutic and I can almost feel the black anvil of guilt lightening on my shoulders.

But I still feel a nagging guilt about Deirdre. After all, I had treated her as shabbily as I'd treated the others.

"Hmmm," Ira muses after I tell him about my dilemma. "That's really a tough nut to crack, Jimmy."

"So what would you advise?" I ask.

Ira lets out a deep breath and probes his ear with an index finger. "You kind of conned her and then dumped her. It wasn't very nice."

"She kind of dumped me too," I reply, "for that gargantuan English teacher."

"True enough," Ira says. "But technically speaking, if you hadn't conned her with the Magic Marker business, you never would have gone home with her that night and you would never have married her; thus she wouldn't have dumped you. Skipping out on her after you slept with her wasn't very nice either. I suppose that's it in a nutshell right?"

"More or less," I say. "So you're saying I *should* apologize?"

Ira shrugs. "Up to you my friend," he says. "The important thing is whether or not you've learned anything from this experience so far."

I give it some thought. "I don't know," I tell him. "Two out of three of them aren't holding any grudges. Maybe I wasn't the colossal asshole I thought I was. Or maybe *everybody's* an asshole at that age."

"I wasn't," Ira says.

"Okay, maybe not everybody then," I say.

"Well then," Ira tells me. "If you still feel you need closure before moving on with your life, apologize to Deirdre."

"Guess I've got nothing to lose," I speculate.

"Know what I think?" Ira says. "I might be wrong, but I get the feeling that the other apologies were just rehearsals for this one."

"Huh?" I say. "That's ridiculous."

Ira puts up both palms. "Just a feeling," he says. "I'm probably dead wrong."

So I decide to bite the bullet and call on Deirdre. The curious thing is, although she now lives up the street, I never see her. I don't spot her watering Dave's lawn or retrieving his mail or jogging down the street with him or getting in her car to go to work. This piques my curiosity. So one evening around dusk, I saunter to the end of the cul-de-sac and knock on Dave's door, fully expecting Deirdre to answer. But when the door opens, it's Dave who stands in the doorway, wearing a sweaty sleeveless T-shirt and gym shorts. The veins in his biceps are bulging and he appears to be slightly out of breath. He's patting his stomach, which I take to mean that he's either just eaten a satisfying meal or he's making sure his abs are still there.

"Well, well, well," he says condescendingly, looking down at me from his doorstep. He's leaning on the jamb, blocking the doorway.

"Well, well, well," I repeat.

"What are you doing in this neck of the woods, Hendricks?" he asks with a smug grin.

"In case you forgot, I *live* in this neck of the woods," I remind him.

"Quite so." He nods somberly for a second. "So what can I do for you, or is this a social visit? Something tells me it's not."

"Is Deirdre here?" I ask.

"I'm afraid not."

"Out shopping?"

"No."

"At the gym?"

"No," Dave says in a bored monotone. "If you must know, she left me."

I take a few seconds to absorb this curious turn of events. Hell, they hadn't even been cohabiting that long.

"When was that?"

"Two days ago."

"Why?"

"She said I didn't have a sense of humor," he tells me with a snort. "Is that a joke or what?"

"A laugh riot," I reply.

"Frankly, she got on my nerves," Dave continues, inspecting his fingernails. "Never cooked or straightened up or did laundry."

"So what you really needed is a maid," I suggest, "or a housewife."

"Plus, if you must know, the sex got weird."

"Really?"

"She kept biting me."

"That's more than I really need to know, Dave."

"Did she used to bite you?"

The answer is no. Deirdre never sank her teeth into my flesh during sex, but I don't want Dave to think she was less passionate with me. "Sure, all the time," I tell him.

"I have goddamn teeth marks all over," he says. "Even several on my fucking *ass*." Then he grins and says facetiously, "Would you care to see?"

"Tempting... " I tell him. "Maybe next time. So where exactly is she?"

He shrugs as if he's not even slightly interested. "I think she's staying at a friend's house," he says. "Some woman named Barbara, not that I really care."

What a sweet guy—they break up after a month and he feels no remorse. But then I'm not entirely innocent of that particular crime myself.

~

Sunday is Deirdre's day off, so I drive over to Barbara's place. When I get there, I stay in the car for about ten minutes, absently listening to an oldies station. I'm stalling because I have no clear idea what I'm going to say.

It wasn't raining when I left the house, but it's pouring now. Bubbly puddles form everywhere almost instantaneously, and

I have no umbrella or raincoat in the car. But I do have an old issue of the local paper rolled up in the back seat and that serves as an impromptu but largely ineffective rain shield. Dodging puddles while holding the newspaper over my head, I sprint up the stone path to Barbara's front door and stamp my feet on the welcome mat.

Deirdre's wearing a silk kimono when she appears in the doorway. She's holding a book in one hand and a remote control in the other. Her hair is tangled from sleeping on it and she's not wearing any make-up, although she's pretty enough without it. From the doorway, I can hear people screaming and applauding on TV.

"Jimmy?" she asks, as if she's unsure of my identity.

"May I come in?"

"Yeah, sure."

"Is Barbara here?" I ask.

"No, she's gone grocery shopping."

She opens the door wider and I step in. Deirdre follows me inside, switches off the TV and gestures for me to sit, so I drop down on the couch while she sinks into a wingback chair, which stands beneath what appears to be a paint-by-number picture of a lighthouse.

"I heard you split up with Dave," I say.

"Was it in the local paper?"

"Banner headlines."

"Must have been a slow news day."

"Actually," I inform her, "Dave told me."

"Somehow I figured that out," she says. "What a jerk."

"Yeah well, sometimes these clandestine affairs don't work out once they're no longer clandestine," I say sagely. "He wasn't your type anyway."

"Oh really? And why is that?"

"I know you, Deirdre. He's a pompous, humorless douchebag."

"Yeah, that pretty much sums it up," she agrees. "But it's over. I saw the light."

She yawns widely and drums her fingers impatiently on the chair arm. I assume she's eager, or at least mildly curious, to know the purpose of my visit.

"You're probably wondering why I'm here," I say.

"To gloat?"

"No, of course not."

"Then why?"

Since I'm not planning on staying long, I take a deep breath and dive right in. "I'll cut right to the chase, Deirdre," I tell her. "I came here to apologize to you."

This announcement evidently throws her because she looks at me dimly. "Apologize for what exactly?"

"For lying."

"Lying about what?"

"The whole Magic Marker story," I say.

She seems amused. "After all these years you're *apologizing* for that?"

"Correct."

"Why?"

"Guilty conscience," I tell her. "Trying to make things right."

"That's it?"

"That's it."

She shrugs. "Okay, I forgive you."

This is unexpectedly sudden. "You do?"

"Jimmy, I knew that was bullshit the whole time. I just played along. Plus, you forget that I've always been a big reader," she reminds me. "A few days after we first made love, I went to the library. The Magic Marker was invented by a guy named Sidney Rosenthal in 1952."

Now I'm confused. "So what are you saying?" I ask, frowning. "That it *wasn't* about the money?"

"Never," she claims.

"But—"

"Jimmy, you didn't lure me into the sack that night," she informs me. "I picked *you* up. I took *you* home. It wasn't my original intent to have sex with you, but one thing led to another and…"

"But why?' I ask. "Why did you take me to your place?"

Deirdre crosses her arms and looks out the picture window. It's still raining, though not as fiercely. Her eyes are still averted when she finally blurts it out. "First off, I felt sorry for you getting stranded there. I truly did. But also, you seemed like a good guy. You were bright and funny. I liked you. There were no men in my life at the time and the only guys I was meeting were creeps. I thought we could… you know… date."

I don't quite know what to say. The last thing on my mind that night had been the idea of dating her.

"But obviously you didn't think I was dating material," she says acidly, looking away again. "I guess I just wasn't good enough for you. Not up to your… standards."

Now I feel worse. "That's not true," I stammer. "It's just that I was already dating someone. I guess I thought it was a one-night stand."

"Maybe it was for you," she says. "You just snuck out the next morning. That was cold. That really hurt me."

"That's another reason why I'm apologizing," I tell her. "I was an asshole. I took your virginity and then I snuck out while you were asleep. Pretty shitty."

Deirdre is quiet for a moment and studies me. "To be honest, I'm not a hundred percent sure about the virginity thing," she confesses.

I frown. "Huh?"

"I probably should have told you this a long time ago," she says. "Not that it really matters, but maybe it'll make you feel better."

I'm eyeing her suspiciously. "Tell me what?"

Deirdre sighs and springs to her feet. "Would you like a lemonade or something, Jimmy?" she asks.

"*Tell me what?*" I repeat.

"Never mind," she says. "It's really not a—"

"Damn it Deirdre," I say forcefully.

She plops back down on the chair, crosses her legs and watches one of her slippers dangling on the toes of her foot. Then she looks up at me. "Okay," she says, taking a deep breath. "I may not have been a virgin when we met. Not technically anyway."

I snort. "Technically?" I ask. "What does that mean exactly?"

"I may have actually lost my virginity before we met," she informs me. "I'm not sure. There was this guy, John or Joe, I don't remember. Anyway, we got smashed, *really smashed,* and went at it in his car. I blacked out almost right away. When I woke up the next morning, I was half-naked in the front seat and he was dressed in the back seat. Neither of us remembered anything."

I look at her, incredulous but unconvinced. "Come on, Deirdre, there must have been *some* evidence," I say.

She shrugs. "I was really hung over," she says. "There was puke all over my lap and sweater. I was dizzy as hell, so when I got home I tossed all my clothes in the washing machine and took a bath."

"No blood?"

"I didn't look."

"But you told me you were a virgin," I say.

"Maybe I was, maybe I wasn't," she says. "I guess the odds were about fifty-fifty. Who knows? What's the difference?"

"So you were kind of *half* a virgin when we met," I conclude, realizing right away how inane that must have sounded.

She squints at me. "*Half* a virgin?" she repeats with a laugh. "That's dumb, Jimmy. How can somebody be *half* a virgin? You're either a virgin or you're not."

"Yes but... never mind... you're right," I tell her. "It doesn't really matter anyway."

"Would it have made any difference if I'd told you I was a virgin before we—?"

"Probably not," I confess.

I think back to that night at Deirdre's apartment and how different my life would have been had I resisted her. My mind is swirling with an onrush of conflicting thoughts and I'm having considerable difficulty sorting them all out. The struggle is making me feel lightheaded, a sensation similar to the realization that you've had one too many drinks and it's too late to turn back. I exhale the exhausted, world-weary sigh of a man who has just learned that he destroyed half of his life simply because he was in the wrong place at the wrong time.

"I'm sorry, Jimmy," she says. "No offense, but I didn't really want to get pregnant and marry you either. It just turned out that way. I swear to God."

"Forget it," I grumble. "It's spilled milk."

"I'm sorry about Dave and how I told you on your—"

"I think we're even on the apology business," I interject. "Why don't we just leave it at that, okay?"

"Okay."

"Anyway, there's someone else in my life now," I tell her, meaning Molly.

"Oh?" she says, trying to force a smile. "Well I guess that's nice for you."

Suddenly, I'm finding the atmosphere in the room unbearably oppressive, so I put my hands on my kneecaps and rise slowly from the couch.

"You can stay for awhile if you want, Jimmy," she offers meekly. "Have a cup of coffee or something. Barbara won't be back for a while."

She gazes up at me, and the vulnerable look on her face almost touches me, but I resist the temptation to stay. Suddenly, I realize I'm feeling more bewildered than angry, but I don't really know why.

"Thanks," I say, softly. "Maybe some other time."

Deirdre walks me to the door. "You know what occurred to me the other day?" she asks me.

"What?"

"I know this is dumb, but I was having dinner with some idiot guy who was droning on about his Porsche or something, so my mind was wandering and I suddenly realized that you and I have spent half our lives together."

"Twenty long years," I say disconsolately.

"Hey, we had some good times," Deirdre says. "Like that time we went kayaking and ended up going down the rapids backwards. Remember?"

"I gotta go, Deirdre," I tell her.

I walk past her through the doorway. On the way to my car, I stop and take a deep breath. The rain has stopped, the clouds have parted and a warm breeze picks up. I bask in it for a moment, then get in my car and drive off, my head filled with visions of Molly.

Part Six

Molly

On the Road Again

A FEW DAYS LATER, I PHONE Morris to beg for another favor. Predictably, he makes a huge fuss, correctly accusing me of trying to take advantage of his good nature, but he finally surrenders to my pathetic whining. I assure him I'll only require his services for half a day this time, and that his sole function will be to provide me with companionship and, should I require it, a shoulder to cry on.

"I can't believe you're dragging me to this," he complains, as he adjusts his headrest. "I can't believe I *agreed* to let you drag me to this."

"It'll be fun," I tell him, in a rousing voice that even I don't find convincing.

"Like a molar extraction," he says. "It's lucky for you it's Sunday."

"Come on, Morris," I continue, struggling to put on a happy face. "Lighten up. It'll be a blast."

"I think you're taking unfair advantage of my religious faith," he scolds, wagging a finger at me. "You're becoming a *mitzvah* abuser."

"I'll do anything you want to pay the debt," I offer.

"Seriously?"

I nod uncertainly.

"Okay," he says, eyeing me skeptically. "I want you to read the Torah at my temple next week. That's my wish."

I glance over to see if he's toying with me, but his face is a blank. "To be honest, I was actually thinking of something a little more within the realm of reality," I confess. "But I'll be happy to take a Berlitz course in Hebrew if you insist."

"Are you kidding? You think you can learn Hebrew in a week?"

"Well, maybe not all of it, but I'm sure I can learn some of the basic words like 'hello' and 'goodbye' and some phrases like 'I'd like the check please'."

"Yeah, there's a lot of that kind of stuff in the Torah," Morris says, rolling his eyes. "God is always asking for the check."

"You're right," I say. "He probably doesn't eat out much."

Morris sighs and shoots me a look. "Never mind," he tells me. "You'd probably drop it on your foot or find some other way to accidentally desecrate it. And anyway, you're not Jewish."

Since neither Morris nor I responded to our invitations, we have to do a little song and dance act for the entry officials, who sit at a long table surrounded by old high school banners. They're skeptical about us at first, although Morris's yarmulke and black suit give him an air of respectability.

Finally, I say to the receptionists, "Why would we want to come to a reunion if we didn't even go to the college?"

That stumps them and, after some whispered consultation, they reluctantly let us pass, but only after we scrawl our first names on a couple of self-adhesive nametags, which, apparently, is mandatory.

The gym, which smells of sweat, is crowded with gaggles of men and women, most of whom I barely recognize. On a makeshift stage, a mediocre three-piece band is blasting out forgettable songs from the year we graduated, so everybody has to shout over the noise. Most of my fellow alumni are holding plastic cups of pinkish punch and laughing uproariously, no doubt over the recollection of some collegiate misadventure. Others are dancing to the uncertain beat of the combo. Dodging elbows, I start weaving my way through the crowd, hoping I don't bump into Samantha, although I suspect that she probably wouldn't deign to mix with this rabble. Meanwhile, Morris stands by the punch bowl, eyeing its contents, most likely wondering whether this mitzvah is important enough to justify a non-kosher alcoholic beverage.

I'm still pushing my way through the throngs when my elbow is suddenly grabbed by a short woman wearing a daringly low-cut blouse which displays a pair of large breasts that appear suspiciously firm and pert. Her fake eyelashes are freakishly long and some of her bright red lipstick has rubbed off on her veneered front teeth.

"Jimmy Hendricks?" she asks excitedly.

"Yes," I say, searching her features for a clue to her identity.

"What, you don't recognize me?" she asks, sounding a trifle peeved. "We dated after you dumped that snob whatsherface."

I'm about to stutter something deliberately unintelligible when her Brooklyn accent tips me off. "Of course I recognize you," I tell her. "You're Amanda Dills."

"You look good, Jimmy," she declares, sizing me up.

"Thanks," I say. "As do you."

"So you married or what?"

"Or what."

"Confirmed bachelor, widowed or divorced?" she asks, finishing off her cup of punch.

"About to be divorced," I tell her. "In the process."

"Me too," she says with a lopsided smile. "My third go around, can you believe it? I keep marrying the same schmucks every single time. Go figure."

I'm only half listening. My eyes keep wandering over her shoulder. Apparently she doesn't notice.

"I've been on Match.com and eHarmony for two years," she moans. "I tried speed dating but that was a joke. Have you tried it yet?"

"Tried what?"

"Speed dating."

"No."

Then someone bumps into her from behind and Amanda stumbles into my arms. She seems to like it there because she doesn't make any effort to move away. "So listen, Jimmy," she says, gazing up at me. "You wanna get together for dinner later? Have a couple of drinks. Catch up on old times?"

I'm thinking: What old times? We dated for three weeks.

Then she winks. "Maybe we could do something else a little later," she suggests. "I got a nice room at the Holiday Inn."

"I'd love to, Amanda," I say, "but unfortunately I already have dinner plans tonight. Maybe we can get together some other time. I'll call you."

She takes a step back. "Yeah right," she says coldly. "I won't hold my breath."

Shaking her head in disgust, either at me personally or men in general or both, she turns around and strolls off into the crowd, unsteady in her four-inch heels. Within a few moments, I spot her sidling up to another guy.

No sooner has she disappeared into the crowd than I feel a tap on the back of my shoulder and swivel around, hoping it's Molly.

"Jimmy Fucking Hendricks," Sanjee says, looking me over through a pair of tinted glasses.

"Sanjee Fucking Pancholy," I say.

"How've you been, man?" he asks as we bump fists. Amazingly, he doesn't seem to have aged a bit, no perceptible weight gain, no other telltale signs of middle age. The only difference is that now his shiny black hair is fashionably moussed up to form a short peak that runs the length of his head and he's sporting a gold rivet in his earlobe. He could pass for twenty-five. Most of the other men in the room are dressed casually in light summer jackets and Dockers, others are wearing Fryman sweatshirts with jeans and running shoes, but Sanjee is decked out in an expensive suit, a conservative silk tie and brown loafers.

"Not bad," I say unconvincingly. "You?"

"Couldn't be better," he tells me with a bright smile. "Making lots of dough, enjoying the good life, getting laid a lot. Did you see the white Porsche out in the lot? That's mine. Drives like a dream. Vintage. Cost me a fucking fortune, but you only live once, right?"

"Actually, that hasn't been definitively proven yet," I say idiotically.

Sanjee smirks. "Still the funny guy," he says.

After a few more minutes of small talk, we head for a quiet corner of the gym and reminisce. Sanjee does most of the talking. Ten years ago, he made a fortune developing some kind of complicated software and although he explains it in detail, I have no clue what he's talking about. No wife, no kids. A townhouse on Fifth Avenue, a place in the Hamptons, a beach house in the Bahamas, a condo in Cabo. Reluctantly, I tell him about my electronics business, but I make it seem as if I own a chain of stores rather than just one, and that we're expanding.

"Can you get me a deal on a state-of-the-art, top-of-the-line sound system?" he asks. "I need a new one for my place in Cabo."

"Sure," I reply, "but you'd be better off buying it on the Internet. Cheaper."

"You're a hell of salesman," he observes.

"Just trying to save you a little cash," I say. "For old time's sake."

"I'd rather throw the business your way," he says. "You never know what you're getting on the Internet. I'll pay top dollar."

Just then, a gorgeous blond in a white, low-cut evening dress, an expensive-looking gold necklace and stiletto heels, pulls up next to Sanjee and grabs his elbow. She smiles at me, revealing a set of perfect teeth.

"Hey babe," Sanjee says. They kiss for a good five seconds while I stand there awkwardly, rocking on my heels, waiting for an introduction. Finally, they separate and Sanjee says, "Avanka, Jimmy. Jimmy, Avanka."

We shake hands. Then, in an accent that sounds vaguely Eastern European, she says, "A pleasure to meet you."

"Likewise," I tell her.

"Is she hot *or what?*" Sanjee says, letting his hand roam around her ass. Avanka smiles shyly, removes his hand from her posterior and nudges Sanjee in the ribs.

"Very," I say.

Avanka turns to Sanjee. "I told you not to say that anymore, baby," she scolds him, although her slight smile indicates to me that she's not entirely annoyed. "It's embarrassing."

"Sorry babe," he says. "You know I can't help myself."

I smile at her. Sanjee looks down at his cup of punch, which is empty. "So listen, Jimbo," he says. "Let's get together sometime. Here's my card."

"That would be really great," I say, trying to sound enthusiastic as I place his card in my pocket.

"We're gonna circulate," he continues. "Great to see you, man. Catch ya later, okay?"

"Sounds good," I say. Then Sanjee takes Avanka's hand and leads her to the buffet table, where a large crowd has gathered.

Once they're gone, I resume my search for Molly, slithering through the throngs of people, trying not to knock over anybody's punch. When the ground level exploration proves fruitless, I climb to the fifth tier of the bleachers and survey the horde. Still no luck. Molly's short, but even with a bird's eye view I can't locate her. Maybe she decided not to come after all. Finally, I give up the search and glumly head for the buffet table where I expect to find Morris ogling, but not indulging in the food. Just before I get there, I hear a familiar voice shout, "Jimmy!"

I turn around and there she is, a vision of loveliness in a tight top and a knee length skirt, standing on her tiptoes, frantically waving at me from about ten feet away. I smile broadly as we approach each other.

"I wasn't sure you were really coming, Jimmy," Molly says.

"The punch was a big draw," I say.

Molly hugs me and I feel a warm flush. "I'm so glad you're here, Jimmy."

"As of this moment, so am I."

"You're sweet," she says, smiling radiantly.

"No, I mean it," I tell her. "I needed to see you again."

There's a pause as Molly cursorily surveys the room. "I hate to say it, but I don't recognize a single soul," she says. "Then again, I didn't expect to recognize anybody You were my only friend at college, except for Morris and Naomi."

"Morris is here somewhere," I say.

"Where?"

"I have no idea," I tell her, looking around the room. "He's probably talking football with some of his old teammates. He was a football star in college, in case you forgot."

"And Naomi?" she asks.

"Naomi stayed home," I say. "They have about forty kids."

"I'd love to say hello to him," she says. Then she searches the room for a moment, but she's too short to see over all the heads even on her tiptoes.

"You look stunning," I say.

"Thanks."

"So listen," I say, my voice wavering a bit. "Can I talk to you in private for a second, Molly?"

"Sure."

I take her hand and lead her to a deserted spot behind the bleachers. I hesitate for a moment, looking at her and wondering whether this is the right place and the right time, but I'm feeling bold and I'm impatient.

"I've been thinking about you a lot since I last saw you," I tell her. "A *lot*."

"I'm glad," she says.

"I keep thinking about how good we were together in college," I continue.

"We were," she says. "But that was a really long time ago."

"I know," I agree. "But that day in your apartment in Providence... when I came to apologize, I felt that maybe there was... I don't know... still a... spark."

"A spark?"

"Yeah," I say. "I mean, you emailed me and you said you wanted to see me again, so I thought maybe we could... I don't know... try again."

I search her face, but she avoids my gaze. "Try again?" she asks. "You mean—"

"I mean start up where we left off," I tell her. "You know, give it another go. See what happens."

She looks at me sweetly, then takes my hand. "Jimmy, we're different people now," she tells me gently. "We've both changed. We were just kids then. It's been twenty years. We don't really know each other at all anymore."

I look away. Somebody in the bleachers laughs. The music stops. My heartbeat, which had been racing, slows down. "Maybe there's still something there," I say desperately. "Maybe we should explore that."

Molly looks at me sadly. "I'm sorry if I led you on Jimmy," she says. "I really didn't mean to. I probably should have told you this but—"

"*There* you are," says a female voice from behind me. "I've been looking all over for you, Mol."

A slightly emaciated woman with a prominent chin walks past me and stands beside Molly. She's wearing round rimless glasses and an ambiguous expression.

"What are you doing back here?" she asks Molly.

"Just talking," Molly says. "Emma, this is my friend Jimmy. I told you about him, remember?"

Emma scrutinizes me. "Ah yes," she says. "You're the college beau."

"Correct," I say.

I extend my hand and shake her bony one. "Pleased to meet you," I say, trying to hide my displeasure at the interruption.

"Likewise."

"I don't recall ever meeting you at Fryman," I say.

"I didn't go to Fryman," she informs me. "I attended Mount Holyoke College."

"So if you didn't go to Fryman, why exactly are you here?" I inquire. "Can't resist a little free punch and some lethal food or did you come for the horrible music?"

For some reason this remark casts a pall over the conversation. Molly gives me a sheepish smile. "Emma's my partner," she says after a moment. "We're... um..."

"Gay," Emma says proudly.

And then, looking at me with an expression that I interpret as pity laced with a trace of hostility, Emma places her arm around Molly's shoulders, a gesture that strikes me as both unnecessarily possessive and slightly belligerent, and then they both smile lovingly at each other.

I'm about to say something, but I stop before the words can form.

Molly fills the silence. "Maybe we can all have dinner together tonight," she suggests brightly, apparently oblivious to my expression of profound discomfort. "We're staying at the Hyatt and I've heard they have a pretty good restaurant."

I glance at Emma who's smirking. "That would be great," I reply, "except I have to take Morris home, like in twenty minutes."

"Does he live far away?" Molly asks.

"Pretty far," I lie. "Connecticut."

Clearly, Emma sees through this lame excuse. She puts her arm around Molly's waist and flashes me a triumphant look.

"Maybe some other time," I say, trying desperately to conjure up a smile to mask the downcast look that threatens to overtake my face. "I'll call you."

I shake Emma's hand again, give Molly a cursory hug and walk off to find Morris, who I spot sitting on a tier of the bleachers, having a lively conversation with Bill Russo, the former captain of our college football team. But before I get there, a tall, skinny guy comes out of nowhere and blocks my path.

"Two words, Hendricks," Robert Arsenault says smugly. "Harvey Blitz."

Tofu Man

AND SO, IT'S BACK TO THE OLD routine. During the day, I put in long hours at the store, where the unsold keyboards are still collecting dust. At night, when I'm not playing poker or warming up a seat at our local movie theatre or having a drink with Ira, who has now become my second best friend, I watch reality shows for the first time and to my surprise, find that some of them are actually halfway interesting, not to mention addictive. You can't beat human theatre and public humiliation for laughs. For dinner, I either order take-out or suffer through packaged foods that just require heating in the microwave—lasagna or coq au vin for one person—although the microwave mystifies me and I often end up with liquefied lasagna or coq au vin that has mysteriously become petrified. Just going to the grocery store and buying this crap is a tiresome errand, so I frequently wind up at Taco Bell, Domino's or Meyer's Deli.

Laura friends me on Facebook and we carry on some lively, flirtatious exchanges for a while, but her messages to me are overpopulated with unnecessary exclamation points, smiley faces and annoying emoticons. I can live with that, but her wall generally contains nothing but the most thoroughly mundane details of her everyday life, most of which her other friends seem to find fascinating. "Kenny has a toothache!!" "I forgot my uncle's birthday!!"

"Kyle cut his elbow playing baseball!!" "I put my shirt on backwards this morning!! LOL (=:)".

Molly doesn't have a Facebook page or a Twitter account so we email back-and-forth for a few months, but we eventually run out of things to say to each other. After a while, I stop hearing from her.

⌒

One Saturday morning, while I'm sitting in an armchair at Starbucks, reading the local paper and sipping a latte, I become conscious of a woman staring at me from the other side of the room. Actually, she's not exactly *staring* so much as looking up from her book from time to time to make eye contact. I furtively give her the once-over. Decked out in a beat-up pair of cargo shorts, dusty hiking boots and a khaki T-shirt, she's an Asian goddess with long silky hair, an athletic body and a sparkling smile. I estimate she's in her late thirties, though she could pass for younger. When she suddenly smiles at me, I smile back. Then I turn back to my paper, but in a moment I look up and she's standing in front of me.

"You're Joey's boss," she says.

"Yup," I respond. "And who might you be?"

"I might be his mother," she says.

"I would've guessed sister," I say, folding up my paper and putting it aside.

"You would've guessed wrong," she says with a smile. "But thanks for the compliment." She extends her hand, the fingers of which are decorated with an odd assortment of colorful, oversized rings, most of them polished nonprecious stones. We shake. Her name is Michelle. "Mind if I sit down?" she asks.

"Please," I say.

She settles into the neighboring armchair, places her book on the table and crosses her legs, which is when I notice the Zen-like tattoo on her ankle. "I have no idea why I ordered hot coffee," she says, fanning her face with a hand. Then she raises her hair from the back of her neck and starts fanning that area. "I just hiked five miles up to the top of Mount Adams and I'm sweating like crazy."

"I'm choking on the odor," I tell her.

"Really?"

"Kidding."

She socks me lightly on the arm, then takes a sip of her coffee, looking at me over the rim. "Joey said you're a kidder," she tells me. "He thinks you're great by the way."

"That's probably because I pay him too much," I say. "But seriously, he's a good kid. Real smart. Knows everything about electronics. I'd go bankrupt in a week without him. Totally broke. I'd be living in a shed."

"He gets that from his Dad," she says, bending over to tie her boot laces. "My ex. My *recent* ex. He's an engineer."

I nod, noting with some guarded optimism that there may be some possibilities here, although my antennae have given me wrong signals on that score more times than not. We talk for about an hour or so. Michelle orders a complex-sounding organic concoction with lots of soy milk and ice. Her eyes are bewitching. Soon we're laughing it up. I'm hoping to stretch this coffee klatch out for a while, maybe let it morph into dinner, but she suddenly looks at her watch and then leaps to her feet.

"Oh shit, I gotta go," she says in a panic "I'm supposed to have a drink over at Milligan's with my friend Sally. She's really depressed. Her German shepherd just died. Christ, I haven't even showered yet. I'd love to stay but—"

"That's okay," I say rising slowly off the plush chair. "Maybe some other time."

"Yeah, sure, that would be nice," she says hurriedly, without much enthusiasm. Then she gives me a mock pout, which is followed by hasty cheek peck. I watch out the window as she dashes to her car.

~

The following Monday, when I get to work, Joey informs me that one of my employees, our resident flat screen expert, Mark Svoboda, is about to quit because his family is moving to Montpelier, where his father has found a more lucrative job. Joey suggests that I hire his older brother to fill the vacancy.

"I didn't even know you had a brother," I tell him.

"I guess I never told you," he informs me. "He plays the piano."

"That's nice, but we don't need a piano player," I say. "It's not actually essential in this business."

"Duh," Joey says.

"Does he have any electronic skills?"

"Kind of."

I wait for Joey to elaborate, but he doesn't. "Okay," I say finally. "What are his electronic skills?"

"Well, he knows a lot about keyboards. He could, like, demonstrate them or something. And since they haven't been selling…"

I put a hand on his shoulder. "Joey, I told you not to worry about that," I say.

"I know," he responds. "But maybe if somebody plays one, like for background music or something that might help. I can teach him about woofers and shit."

I nod. "Will he work for ten bucks an hour plus commission?"

"Yeah," he says. "He really needs a job right now."

"Okay, I'll fill out the paperwork," I say. "He can start tomorrow."

Joey thanks me and I'm about to walk off, when he stops me. "One other thing, boss," he says. "I forgot to tell you. He's retarded."

"We don't use that word anymore, Joey," I scold him. "It's insulting."

"Okay," Joey says, rolling his eyes. "He's whadaycallit… developmentally-challenged."

"So what?"

Joey gives me a surprised look. "You're okay with that?" he asks.

"Sure," I tell him. "Why wouldn't I be?"

"Cool."

"What's his name?"

"Walter."

"How old?"

"Eighteen I think," Joey says.

"You *think?*"

"We're not close," he explains.

I squint at Joey for a moment, trying to determine whether or not he's serious, but his face is a blank. I look at my watch. Three fifteen. The store is empty, not a customer in sight.

"You can have the rest of the afternoon off," I tell him. "Go swim in the lake or hang out at the mall."

"For real?"

"Go."

"Thanks boss!" he exclaims, pulling off his store T-shirt and handing it to me. In a moment, he's out the door and I watch him delicately place his motorcycle helmet over his coif. A second later, the bike vrooms a few times and screeches out into the street.

~

The next day, I get to work early to see how Joey's brother is doing, but he doesn't appear to be in the showroom. I walk the aisles until I find Joey taking a picture of himself with one of our new digital cameras.

"What's up, Mr. H?" he asks. "Want me to take your picture?"

"Not really."

Joey snaps one anyway and shows it to me.

I look around. "So where's Walter?" I ask. "I thought you told me he was starting today."

"He's getting me a mocha frap at Starbucks."

"Excuse me?"

"Hey, I'm the manager, right?"

"You're having your own brother get you coffee?"

"Like I said, we're not close."

"But he's eighteen and you're seventeen."

"And your point is?"

Although I like Joey, I often find him exasperating. This is one of those times. "Never mind," I tell him with a sigh. "I'll be in the office if you need me."

"Wait a sec, Mr. H," he says.

I swivel. "What?"

"My Mom says she met you at Starbucks."

"Yeah," I say. "Nice lady."

"Yeah well... the thing is... I hope you don't mind since it's kinda private and all, but I gave her your cell number," he says, a little sheepishly. "She said she wanted to send you some link to some article or something. Are we cool with that?"

I shrug. "Sure, we're cool with that," I say. "Just don't make it a habit."

I have no idea what article he's talking about, so I retreat to the peace and quiet of my office, lock the door and watch some free porn video clips. This gets boring fast (how many blowjobs can you watch?) so I decide to get an early start on tabulating the month's billings. This is my favorite part of the job, as long as the number at the bottom of the profit column is higher than the one at the bottom of the loss column, which it usually is. For some reason, I love using calculators.

I'm in the middle of figuring out the month's service and in-stallation charges, when my cell vibrates. It's a text. "Thanks for hiring Walter," it says. "Love, Michelle. P.S. Here's your reward."

The phone buzzes again. Another message from Michelle, only this one's not a text. It's a photo of her from the waist up.

Nude.

~

We don't waste any time with formal dating. Michelle invites herself to my place and the festivities begin. Later, after we're both spent, we lie in bed and talk about things we have in common, such as how we both dislike the bland, conservative town we happen to live in, a subject that brings out enough humor to bond us for life. People in town, she tells me, think she's a little quirky and I respond that I like women who are a little quirky. She has an easy, contagious laugh. Her energy seems boundless, her serotonin level annoyingly high. After a short time, Michelle and I develop an easygoing conversational style, although I'm not entirely certain that she understands sarcasm. No matter. This is all new to me, but I like it, and we seem to hit it off right from the start.

Of course, we try to keep our little romance a secret from Joey and Walter, hoping to spare ourselves the embarrassment of their total revulsion. (Fortunately, her sons live with their father in one of the tracts.)

One Monday afternoon, she invites me over to her place, so we caravan up a winding dirt road I never even knew existed. Her house is a small, weather-beaten affair in the middle of a secluded pine forest. Four sets of wind chimes hang from the roof beams over the porch and an organic garden, surrounded by a high chicken wire fence, graces most of the front yard. Before we go in, Michelle identifies the various fruits and vegetables she's growing, picks a large ripe strawberry and puts it to my lips.

"Mmmmm," I say.

It's dark inside. Beaded curtains separate the living room from the kitchen and a huge framed painting of the Himalayas dominates the wall above her bed. As it turns out, Michelle is a Buddhist. A jade statue of the Holy Man sits on her mantle surrounded by a semi-circle of incense stalks, several of which she lights.

"Can I get you something to drink?" she asks on the way to the kitchen.

"Coke?"

"Don't have any," she says. "Too many chemicals."

"Beer?"

"Sulfites."

"Wine?"

"Ethanol."

"Okay," I say, "what *do* you have?"

"Soy milk and some homemade organic smoothies," she tells me.

"Smoothie sounds good."

Later, after I've consumed the bland concoction, we smoke half a joint. Then she instructs me to remove my shoes and assume a yoga position on a bamboo mat. I do the best I can, and she sinks to the floor beside me. She closes her eyes and, taking the cue, I close mine. We sit there for half an hour, by which time I have a serious cramp in my left thigh and a strong desire to take a nap.

"Okay," she says, rising to her feet. "Enough of that. I feel great. Let's fuck."

Smiling, she grabs a copy of the *Kama Sutra* from a table and we head for the bedroom. She flips through a few pages, some of which are dog-eared, shows me a few illustrations, takes off her clothes and then strips off mine. After assuming five or six different positions, all of which require an unpleasant series of nearly impossible contortions, we lie naked on her sundeck chaises and smoke the rest of the joint. I make a mental note to see a chiropractor the next day.

"Are you okay?" she asks me.

"Sure, I'm fine," I lie. "Never better."

She glances over at me. "You seem to be grimacing a lot."

"Marijuana causes me to make funny faces," I tell her. "It's a quirk."

"Weird."

Since Michelle's a vegetarian, the following night I take her to dinner at The Greenery, my town's only health food restaurant, where I lavish praise on the wonders of tofu, green tea and alfalfa sprouts. I actually despise alfalfa spouts because they're tasteless and remind me of used dental floss.

Michelle loves Salsa dancing and, although I'm not exactly Mr. Twinkle-Toes, she insists on teaching me a few steps. I've never been agile or rhythmically gifted enough to effectively trip the light fantastic, but after a few sessions of struggling to keep from resembling a panic-stricken drowning victim, I manage to force my limbs to cooperate, although I still have to count the tempo out loud and keep my eyes on my shuffling feet at all times. She finds this ungainly spectacle comical, but manages to keep from laughing. Sometimes when we dance close, I can smell the organic perfume on her neck and it practically makes me delirious with desire, even though it actually smells like hay.

Michelle is a free spirit. Turn on a little music and she suddenly becomes an exhibitionist. It's quite amazing really. If the band's playing and there's nobody on the dance floor, she has no inhibitions about going it solo, oblivious to the whoops and encouraging whistles coming from the single guys. I can barely stand to watch her gorgeous posterior, swaying, thrusting and gyrating to the music, especially when she wears her favorite cut-off blue jeans, the ones that reveal almost everything.

One blisteringly hot afternoon, she packs a lunch of organic cheese, tasteless whole wheat French bread and homemade honey wine, and drags me on an endless hike, mostly uphill, to a hidden waterfall for a picnic. Another time, she appears at my doorstep with two bikes strapped to the trunk of her perpetually dusty Jeep Cherokee and we pedal to the next town and back, which I find thoroughly exhausting. The next day, she talks me into joining a health club, which is something I've been strenuously trying to avoid for most of my life, given my lack of motivation to pull a tendon. At Michelle's urging, I find myself signing up for yoga, Zumba and Pilates.

At some point, I realize that I'm dying to show her off to Deirdre, to make my soon-to-be ex-wife squirm a little. Since Deirdre spends half her day at the gym, instructing shapeless men and women on how to work the Stairmasters and treadmills, I'm relatively sure that one day Michelle and I will bump into her. I know it's infantile, but I can't resist taking a little revenge for Deirdre's dalliance with Dave.

One afternoon, it finally happens. Deirdre is unlocking her car as Michelle and I head out of the gym and into the parking lot.

"Hi Deirdre," I say as she slings her gym bag into the backseat of her Lexus.

Michelle turns to me and whispers, "Is that your wife?"

"Soon to be *ex* wife," I correct her.

Deirdre turns. "Hi Jimmy," she says pleasantly, sizing up Michelle but trying not to be too obvious about it. She raises her Nike-clad foot to the bumper of her car and reties her laces.

"This is Michelle," I say beaming.

"Hi," Michelle says, putting out her hand. Deirdre shakes it and says, "I'm Deirdre."

"Nice to finally meet you," Michelle says.

"Same here," Deirdre says. "I've been wanting to meet the woman who got this lug to join a health club. I tried for years and got nowhere."

Michelle shrugs. "It wasn't that hard actually," she says. "He does yoga and Pilates too."

"And Zumba," I add proudly.

Deirdre ignores me and gazes admiringly at Michelle's body. "Looks like you work out a lot," she observes. "You've got some impressive biceps there, nice tight ass too. Good abs."

"Thanks!" Michelle says. "You look amazing yourself."

This is not at all how I was expecting it to go. I was hoping for awkwardness, maybe a little concealed jealousy from Deirdre, but if this dialogue continues, they'll be having lunch together soon.

I look at my watch. "We're about to grab some lunch," I say. "It was nice seeing you Deirdre."

"Great meeting you," Michelle adds.

"Maybe we can work out together sometime," Deirdre offers. "I know a few new stretching techniques that really work."

"I would love that," Michelle says. "I get these thigh cramps sometimes. They kill."

Deirdre pulls a business card out of her Spandex waistband. "Call me," she says, handing it to Michelle.

"I will!" Michelle says.

Michelle seems to be oblivious to my sighs and grimaces, so I grab her hand. "Let's go," I say, pulling her slightly. "I'm famished."

"Okay."

"See you around, Jimmy," Deirdre says. And then she climbs into her car and starts to back out of her space.

～

Of course, all my poker buddies are bursting with envy and encouragement at my good fortune. Since dating Michelle, I'd missed three of our gatherings, but all the guys understand. When it comes to poker versus sex, there's little question which activity will prevail. It's an unwritten law.

"Does she have a sister?" Jack McPhee asks me one night. The only reason I'm at the game is because Michelle has the flu, which she's treating with a wide variety of herbs and natural teas, none of which have worked.

"I don't think so," I reply. "I'll ask her."

"Okay, how about a cute friend?"

"I'll ask her that too."

"So how's the sex?" Jack boldly inquires. The others look at me expectantly as if I'm about to reveal the meaning of life.

"Isn't that kind of personal guys?" I ask.

They all just look at me.

"Okay fine. Let me put it this way," I say with a mock groan, "I'm single-handedly making my chiropractor a wealthy man."

Even Ira is delighted. He follows me into the kitchen where I've gone to round up another bag of Fritos. "I'm proud of you Jimmy," he tells me. "You seem to have pulled yourself out of the doldrums."

"I'm a new man Ira," I say happily, as I reach into the pantry. "My conscience is clear, my guilt is gone."

Ira squeezes my shoulder. "You've moved on," he adds. "That's an important step in your life."

"And the good thing is that I'm not bitter anymore," I say proudly.

"Excellent."

There aren't any Fritos, so I grab a tube of Pringles. "I'm not sure I could have done this without you Ira," I say, turning to face him. "You helped rescue me and I'll always be grateful."

"My pleasure," he says, beaming. "And this woman, Michelle, she makes you happy?"

"She's quite a woman," I reply.

"Good," Ira says. "But you didn't answer my question."

"Do you think we need more dip?" I ask him, pulling open the fridge door.

"Is she making you happy?" Ira repeats.

"Onion or cheese?" I ask, staring at the two brands of dip on the fridge shelf. "I can't decide."

Ira moves in closer. "Is she making you—?"

"YES," I finally say crossly. "She makes me happy. Very happy. Now what's it going to be, Ira? Onion or cheese? The guys are waiting."

Ira shrugs. "Who cares," he says. "Bring them both."

Friends and Enemas

ABOUT A MONTH LATER, I DEVELOP a case of constipation so acute that it refuses to submit to the usual over-the-counter remedies, nostrums and elixirs, not to mention a gallon of prune juice. Overcome with frustration at not being able to relieve myself for five days, I drive down to our local Rite Aid at one o'clock in the morning in search of a Fleet enema. I've never actually administered a Fleet enema and it doesn't sound like an enjoyable way to spend the early morning hours, but I'm a desperate man. If I don't release something substantial very soon, my large intestine will swell up like a helium balloon and explode.

After walking down every aisle twice, I can't seem to locate the Fleet enemas (for some odd reason, they're not in the laxative section), so I am forced to consult one of the clerks, who spots the manager at the other end of the aisle and says, "Hey Connie, where are the Fleet enemas?"

Now that I've been identified as a man in need of an enema to the eight yawning night prowlers standing in line at the check-out counter, several of whom cannot resist chuckling, Connie performs an impromptu impersonation of a carnival barker and belts out, "Fleet enemas should be on aisle six."

"Thanks a lot," I mutter quietly and slink for cover behind the nearest aisle, where I happen to find Deirdre intently reading the text on a bottle of cold medicine. I haven't seen her in weeks and the next thing I notice is the pair of reading glasses perched on the tip of her nose.

"Finally given in on the glasses issue," I observe, pulling up beside her.

Startled, she looks up and nearly coughs in my face. "Jimmy!" she exclaims in a hoarse, nasally voice. "Hi!"

"They look good on you, the glasses."

"Do you really think so?"

"Definitely," I say.

"The other day I had trouble reading the fine print on the back of a bottle of mouthwash," she tells me. Then she adds facetiously "I *think* it was mouthwash."

I laugh. "I figured you'd come around sooner or later."

Her response is a short, high-pitched sneeze, followed by another.

"Got a cold huh?" I ask dumbly.

"No, I'm practicing for the sneezing Olympics," she says.

I grab a giant box of Kleenex and drop it into her basket. "My treat."

"So what brings you here at this ungodly hour?" she asks, struggling to stifle another sneeze.

"You don't want to know."

She looks at me intently. Evidently, she hasn't heard about my break-up with Michelle, because the next thing she says is, "The Trojans are on aisle five."

"Is that so?" I say. "How do you know?"

She shrugs and pulls a bottle of decongestant off the shelf. "I was in charge of balloons for the gym's last Christmas Party," she tells me. "Do you have any idea how expensive real balloons are? Especially Mylar."

We look at each other for a moment, and then we both crack

up. "I'm not here to buy Trojans," I inform her. Then I lean in to whisper in her ear. "If you really want to know, I'm looking for the elusive Fleet enema."

"Ooooh," she says humorously. "Got a little intestinal gridlock?"

"Could you say that a little louder?" I mutter, glancing around. "I don't think they heard you in the parking lot."

It occurs to me then that there isn't a single other woman on earth with whom I would even consider sharing an update on the state of my bowels.

"How bad is it?" she says. "If you don't mind me asking."

"Think Hoover Dam."

Deirdre laughs. "Come on, I'll help you look," she says, putting two bottles of Extra Strength Tylenol into her basket beside the box of tissues. "Follow me."

I walk a few steps behind her as she strides down the aisle, and I can't seem to take my eyes off of her long, slender legs, which are sheathed in a pair of skin tight corduroys. In spite of the unappetizing object of our search, I suddenly realize that I'm ogling my soon-to-be ex-wife.

Perhaps one of the drugstore clerks thought that only women get constipated because, for some inexplicable reason, the enemas are located in the feminine hygiene aisle next to several industrial-sized packages of Tampax and Stayfree Minipads. There are two choices and they appear to differ only in color.

"What's it going to be?" Deirdre asks. "Blue or green?"

"What would you recommend?"

Deirdre plucks one off the shelf and examines it. "Blue matches your eyes," she says and we head for the cashier. Deirdre has a coughing fit as she hands the checker a twenty dollar bill. A few of the customers near us take a step or two back to avoid the spray of germs she has just unleashed.

After I pay for the Kleenex and the enema and politely decline the checker's offer to carry the eight ounce package outside, Deirdre and I exit and head for her car. It's an unseasonably frigid September night and I turn up the collar of my denim jacket. Shivering, Deirdre grabs my upper arm and we run awkwardly through the parking lot. She beeps open her car door but doesn't get in right away.

"I haven't seen you at the gym lately," she says. "What happened? Did Michelle give up on you?"

"We're not seeing each other anymore," I inform her. "It was a mutual decision."

"Oh?" she says. "I hadn't heard. What happened?"

I just shrug.

"I'm sorry," Deirdre says. "It's none of my business."

"No, that's okay," I tell her. "Let's just say I developed an allergy to sprouts and soy milk. One day she caught me with a box of Dunkin' Donuts and it was all over. We really didn't have much in common anyway."

"To be brutally honest, I didn't think she was really your type," Deirdre says.

"Why is that?"

Deirdre just shrugs. "I know you pretty well, Jimmy," is all she says.

We stand there for a moment looking at each other, her face eerily ashen from the light of the full moon.

"So are *you* seeing anybody?" I ask. "Just curious."

"No. I decided to take a break from dating," she says. "The guys I've met are boring or dense or too into themselves or just looking to get laid. Nobody really gets me. What about you?"

I shake my head. "After Michelle and I split up, I went out with a few women, but nothing clicked. I felt like I had to keep pretending I was someone else just to please them."

"Yeah, I know what you mean," she tells me.

"It was like… something was missing," I reflect.

"Same here," she says.

For a moment we just look at each other. Then I pat my belly. "But at least Michelle got me in shape."

"I see that," Deirdre says, smiling. "You look good."

"Thanks."

Deirdre nods and zips up her parka. "Well, it was nice to see you, Jimmy."

"Likewise," I say. "By the way, I haven't signed the divorce papers yet."

"Neither have I," she tells me. "I keep meaning to."

After a moment, she turns to grab the door handle, but I touch her arm and say, "Look, maybe we can have lunch or something one day."

She stops and faces me. "What?"

"Lunch," I repeat. "I mean, if you're not too busy."

She pulls off her glasses. "Do you have a hanky?" she asks. "My glasses are kind of wet."

I dig into my back pocket and produce a wad of tissue paper. "Thanks."

I watch as she wipes the lenses. "So how about it?" I ask her again. "Lunch? It doesn't have to be lunch. It could be—"

"Okay," she says.

"Great."

"Call me on my cell," she instructs me, "if you still have the number."

"I do."

Deirdre carefully slips her glasses back on and is about to hand me back my hanky, when she suddenly throws her head back and erupts with a violent sneeze, covering her nose just in time with the tissue.

"I should go," Deirdre says, dabbing at her nostrils. "It's late. I have to be at the gym at six tomorrow."

"You should stay home and nurse that cold," I advise her.

"I'll probably be better after a good night's sleep," she says. "But thanks for your concern, doc."

"I guess I should go too," I say, stamping my feet to ward off the chill. "So I'll call you?"

"Sure," she says.

I open her car door for her and she slips in. She turns the ignition, but before pulling out of the space, she lowers her window and says something that no human being has ever said to me before or since: "Good luck with that enema."

The End

Acknowledgments

THANKS...

TO MY VERY TALENTED sister, Stephanie Blumenthal, for designing the perfect cover.

To Pete Masterson for his skill in putting the book together and his tireless, though mostly futile attempts at trying to educate me about the intricacies of ebook publishing.

To Patricia A. Smith, writer, artist, restaurant critic and overall Renaissance woman, for tirelessly proofreading and editing several versions of the book without strangling me for my frustrating lack of comma sense.

To my wife, Ingrid, for putting up with my moodiness, and for not objecting too strenuously whenever I release my frustrations on household appliances and drywall.

To my handyman, who doesn't charge that much for repairing household appliances and drywall.

To Linda A. Black, who is good at fixing things, for making last minute corrections while repairing my vacuum cleaner, and for providing much-needed encouragement.

To my daughters, Julia and Lizzie, who serve as a constant reminder that I actually did *something* right.

To Bernadette Turowitz for being the most generous, kind-hearted person I have ever met.

About the Author

A FORMER *PLAYBOY* MAGAZINE editor, John Blumenthal is the author of seven books and numerous magazine articles. He has also written for television and is the co-author of the movies *Blue Streak* and *Short Time*.

CPSIA information can be obtained at www.ICGtesting.com
Printed in the USA
LVOW081802010212

266575LV00001B/56/P